HENRY WILLIAMSON

Tarka the Otter

ILLUSTRATED BY ANNABEL LARGE

PUFFIN BOOKS

PUFFIN BOOKS

Published by the Penguin Group
Penguin Books Ltd, 27 Wrights Lane, London W8 5TZ, England
Penguin Books USA Inc., 375 Hudson Street, New York, New York 10014, USA
Penguin Books Australia Ltd, Ringwood, Victoria, Australia
Penguin Books Canada Ltd, 10 Alcorn Avenue, Toronto, Ontario, Canada M4V 3B2
Penguin Books (NZ) Ltd, 182–190 Wairau Road, Auckland 10, New Zealand

Penguin Books Ltd, Registered Offices: Harmondsworth, Middlesex, England

First published 1927
Published in Penguin Books 1937
Reprinted in Puffin Books 1949
Reprinted with revisions by the author 1962
Reprinted with map 1963
This edition published in Puffin Books 1995
9 10 8

Typeset by Datix International Limited, Bungay, Suffolk
Set in 12/15pt Monophoto Bembo
Printed in England by Clays Ltd, St Ives plc

Tarka the Otter

Henry Williamson was born on 1 December 1895 at Brockley, London and was educated at Colfe's Grammar School, Lewisham. His experiences during the First World War cast a shadow over the rest of his life. He had witnessed the fraternization between the English and German troops on Christmas Day 1914 and as he then wrote, this changed his entire outlook on life. Ever after he hoped for the union of Europe.

Until he went to war, Henry Williamson had a passion for wildlife, and it was because of this feeling that in peacetime he wrote his stories of the creatures of the English countryside. He also wrote novels, which were not immediately successful, but after a spell of journalism, he published his first book in 1921, *The Beautiful Years*. In 1927, *Tarka the Otter* was published and won the Hawthornden Prize. Though to him it was the least important part of his prestigious output, it is *Tarka the Otter* for which he is most widely known. He was also a farmer – reclaiming derelict land, building barns, cottages and roads and planting trees in both Norfolk and Devon. As well as writing books, for a short time he also edited *The Adelphi*, a literary magazine. He was married twice and had eight children. He died in August 1977.

Once you have finished reading *Tarka the Otter* you may be interested in reading the Afterword by Eleanor Graham on page 272.

To
William Henry Rogers

A map of Tarka's journey will be
found on pages 268–9

A glossary of local
words and phrases
is on page 270

The First Year

*T*wilight over meadow and water, the eve-star shining above the hill, and Old Nog the heron crying *kra-a-ark!* as his slow dark wings carried him down to the estuary. A whiteness drifting above the sere reeds of the riverside, for the owl had flown from under the middle arch of the stone bridge that once had carried the canal across the river.

Below Canal Bridge, on the right bank, grew twelve great trees, with roots awash. Thirteen had stood there – eleven oaks and two ash trees – but the oak nearest the North Star had never thriven, since first a pale green hook had pushed out of a swelled black acorn left by floods on the bank more than three centuries before. In its second year a bullock's hoof had crushed the seedling, breaking its two ruddy leaves, and the sapling grew up crooked. The cleft of its fork held the rains of two hundred years, until frost made a wedge of ice that split the trunk; another century's weather wore it hollow, while every flood took more earth and stones from under it. And one rainy night, when salmon and peal from the sea were swimming against the brown rushing water, the tree had suddenly groaned. Every root carried the groans of the moving trunk, and the voles ran in fear from their tunnels. It rocked until dawn; and when the wind left the land it gave a loud cry, scaring the white owl from its roost, and fell into the river as the sun was rising.

Now the water had dropped back, and dry sticks lodged on the branches marked the top of the flood. The river flowed slowly through the pool, a-glimmer with the clear green western sky. At the tail of the pool it quickened smoothly into paws of water, with star-streaming claws. The water murmured against the stones. Jets and rills ran fast and shallow to an island, on which grew a leaning willow tree. Down from here the river moved swift and polished. Alder and sallow grew on its banks. Round a bend it hastened, musical over many stretches of shillet; at the end of the bend it merged into a dull silence of deep salt-water, and its bright spirit was lost. The banks below were mud, channered by the sluices of guts draining the marsh. Every twelve hours the sea passed an arm under Halfpenny Bridge, a minute's heron-flight below, and the spring tides felt the banks as far as the bend. The water moved down again immediately, for the tide's-head had no rest.

The tree lay black in the glimmering salmon-pool. Over the meadow a mist was moving, white and silent as the fringe of down on the owl's feathers. Since the fading of shadows it had been straying from the wood beyond the mill-leat, bearing in its breath the scents of the day, when bees had blended bluebell and primrose. Now the bees slept, and mice were running through the flowers. Over the old year's leaves the vapour moved, silent and wan, the wraith of waters once filling the ancient wide river-bed – men say that the sea's tides covered all this land, when the Roman galleys drifted up under the hills.

Earth trickled by the gap in the bank to the broken roots below. Voles were at work, clearing their tunnels, scraping new shafts and galleries, biting the rootlets which hindered them. An otter curled in the dry upper hollow of the fallen oak heard them, and uncurling, shook herself on four short legs. Through a wood-pecker's hole above her she saw the star-cluster of the Hunting Dogs as faint points of light. She was hungry. Since noon the otter had lain there, sometimes twitching in sleep.

The white owl alighted on the upright branch of the tree, and the otter heard the scratch of its talons as they gripped the bark. She looked from the opening, and the brush of her whiskers on the wood was heard by the bird, whose ear-holes, hidden by feathers, were as large as those of a cat. The owl was hearkening, however, for the prick of the claws of mice on leaves, and when it heard these tiny noises, it stared until it saw movement, and with a skirling screech that made the mouse crouch in a fixity of terror sailed to the ground and clutched it in a foot. The otter gave but a glance to the bird; she was using all her senses to find enemies.

She stood rigid. The hair on her back was raised. Her long tail was held straight. Only her nose moved as it worked at the scents brought by the mist from the wood. Mingled with the flower odours, which were unpleasant to her, was the taint that had given her a sudden shock; causing her heart to beat quickly, for power of running and fighting if cornered: the taint most dreaded by the otters who wandered and hunted and played in the country of the Two Rivers – the scent of Deadlock, the great pied hound with the belving tongue, leader of the pack whose kills were notched on many hunting poles.

The otter had been hunted that morning. Deadlock had chopped at her pate, and his teeth had grooved a mark in her fur, as she ran over a stony shallow. The pack had been whipped off when the Master had seen that she was heavy with young, and she had swum away down the river, and hidden in the hollow of the water-lapped trunk.

The mist moved down with the river; her heart slowed; she forgot quickly. She put her head and shoulders under water, holding her breath, and steadying herself by pressing her tail, which was thick and strong and tapered from where her backbone ended, against the rough bark. She was listening and watching for fish. Not even the voles peeping from their holes again heard the otter as she slid into the water.

Her dark form came within the inverted cone of waterlight wherein movement above was visible to a trout waving fins and tail behind a sunken bough. While the otter was swimming down to the rocky bed, she saw the glint of scales as the fish sped in zigzag course to its cave. The otter was six feet under the surface, and at this depth her eyes, set level with the short fur of the head, could detect any movement above her in the water lit by star-rays. She could see about four times her own length in front, but beyond all was obscure, for the surface reflected the dark bed of the river. Swimming above the weeds of the pool, she followed the way of the trout, searching every big boulder. She was way-wise in the salmon-pool. In under-water pursuit her acute sense of smell was useless, for she could not breathe.

She peered around the rocks, and in every cave in the bank. She swam without haste, in a slow and easy motion, with kicks of her thick webbed hindfeet, and strokes of her tail which she used as a rudder to swing herself up or down or sideways. She found the fish under an ash-tree root, and as it tried to dart away over her head, she threw herself sideways and backwards and seized it in her teeth. By a bay in the bank, broken and beaten by the hooves of cattle going to drink, she ate her prey, holding it in her fore-paws and crunching with her head on one side. She ate to the tail, which was left on a wad of drying mud cast from a hoof; and she was drinking a draught of water when a whistling cry came from under Canal Bridge. It had a thin, hard, musical quality, and carried far down the river. She answered gladly, for it was the call of the dog-otter with whom she had mated nearly nine weeks before. He had followed her down from the weir by the scent lying in her seals, or footprints, left on many scours, and on the otter-path across the meadowland of the river's bend. He swam in the deep water, hidden except for his nose, which pushed a ream on the surface placid in the windless night.

As she watched, the ream became a swirl. The otter on land heard the instant hiss of breath in the nostrils before they sank. Immediately she slipped into the river with the least ripple tracing where she had entered. The dog-otter had sniffed the scent of a fish.

Bubbles began to rise in the pool, making two chains with silver-pointed links, which moved steadily upstream. Twenty yards above the swirl, which lingered as the sway of constellations between black branches, a flat wide head fierce with whiskers looked up and went under again, the top of a back following in the down-going curve so smooth that the bubbles rising after it were just rocked. Time of breathing-in was less than half a second.

The bubbles, eking out of nostrils, ran over pate and

neck and shook off between the shoulders, to rise in clusters the size of hawthorn peggles; the dog-otter was swimming with his forelegs tucked against his chest. Near the bridge the bubbles rose large as oak-apples; he was kicking four webs together, having sighted the fish. The bubbles ended in another swirl by a weed-fringed sterling, and a delicate swift water-arrow shot away between the two piers of the middle arch – the peal, or sea-trout, had gone down, passing three inches off the snapt jaws.

The river became silent again, save where it murmured by root and rock. Old Nog the heron alighted by a drain behind the sea-wall of the marsh two miles below Halfpenny Bridge, whither he had straightly flown. The white owl had just caught by an old straw rick its second mouse, which, like the first, caught five minutes before, was swallowed whole.

Where water clawed the stones at the tail of the pool the peal leapt to save itself from the bigger enemy ever trudging and peering behind it. It fell on the shillets, on its side, and flapped, once, then lay still, moving only its gills. Then the dog-otter was standing by it, holding up his nose to sniff the air when a thin, wavy, snarling cry rose out of the water. It was the bitch's yinny-yikker, or threat. She ran upon the fish, pulled it away from the dog, who was not hungry, and started to eat.

While she was chewing the bones and flesh of the head the dog played with a stone, and only when she had turned away from the broken fish did he approach and lick her face in greeting. Her narrow lower jaw dropped in a wide yawn which showed the long canine teeth, curved backwards for holding fish, and kept white by the strength of bites. The yawn marked the end of a mood of anxiety. The dog had caught and eaten a peal on his journey, and was ready for sport and play, but the bitch did not follow him into the river. She felt the stir of her young, snarled at the dog in sudden fear, and turned away from the water.

She ran over the bullock's drinking-place and passed through willows to the meadow, seeking old dry grasses and mosses under the hawthorns growing by the mill-leat, and gathering them in her mouth with wool pulled from the over-arching blackberry brambles whose prickles had caught in the fleeces of sheep. She returned to the river bank and swam with her webbed hind-feet to the oak tree, climbed to the barky lip of the holt, and crawled within. Two yards inside she strewed her burden on the wood-dust, and departed by water for the dry, sand-coloured reeds of the old summer's growth which she bit off, frequently pausing to listen. After several journeys she sought trout by cruising under water along the bank, and roach which she found by stirring up the sand and stones of the shallow wherein they lurked. The whistles of the dog were sometimes answered, but so anxious was she to finish making the couch in the hollow tree that she left off feeding while still hungry, and ran over the water-meadow to an inland pond for the floss of reed-maces which grew there. On the way she surprised a young rabbit, killing it with two bites behind the ear, and tearing the skin in her haste to feed. Later in the night a badger found the head and feet and skin as he lumbered after slugs and worms, and chewed them up.

The moon rose up two hours before dawn, and the shaken light on the waters gladdened her, for she was young, and calling to the dog, with a soft, flute-like whistle, she swam to the high-arched bridge upriver and hid among the sticks and branches posited by the flood on the bow of the stone cutwater. Here he found her, and as he scrambled up she slipped into the river and swam under the arch to the lower end of the cutwater, meeting him nose-to-nose in a maze of bubbles, and swimming back under the arch. They played for half an hour, turning on their backs with sideway sweeps of rudders, and never touching, although their noses at each swirling encounter were but a few inches apart. It was an old game they played, and it gave them delight and made them hungry, so they went hunting for frogs and eels in a ditch which drained the water-meadow.

Here they disturbed Old Nog, who was overlooking one of his many fishing places along the valley. *Krark!* He flapped away before them, his long, thin, green toes scratching the water. The otters hunted the ditch until the moon paled of its gleam, when they went back to the river. They played for a while, but jackdaws were beginning to talk in soft, deep, raven-like croaks in the wood, as they wakened and stretched wings and sought fleas. A lark was singing. The dog turned east, and ran along the otter-path used by otters long before the weir was made for the grist-mill below Leaning Willow Island. His holt was in the weir-pool. The bitch drifted lazily with spread limbs, over shallow and through pit, to the rippled water by the hollow tree, into which she crept. Cocks crew in the distant village as she was licking herself and when she was clean she turned in the couch and made a snug sleeping place, and resting chin on rudder, was asleep.

The rising sun silvered the mist lying low and dense on the meadow, where cattle stood on unseen legs. Over the mist the white owl was flying, on broad soft wings. It wafted itself along, light as the mist; the sun showed the snowy feathers on breast and underwings, and lit the yellow-gold and grey of its back. It sailed under the middle arch of the bridge, and pulled itself by its talons into one of the spaces left in the stonework by masons. Throughout the daylight it stood among the bones and skulls of mice, often blinking, and some-times yawning. At dimmity it flew down the right bank of the river and perched on the same branch of the fallen oak and skirred to its mate, who roosted by day in a barn near the village.

It flew away; it fluttered down upon many mice in the fields; but the otter did not leave the holt. The instincts which had served her life so far were consumed in a strange and remote feeling that smouldered in her eyes. She lay on her side, in pain, and a little scared. The song of the river, hastening around Leaning Willow Island, stole into the holt and soothed her; the low whistles of her mate above the bridge were a comfort.

When the moon gleamed out of the clouds in the east, pale and wasted as a bird in snow, the occasional whistles of the dog ceased. She did not care, for now she needed no comfort. She listened for another cry, feeble and mewing, and whenever she heard it, she rounded her neck to caress with her tongue a head smaller than one of her own paws. All the next day and night, and the day after, she lay curled for the warming of three blind cubs; and while the sunset was still over the hill, she slid into the water and roved along the left bank, looking in front and above her, now left, now right, now left again. A glint in the darkness! Her back looped as the hind legs were drawn under for the full thrust of webs, and bubbles wriggled off her back larger than oak apples; she was only a little slower than when she had last chased a trout. Her rudder, about two-thirds as long as her body and two inches thick at the base, gave her such a power of swiftness in turning that she snatched the fish two feet above as it flashed over her head.

She ate it ravenously, half-standing in shallow water, yinnying at shadows as she clawed and swallowed. After four hasty laps she went under again. She caught an eel, ate the lower part of it and returned to the holt. But she was still hungry and left them a second time, running up the bank to stand upright with the breeze drawing across her nostrils. Blackbirds in the wood were shrilling at tawny owls which had not yet hooted. The otter dropped on her forepads and ran to water again. The weight of her rudder dragging on a sand scour enabled her to immerge noiselessly while running.

The eldest and biggest of the litter was a dog-cub, and when he drew his first breath he was less than five inches long from his nose to where his wee tail joined his backbone. His fur was soft and grey as the buds of the willow before they open at Eastertide. He was called Tarka, which was the name given to otters many years ago by men dwelling in hut circles on the moor. It means Little Water Wanderer, or, Wandering as Water.

With his two sisters he mewed when hungry, seeking the warmth of his mother, who uncurled and held up a paw whenever tiny pads would stray in her fur, and tiny noses snuffle against her. She was careful that they should be clean, and many times in the nights and days of their blind helplessness she rolled on her back, ceasing her kind of purr to twist her head and lick them. And sometimes her short ears would stiffen as she started up, her eyes fierce with a tawny glow and the coarse hair of her neck bristling, having heard some danger sound. By day the dog was far away, sleeping in a holt by the weirpools which had its rocky entrance underwater, but in the darkness his whistle would move the fierceness from her eyes, and she would lie down to sigh happily as her young struggled to draw life from her.

This was her first litter, and she was overjoyed when Tarka's lids ungummed, and his eyes peeped upon her, blue and wondering. He was then eleven days old. Before the coming of her cubs, her world had been a wilderness, but now her world was in the eyes of her firstborn. After a day of sight-seeing he began to play, tapping her nose with a paw and biting her whiskers. He kicked against the other cubs, growling lustily, and his eyes darkened, and he tried harder than ever to bite his mother's whiskers, which tickled him when he was being held between her paws and washed. Once, when he was milk-happy and had snarled his first snarl without frightening her into stopping the licking of his belly, he was so furious that he tried to bite off her head. She opened her mouth and panted, which is the way otters laugh among themselves, while he kicked and struggled, and she pretended to bite through his neck. Tarka was not afraid, and clawed her whiskers and struggled to be free. His mother released him very gently; on wobbly legs he returned to the assault of her head, but he snarled so much that he was sick; and when she had tidied him he fell asleep under her throat.

When his eyes had been opened a fortnight, Tarka knew so much that he could crawl as far as a yard from her, and stay away although in her anxiety she mewed to him to return. She was afraid of the daylight by the opening of the holt, but Tarka had no fear. He liked to stare at the waterflies dancing their sun-dance over the ripples. One morning as he was blinking away the brightness a bird about the size of a sparrow alighted on a twig over the hole. A sparrow in size, but not in colour! It may have been that the Quill Spirit had painted the bird with colours stolen from rock and leaf and sky and fern, and enriched them by its fervour, for the bird's feet were pinker than the rock-veins in the cleaves of Dartmoor, his wings were greener than opening buds of hawthorn, his neck and head were bluer than the autumn noonday sky, his breast was browner than bracken. He had a black beak nearly as long as his body. He was Halcyon the kingfisher. His feathers were now at their brightest, for his mate had just laid her seven glossy white eggs at the end of a tunnel in the bank.

Halcyon peered with a bright brown eye at Tarka, who wanted the bird to play with. A wind ruffled one of the emerald feathers, and Halcyon crouched to peer into the water. Tarka mewed to him to come and be played with, and at the sound the bird gave a sudden piercing whistle and flew upriver, leaving Tarka creasing his nose as he blinked at the perching place, unable to understand why it was not there.

He went back to his mother and played the biting-game with her, after which he slept. When he awoke again, he saw one of his sisters playing with something and immediately wanted it. The cub was patting it with one paw, holding her head sideways; but as it did not run, she patted it with the other paw, while holding her head to that side. Tarka was slowly crawling towards it, meaning to take it for himself, when he noticed that it was looking at him. The look frightened him as he tissed at it. The other cub jumped back and tissed as well, and the noise awakened the youngest cub, who spat at her mother. The mother licked its face, yawned, and closed her eyes.

Again Tarka crawled towards the thing looking at him. He sniffed at it and crept away. He crept back to it, but the other cub tissed and so he returned to his mother. When next he went towards it, the look in its eyes had changed, and he boldly touched it with his nose and shifted it with a paw. It looked at him no longer, for it was only the skull of a field-vole, and light coming down the woodpecker's hole from above had put shadows into its empty eyes. Tarka moved it between his paws; some of its teeth dropped out and rattled inside the hollow. The sound pleased him. He played with the skull until he heard one of his sisters mewing in hunger, when he hurried back to his mother.

One evening, while the cubs were alone, Tarka was playing with his rattle when he saw a live vole, that had come into the holt through an opening by the roots. As the way was large enough for a rat to pass, he crept easily along the tunnel, up which the vole had fled in fright as soon as it smelled him. The tunnel ended at the broken roots, to which part of the earth that had nourished them still clung. Little green leaves were growing out of this earth, for the oak's disaster had been as a blessing to many seeds of charlock which had been lying buried in the cold earth long before the acorn had sprouted.

Voles, which are the red mice of the fields, were squeaking among the roots as they hurried to their holes; for the explorer ran among them, crying the alarm that a great weasel was coming. Tarka did not know that his scent had filled them with terror; indeed, he did not know what a vole was. He had seen movement and gone to it, for he was already ready to play, and play was movement. The squeaks ceased.

All was quiet and he heard, for the first time, the jets and rills on the stones which made the ancient song of the river. He wanted to get nearer to the sounds and crawled along a root. When he was half-way along it, he saw that there was nothing on either side of him. He was alone on the root. He tried to turn back, but the claws of one hindfoot slipped and there he clung, curved across the wood, unable to go up or down. He mewed to his mother, but she did not come. His cries grew more and more plaintive as he became colder.

About five minutes afterwards a ream passed under the stone bridge and moved into deeper and quieter water where its raised lines were carried to the banks before being smoothed away by the flow. The angular wave pushed steadily down the river. The bitch was returning. She had caught and eaten six small trout and two eels during the uneasy half-hour she had been away. When nearly opposite the holt she turned across the current, and had almost reached it when she flung head and shoulders out of the water. While rising she was staring, sniffing the air, and listening; and before all the drops running off her whiskers had splashed, her head was underwater and her body doubling with the effort of thrusting four webs together. Then more drops splashed by the holt. A pebble rolled down the bank.

The bitch had heard Tarka's cries, and fear had shocked her into the swiftest movements. She was in the root-pit beside Tarka while the stars were still shaking in the undulation of the old ream. He trembled with cold. A score of hearts under browny-red coats beat faster at the otter's chiding yikker as she picked up her cub by the neck and carried him to the shore. She swam with her head held high and carefully, lest the water should touch him. Afterwards, lying on the warm couch, she forgot her fright and closed her eyes in enjoyment of her young.

The next night Tarka crept along the root again, and fell in the same way. He was crawling around, when a strange-smelling animal leaned over him, wetting him with drops from its jowl. He tissed at it and tissed again when he heard the yinny-yikker of his mother and the snap of her teeth as the animal was driven away. Then something bit the back of his neck and lifted him up. With the cub dangling from her mouth, the bitch threatened the dog, who had followed her in curiosity to the holt. The dog tried to look into the tree on the following night, but the bitch dragged him down by the rudder as though she would drown him. The dog thought this was fun, and ragrowstered with her under and on the water all the way to Leaning Willow Island, where she left him, remembering Tarka.

CHAPTER 2

*I*n mid-May the buds of the fallen oak began to open hopefully and to show their ruddy leaves. Seven small kingfishers perched on an alder branch outside the entrance of their tunnel, while the wind stirred the fledgeling down between their feathers, and they waited for loach or beetle or shrimp or elver or troutling. At sunset seven beaks were laid on shoulders, sometimes to lift at a whistle shriller and louder than the whistle of their parents; but the night was to other hunters.

While the moon was full and bright the otters went to hunt the fish lying in the Tunnel Pool below Halfpenny Bridge – bass, grey mullet, and flukes, or flatfish. The cubs were two months old and they had learned to squeeze through the inner opening of the holt and run along the root, in order to play on the grassy bank. One night as they were playing rough-and-tumble round the base of an ash tree, they heard their mother's whistle. This cry was not as piercing as the dog's call to his mate, but like wet fingers drawn down a pane of glass. Immediately Tarka stopped biting the tail of his younger sister, and the third cub ceased to gnaw his neck. As fast as they could they ran across the root and into the holt. The bitch was waiting for them, with a trout in her mouth. Tarka sniffed at it as she was breaking it up, then turned away, for he did not like the smell of it. The cubs struggled for their own food, so the bitch lay down and fed them with her milk until she grew tired of them. Shaking them off, she went away with the dog, who had swum upriver with her.

When next she returned, she brought two skinned frogs, which she had caught in the reed-grown, marshy bed of the old canal. She dropped them in the holt and slid back into the river, heedless of the cubs' cries. Tarka licked a frog and liked the taste of it; he bared his milk teeth at his sisters, but he did not eat it. They rolled and snarled and played until their mother's return, when they ran to her. She had brought an eel, which she bit into pieces, beginning near the tail, but leaving the head above the paired fins. Tarka swallowed little pieces of the fish and licked his small sister's head afterwards, because it tasted nice. Then he licked his own paws. He was cleaning himself for the first time.

The new food changed them almost at once. They grew swift and fierce. Their frolics on the bank often ceased at the cry of a night-bird, or the distant bark of a cattle dog in the village. They started whenever their mother started. They began to fear. Sometimes at sunset, when their mother left the holt, they ran on the bank and mewed to her as she hunted upstream. She would leave the water and chase them back again to the holt. Her smooth movements near them on land were often broken; she would stand still and uncertain, or run on, jerky with fear. Many times she stood upright and listened, her nose towards the village. People occasionally walked over Canal Bridge, which now carried a drive to a house near the weir; and whenever she heard voices she ceased to hunt, and swam down the river to be near the cubs. Human voices frightened her; but the thunderous noise of trains in the valley and the long, whisking lights of motor-cars on the road beyond the railway were ignored because she was used to them, and knew them to be harmless.

The buds of the ash, sullen for so long in their coverings shaped like the black hooves of cattle, broke into browny-green sprays. The cuckoo sang all night. Reed-buntings chattered among the rising green, water-holding stems of balsam; soon Antares would burn dull red in the low southern night sky.

One warm evening when the river was low, the

mother swam down to the holt and called the cubs into the water, and although they were ravening, she did not climb up, but waited for them with a fish below the tree. They whimpered and peered, moving their heads sideways and telling her that below was fearful. She lay on her back in the water and let the fish go, in order to catch it, and rise with it gleaming again. The two youngest cubs ran back over the damp, trodden couch to get through the tunnel, but they were too fat to squeeze through. Perhaps Tarka would have gone with them, if he had not wanted the fish so much. His eyes were on it, he smelled it, his mouth filled with eat-water. He mewed, he yikkered, he tissed, but there was no fish. The otter swam on her back and called him into the water.

Tarka watched her. He wanted the fish, but he dared not let go with his feet. The fish came no nearer, so he dropped down into the black, star-shivery water. He was clutched in a cold and terrible embrace, so that he could neither see nor breathe, and although he tried to walk, it smothered him, choked him, roared in his ears, and stifled every mew for help, until his mother swam under him, pressing pads and tail against her back. Tarka was carried to the stony margin of an islet, where the closed flowers of the water-crowsfoot were floating among their leaves. He spluttered and sneezed and shook water out of his eyes, and saw the stars above him, and felt his mother's tongue on his head.

When he had eaten the fish, Tarka began to enjoy the strangeness. He was playing with the fish-tail when he heard the whistle so often listened to from the holt. When he saw the animal with the wide flat head and great bristling whiskers that had loomed over his head once before, Tarka tissed and snarled at it and ran for his mother. He snapped at the nose sniffing at him. The dog turned on his back and tried to touch Tarka with his paws, in play. Tarka watched him and wanted to roll as well, but he was awed by the stranger's size.

An hour later, the three cubs had eaten their fish happily on the stones. The bitch had grown tired of coaxing the other cubs to enter the water and had dragged them by their scruffs out of the holt and dropped them into the river.

The first otter to go into deep water had felt the same fear that Tarka felt that night; for his ancestors, thousands of years ago, had been hunters in woods and along the banks of rivers, running the scent of blooded creatures on the earth, like all the members of the weasel race to which they belonged. This race had several tribes in the country of the Two Rivers. Biggest were the brocks, a tribe of badgers who lived in holts scratched among the roots of trees and bushes, and rarely went to water except to drink. They were related to the fitches or stoats, who chased rabbits and jumped upon birds on the earth; and to the vairs or weasels, who sucked the blood of mice and dragged fledgelings from the nest; and to the grey fitches or polecats, so rare in the forests; and to the pine-martens, a tribe so harried by men that one only remained, and he had found sanctuary in a wood where a gin was never tilled and a gun was never fired, where the red deer was never roused and the fox never chased. He was old; his canine teeth worn down. Otters knew the ponds in this wood and they played in them by day, while herons stalked in the shallows and nothing feared the old lady who sometimes sat on the bank, watching the wild creatures which she thought of as the small and persecuted kinsfolk of man.

Long ago, when moose roared in the forest at the mouth of the Two Rivers, otters had followed eels migrating in autumn from ponds and swamps to the seas. They had followed them into shallow water; and one fierce old dog had run through the water so often that he swam, and later, in his great hunger, had put under his head to seize them so often that he dived. Other otters had imitated him. There was a web of skin between the toes, as in the feet of wolves and dogs, and generations of swimming otters had caused the spread of the toes to increase and the web of skin to widen between them. Claws grew shorter. Tails used as rudders became longer, thicker, and powerful with muscles. Otters became hunters under water.

The moose are gone, and their bones lie under the sand in the soft coal which was the forest by the estuary, thousands of years ago. Yet otters have not been hunters in water long enough for the habit to become an instinct. And so the original water-fear was born with Tarka, whose mind had to overlay a weak instinct with habit, just as his ancestor had done when he was hungry.

When he went into the water the next night and tried to walk towards his mother, he floated. He was so pleased that he set out across the river by himself, finding that he could turn easily towards his mother by swinging his hindquarters and rudder. He turned and turned many times in his happiness; east towards Willow Island and the water-song, west towards the kingfisher's nest, and Peal Rock below Canal Bridge, and the otter-path crossing the big bend. North again and then south-west, where the gales came from, up and down, backwards and forwards, sometimes swallowing water, at other times sniffing it up his nose, sneezing, spitting, coughing, but always swimming. He learned to hold his nose above the ream, or ripple, pushed in front of it.

While swimming in this happy way, he noticed the moon. It danced on the water just before his nose. Often he had seen the moon, just outside the hollow tree, and had tried to touch it with a paw. Now he tried to bite it, but it swam away from him. He chased it. It wriggled like a silver fish and he followed to the sedges on the far bank of the river, but it no longer wriggled. It was waiting to play with him. Across the river Tarka could hear the mewing of his sisters, but he set off after the moon over the meadow. He ran among buttercups and cuckoo-flowers and grasses bending with bright points. Farther and farther from the river he ran, the moonlight gleaming on his coat. Really it was brown like the dust in an October puff-ball, but the water sleeked the hair.

As he stopped to listen to the bleat of lambs, a moth whirred by his head and tickled him. While he was scratching, a bird flying with irregular wingbeats and sudden hawk-like glidings took the moth in its wide gape and flew out of his sight. Tarka forgot the moon-play. He crouched in the grasses, which rose above his head like the trees of a forest, some with tops like his rudder, others like his whiskers, and all whispering as they swayed. The nightjar returned, clapping its wings over its head with the noise of a dry stick cracking. Tarka was glad to hear his mother calling him. He mewed. He listened and her whistle was nearer, so he ran away in the wet grasses. The cub did not know how alarmed his mother was nor did he know that less than fifty flaps away a bird with great eyes and wings spanning a yard was flying upon him. The nightjar had seen the bird, too, and had clapped its wings as a danger signal to its mate whose two eggs were laid among ferns in the woods.

The nightjar twirled and planed away; Tarka scampered on. The great bird, who had raised two tufts of feathers on its head, dropped with taloned feet spread for a clutch. The otter saw it drop and ran forwards so swiftly that the sound of her going through the grasses was like the first wind which uncoils as it runs before the south-westerly gale. The bird, which was a short-eared owl, thought that Tarka was a small rabbit, and fanned above him while it considered whether or not he was small enough to be attacked. It did not hesitate longer than the time of six flaps, but stopped, while screaking to terrify and subdue its prey. But Tarka came of a family fiercer and quicker in movement than the owl. Tissing with rage, he jumped and bit his assailant as a foot grasped his back and four talons pierced his skin. The other foot of the bird grasped grasses and it had turned with clacking beak to peck the base of the cub's skull when the paw-stroke of the bitch tore half the feathers from its breast. She stood on it, bit once, twice, thrice, in a second of time, and so the owl died.

Tarka was nipped in the neck, shaken, picked up, bumped all the way back to the bank, scraped over the stones, and dropped into the water. Obediently he followed his mother across the river, to where the dog was lying on his back and gravely watching two cubs playing with the tip of his rudder.

Fish were brought alive to the cubs when they had been swimming about a fortnight, and dropped in the shallowest water. And when they were nearly three months old their mother took them downstream, past Leaning Willow Island, and across the bend, to where the banks were glidden into mud smothered by the sea. The tide had lapsed from the mud, leaving fresh water to tear the rocky bed below.

Tarka galloped through the tall green reeds to the river, stopping by a gut to sniff at the tracks of a curlew, which had been feeding there during the ebb-tide. Near the water he found another track, of five toes well spread, and the prick of five claws. The dog had walked there. Just above Halfpenny Bridge they saw him, half out of the water, and chewing a fish which he did not trouble to hold in his paws. He crunched it from the head downwards, gulping his bites quickly, and as soon as the tail was swallowed, he turned and went underwater for more.

The bitch took her cubs to a pool below the bridge and walked with them across a shallow tail of water. She stared at the stones, brown and slippery with seaweed, and the cubs stared also. They watched the glimmers in the claws of water, sometimes trying to bite them. While they were watching the mother ran along the bank to the top of the pool and slid into the water. More often than usual her head looked up as she swam from bank to bank, for she was not hunting, but driving the fish down to the cubs. Tarka became excited and, seeing a fish, he swam after it and went underwater to get it. In order to travel faster, he struck out with all four webs together, and lo! Tarka was swimming like an otter near a fish. It was the biggest fish he had seen, and although he kicked after it at the rate of nearly two hundred kicks a minute, he lost it after a yard. He yikkered in his anger, and oh! Tarka was no longer swimming like an otter, but gasping and coughing on the surface, a poor little sick-feeling cub mewing for his mother.

He felt better when he had eaten a mullet caught by his mother. The fish had come up with the tide and remained in the still pool. Later in the night Tarka caught a pollywiggle, or tadpole, in a watery hoof-hole and thought himself a real hunter as he played with it, passing it from paw to paw and rolling on his back in the mud. He was quite selfish over his prey when his mother went to see what he was doing, and cried, *Iss-iss-ic-yang!* an old weasel threat, which being interpreted, means, Go away, or I will drink your blood!

Old Nog, the heron, beating his loose grey wings over Leaning Willow Island as the sun was making yellow the top of the tall tree, saw five brown heads in the salmon-pool. Three small heads and a larger head turned to the left by the fallen tree, and the largest head went on upriver alone. The cubs were tired and did not like being washed when they were in the holt. Afterwards Tarka pushed his sister from his mother's neck, the most comfortable place in the holt, and immediately fell asleep. Sometimes his hindlegs kicked, gently. He was trying to catch a shining fish that wriggled just before his nose, when he was abruptly flung awake. He yawned, but his mother, tissing through her teeth, frightened him into silence. The day was bright outside the hole.

Halcyon the kingfisher sped down the river, crying a short, shrill *peet!* as it passed the holt. The otter got on her forelegs and started towards the opening. Soon after the kingfisher had gone, a turtle dove alighted on the ash tree above the holt and looked about her; she had just flown off her two eggs, nearly dropping through a loose raft-like nest in a hawthorn by the weir. The bird held out a wing and began to straighten the filaments of a flight-quill which had struck a twig during her sudden flight out of the bush-top. She drew the feather through her beak thrice, shook her wings, listened, and went on preening.

Tarka closed his eyes again, breathed deeply and settled to sleep on the youngest cub's neck. He looked up when his mother ran to the opening. The otter was listening to a sound like the high, thin twang of a mosquito. Hair bristled on her neck. From far away there came a deep rolling sound, and a screaming cheer. The otter instantly returned to her cubs and stood over them in a protective attitude, for she knew that hounds were hunting the water.

Tarka crouched down, listening to the cries. They became more distinct. Always a deeper, gruffer note was heard among them. The sounds, almost continuous, became louder and louder. Nearer came another sound – the wings of the dove striking against twigs as it flew away.

A minute later the pair of cole-tits that had a nest in a hole of the ash tree began to make their small, wheezy notes of alarm. The white owl had flown from the bridge and was perched against the ivy of the trunk, turning its head from side to side and blinking. One cole-tit, about as long as a man's finger, flittered with rage on the twigs a few inches from the gold-grey head. The owl blinked slowly; the baying swelled under the bridge; it swung its head round without moving its body and stared straight behind it. *Chizzy-chizzy-chizzy-te!* wheezed the cole-tit as the owl floated away. Tarka was used to this sound, for usually it greeted him whenever he looked out of the holt in daylight.

Chizzy-chizzy-chizzy-te! the bird wheezed again, and then Tarka saw the big head of the dog-otter by the opening, and his wet paws on the bark. The bitch tissed at him, her teeth snapped at his head, and the dog was gone.

The cries were now very loud. Tarka heard thuds in the wood all around him. The cubs crouched in the darkest corner. Nearer came the shouts of men, until the thuds of running feet ceased on the bank. The water began to wash against and lap the half-drowned trunk, claws scraped the wood, the opening grew dark and the tongue he had heard above the others boomed in the hollow. The otter crouched back, larger than usual, for her body was rigid and all the hair of her back stood straight. Swish, swish swept her rudder. She recognized another sound and tissed every time it cried the names of hounds, in a voice thin and high as though it were trying to become as the horn which so often took its rightful breath. The voice ceased. The horn sang its plain note. Whips cracked.

By their big feet hounds pulled themselves out of the water, except the one who threw his deep tongue at the holt opening. He was all black-and-white, with great flews, and the biggest stallion-hound in the pack. He was black from nose to neck except for the pallid nicks of old quarrel scars on his muzzle and head. No hound quarrelled with him now, for Deadlock was master of all. In his veins ran the blood of the Talbots, and one of his bloodhound ancestors had eaten man. He had mastiff in him. His dam and sire had pulled down many a deer at bay in the waters of the moor, and died fireside deaths after faithful service to red coats. A pink weal ran down his belly, for in his second stag-hunting season the great pied hound had been ripped open by the brow-point of a stag; and his pace had gone from him afterwards. The otter-hunters bought him for a guinea, liking his long legs, and now Deadlock was the truest marking hound in the country of the Two Rivers.

He held by his paws, and his teeth tore at the sodden tinderwood. He could thrust in only his head. While he was kicking the water for a foothold, the otter ran forward and bit him through the ear, piercing the ear-mark where the blue initial letters of his original pack were tattooed. Deadlock yarred through his bared teeth. Three small mouths at the other end of the holt opened and tissed in immense fright.

Then Tarka heard a cry which he was to hear often in his wanderings; a cry which to many otters of the Two Rivers had meant that the longest swimmings, the fastest land-looping, the quietest slipping from drain or holt were unavailing.

Tally Ho!

The cry came from down the river, just above Leaning Willow Island, from the throat of an old man in a blue coat and white breeches, who had been leaning his bearded chin on hands clasping a ground-ash pole nearly as long and as old as himself. From his look-out place he had seen something moving down like brown thong-weed just under the clear and shallow water. Off came the hat, grey as lichen, to be held while he cried again.

Tally Ho!

The horn of the huntsman sang short and urgent notes; the air by the holt was scored by the names of hounds as he ran with them to where, amidst purple-streaked stems of hemlock, the old man was standing on the shillets.

Soon afterwards the horn sounded again near the holt and the baying of hounds grew louder. Footfalls banged the wood above Tarka's head, as a man climbed along the trunk. The water began to lap: hound-taint from a high-yelping throat came into the holt: the bitch grew larger along her back when, above her head, a man's voice cried snarlingly, *Go'rn leave it, Captain! Go'rn leave it!* A thong swished, a lash cracked. *Go'rn leave it, Captain!*

The high yelping lessened with the taint of breath. The cries went up the river. The rudder of the bitch twitched. The hair on her back fell slanting; but it rose when something scratched above. Her nose pointed, she breathed through her mouth. She moved away uneasily. Tarka sneezed. Tobacco smoke. A man was sitting in the branches over them.

After half an hour the cries came down to the holt again. They passed, and then Tarka heard a new and terrible noise — the noise as of mammoth iron-toed centipedes crossing on the stones, or shillets, at the tail of the pool.

Tally Ho! Look out, he's coming down!

Iron toes scraped the shillets faster. Here, across the shallow, a dozen men and women stood almost leg-to-leg in the water, stirring the stream with their ironshod poles to stop the dog-otter passing down to the next pool.

Tarka and the cubs breathed fast again. Deadlock's great bellow swam nearer, with the high yelping of Captain. Many wavelets slapped against the tree. A dozen hounds were giving tongue between Canal Bridge and the stickle above Leaning Willow Island. A shaggy face looked into the holt and a voice cried just over Tarka's head, *Go'rn leave it, Dewdrop! Go'rn leave it!* Boots knocked on the trunk. *Is-isss-iss! Go'rn leave it!* And Dewdrop left it, bitten in the nose.

Unable to break the stickle, the dog-otter went back under the bridge. Baying became fainter. The notes of the cole-tits in the ash tree were heard again.

In the quiet hollow the otter unstiffened and scratched for ticks as though the hunt had never come there. Hounds and men were above the bridge, where another stickle was standing. The water flowed with small murmurs. She heard the rustling clicks of dragon-flies' wings over the sun-splashy ripples. Silence, the tranquil *chee-chee* of a cole-tit seeking a grub in an oak-apple, and the sunbeam through the woodpecker hole roving over the damp wood dust on the floor. The otter lay down, she dozed, she jumped up when sudden cries of *Tally Ho!* and a confused clamour arose beyond the bridge. Now all the sounds of the past hours were increasing together, of tongues, and horns, and cheers; and very soon they were overborne by a deep new noise like the rumbling of the mill when the water-wheel was turning. Then with the deep rumbling came the prolonged thin rattle of the horn, and the triumphant whooping of whips and huntsmen. The sounds slowed and ceased, except for the lone baying of a hound; they broke out again, and slowed away into silence; but long afterwards the strange blowing noises made by their mother frightened the huddled cubs.

Sometimes the slits of the owl's lids opened, and dark eyes would watch a drop of water falling from one of the thin horns of lime hanging from crevices between stones of the arch. Yellow ripple-light no longer passed across the stonework of Canal Bridge. The sun made shadows on the meadow slightly longer than the trees were tall. For more than an hour the water had been peaceful. A blackbird sang in the sycamore growing by the bridge. The otter looked out of the holt and listened. She feared sunlight on the field less than the taint of hounds still coming down on the water, and, calling her cubs, she slid into the river and ran out under the bank, and to the grass. *Iss-iss-iss!* The ground in patches was damp with the water run off hounds' flews, flanks, and sterns. Only a carrion-crow saw them hastening across the meadow to the leat, and its croaks followed them into the wood where bees were burring round purple spires of foxgloves, and chiffchaffs flitted through honeysuckle bines. Otter and cubs passed low and swift among the green seedheads of the bluebells; and uphill over blackening leaves, until they saw the river again below them, where the sun-points glittered, and a young kingfisher, one of the sons of Halcyon, drew a blue line in the shade of oak trees.

CHAPTER 3

*T*he shock-headed flowers of the yellow goat's beard, or John-go-to-bed-at-noon, had been closed six hours when a grey wagtail skipped airily over the sky-gleams of the brook, flitting from stone to stone, whereon it perched with dancing tail and feet. In the light of the sun more gold than at noon the drakeflies were straying low over the clear water, and the bird fluttered above its perch on a mossy stone, and took one. The water reflected the colour of its breast, paler than kingcups. It did not fly, it skipped through the air, calling blithely *chiss-ik-chiss-ik*, until it came to the verge of a pool by a riven sycamore. On a sandy scour it ran, leaving tracks of fragile feet and dipping as it took in its beak the flies which were crawling there. It skipped to the ripple line and sipped a drop, holding up its head to drink. Two sips had been taken when it flew up in alarm, and from a branch of the sycamore peered below.

The brook swirled fast by the farther bank; under the sycamore it moved dark and deep. From the water a nose had appeared and the sight of it had alarmed the wagtail. Two dark eyes and a small brown head fierce with whiskers rose up and looked around. Seeing no enemy, the otter swam to the shore and walked out on the sand, her rudder dripping wet behind her. She stopped, sniffing and listening, before running forward and examining all entrances under the bared roots of the sycamore tree in the steep bank. The otter knew the holt, for she had slept there during her own cub-hood, when her mother had left the river and followed the brook to get to the White Clay Pits.

The wagtail was still watching when the otter came out of the holt again. It flew away as she whistled. Two heads moved across the pool and a third behind, slightly larger, for Tarka followed his sisters. The cubs crawled into the holt, leaving seals, or marks of five toes and running pad, in the sand with the prints of the wagtail.

The sycamore was riven and burnt by lightning, yet sap still gave it a few leaves for summer. Its old trunk was beloved by two mouse-like birds which crept up the whitest tinder and held themselves by their spread tails as they looked in the cracks for woodlice and spiders. Every spring this pair of treecreepers made a nest between the trunk and the loose bark, of twigs, tinderwood, dry grasses, and feathers. Here burred the bumblebees to their homes in the crannies, and when the first frosts stiffened the grasses they tucked their heads under their fore-legs and slept, if they did not die, until the primroses came again. Here, when the trees were nearly bare, waddled Iggiwick, the grunting vuz-peg, or hedgehog, with a coat of the tree's dry leaves, black-patched with autumn's falling mark, and on the earth he curled and closed meek eyes and dozed into a long rest. The tree was the friend of all, and it had one human friend, who as a child had seen it first when trailing in summer after her father hunting the otters of the brook. She had imagined that the old charred sycamore was a giant with many legs, who had been burnt in a fire and had rushed to the bank to cool himself, and that its roots, bared by floods, were thin legs bent at wooden knees and fixed in the water. The brook was determined to drown the giant, who was burrowing his toes for a hold. The maid grew tall and beautiful, but still the old giant sat cooling his thirteen legs, and every June when she passed by with her father, following the otter hounds, he wore a fresh green wig.

Many otters had slept in the cave behind the roots; some had died there, and the floods of the brook had taken their bones away.

Mother and cubs curled up together against the dry

earth of the holt's end, five feet away from the water. The cubs fell into a deep sleep, torn with dreams wherein an immense black face showed its long fangs. Tarka slept with his small paws on the neck of his mother, and her paw held him there. They snuggled warm in the holt, but the bitch did not sleep.

At dimpsey, when day and night hunters see each other between the two lights, she heard the blackbirds scolding the wood owls; and when the blackbirds were silent, roosting in thorn or ivy with puffed feathers, she heard a badger drinking and grunting as he swallowed. The owl's bubbling quaver settled into the regular hunting calls; then the otter yawned and slept.

She awoke when the wood owl had made a score of journeys with mice to the nestlings in the old eyrie of a trapped buzzard, when the badger had walked many miles from its earth in the oakwood. She was hungry. Leaving her cubs asleep, she crept out of the holt. At the water edge, she listened nearly a minute. Then she turned and climbed the bank, running into the meadow where cows snuffled at her as she stood on her hindlegs. Hearing no danger sound, she went down to the river, entered quietly and swam across to the shallows. She walked through a matted and floating growth of water-crowsfoot, and came to summer plants growing out of stones – figwort, angelica, water-hemlock. Returning through the jungle with a crackling of sappy hollow stems and the breaking of rank florets and umbels, she walked among nettles which stung her nose and made her sneeze. Thence she passed under branches of blackthorn, which combed her back as she ran into the marshy field. As in the meadow, she explored as far as the centre, rising to her full height to listen. She heard the munching of cattle, and the harsh *crake crake* of a landrail throwing its voice about the uncropped bunches of marsh grasses and the bitten clumps of flowering rush. Then swiftly back to the brook by another way, through tall balsam stalks to the water, where she climbed on a boulder and lay across it, her head near the stream. She clung by her rudder to the reverse side of the stone, and whistled for the cubs.

Tarka had been peering from the holt and, at the first whistle, he moved forward into the water, making hardly a ripple. He swam across the pool with his fore-legs tucked under him, kicking with the hindlegs only. The toes were spread at the thrust, so that two webs drove him forward with one kick. Behind him swam the cubs, the arrowy ripples pushed from their noses breaking against each other. They followed Tarka across the floating crowsfoot flowers and reached their mother who lay so still. They spoke to her, nuzzling her with their heads and mewing their hunger. When she would not speak to them they bit her rudder, they cajoled and wheedled, they made angry tissing noises, but she did not move. They left her; and suddenly she sprang up with an otter-laugh, which was not so much a sound as the expression of lips curled back from teeth, and the rolling of the head. She was boisterous with joy after the day's fright, and had been shamming death in fun. Calling the cubs to follow her, she sank into the water and swam upstream.

The cubs knew that she was looking for fish, and they followed her by scent in the line of bubbles that was breaking along on the surface. She looked up with a fish in her mouth and they raced for it, yikkering threats to each other. The otter led them out of the pool and to a shallow; she dropped the fish, a trout of three ounces, and went to the gravelly bank where the water was deeper. Tarka picked up the live trout and took it on to a mossy boulder, where he ate it in less than a minute.

The otter caught small fish so quickly in the narrow water that Tarka was soon gorged; and the other cubs in their quick hunger were able to snatch a fish from him while he was rolling on his back in order to have the pleasure of clawing it over his head. The bitch cubs were smaller than Tarka, but quicker in movement. Sometimes they swam along the bank underwater, looking left and right; but their mother had scared the fish before them and they rarely saw the gleam which was a fish curving back over her head. Often they snapped at stones or roots, mistaking them for trout.

At the end of the night, Burnt Sycamore Holt lay a mile and a half behind them. It was time to hide when buzzards were seen soaring above the oak and larch woods. The bitch led them out of the water, through willows and ash trees and brambles, and across a narrow-gauge railway track to a fir plantation. Two years before her mother had taken her to a large rabbit bury near the edge of the quarry, and now she led her own cubs there. A scent strange to Tarka was on the dry soil before the tunnel but his mother did not heed it. She ran down the tunnel and immediately a fox crept out of it by another way, not wanting to meet a bitch otter with cubs underground, or indeed anywhere.

While the otters were cleaning themselves, the fox was sitting down outside the hole, sometimes yawning; he had within him a fill of mice, beetles, and young rabbits. He was drowsy. He remembered his scratching post, the stump of a sapling larch, and walked there, to rub his flanks against it. Reddish hairs lay around it on the ground; one side was polished. When he had scratched enough he walked to a grey stone wall behind a cattle shippen and climbed upon it, waiting for the sun.

The disused rabbit bury was dry and echoed the greater noises of day – the screeching of whistles as light engines, drawing trucks of white clay from the pits on the moor where the brook took its source, slowly approached the crossing of the lane below; the voice, up the valley, of a man chaunting *coo-coo-coo-coo-coo*, and the barks of a dog running round a field while cows swung in a file along a narrow, trodden way, to the milking shed; the buzz, like a blowfly in a spider's web, of a motor-car passing slowly over the little bridge and the rails beyond; the wheeooing of buzzards and the croaking of crows above the larch wood. These noises did not disturb the otters.

At dimmit light they went down to the brook again, meeting the fox, who was quietly lapping to quench his thirst made by swallowing the fur of so many mice. He looked at the otter; the otter looked at him. The fox went on lapping until the water was spoiled by their musky scent, when he went up the hill to sniff in his earth. For ten minutes he sniffed and pondered, until his curiosity was satisfied, and then he started his nightly prowl – after a little scratching against his post.

The otter took her cubs up the brook and over a field. Away from water her movements were uneasy. Often she stopped in her low running to stare with raised head and working nostrils. A galvanized iron chicken coop in a field caused her to make a wide loop – the scent of man was there. A pair of boots left by a tramp in a hedge made Tarka tiss with fear, turn about, and run away. The cubs were now as active and alert as their mother.

At last they reached the ditch remembered by the otter. She leaned down to the brown-scummed water, clinging to the bank by her rudder. Bull frogs had been croaking a moment before she arrived there, but now they were silent and burrowing in the mud. With paw and nose she sought under the weed, nipping them and dropping them on the grass. The cubs seized them and turned away, yikkering; and when she had caught all she could find, the otter ran back to the cubs and began to flay the frogs for their skins were tough.

They left some of the frogs uneaten, for there were eels in the ditch. Iggiwick, the vuz-peg – his coat was like furze and his face like a pig's – found the remains, and was gleefully chewing when a badger grunted near. With a squeak of terror the vuz-peg rolled himself in a ball, but the badger bit through the spines as though they were marram grasses. Iggiwick squealed like marram grass in flame. Later in the night nothing was left except the trotters, teeth, and spiny coat of poor Iggiwick.

They were too far off to hear the dying squeals of the vuz-peg, for during the half-hour before the badger caught him they had travelled a mile up the brook. The otter swam in front, the cubs scrambling behind her. Often a fish would dodge back by her whiskers, missing the snap of her teeth by the space of a fin, and the cubs would bump into one another in their eagerness to get it. When this happened, the otter would turn again to her prowling from bank to bank, and leave the fish to be caught by them.

The brook became smaller and narrower, and at the end of the night it was less than a yard across. The next evening they left the rushes in the wet ground where they had been sleeping, and crossing a road, came to a bog tract where curlew and snipe lived. Tarka ran over the line of a hare, and followed it in curiosity until his mother called him back. Mosses made the way soft and held many scents – of marsh orchid, stinking iris, bog pimpernel; of wild duck, stoat, short-eared owl, magpie, and, once, the rank-smelling flight-quill of a raven.

They reached a thread of water and followed it downwards until it was joined by another thread. The two made a stream, which hastened under whitish banks of clay. The otter sought for fish, but finding none, climbed out of the channel by a slanting otter-path and crossed the railway track near a tall, dark chimney that rose out of buildings. It was a brick factory. An otter had travelled before them, and in a hollow behind birch trees about a quarter of a mile on they heard a whistle; and running towards the call, they came to a deep, reedfringed pond, on the clay side of which a grown dog-otter was playing with the wings of a drake. Tarka kept behind his mother, being frightened of the stranger. He had a split ear, done in a fight two years before. Mother and cubs went into the pond, leaving him rolling on the bank and tossing the wings with his paws.

The pond was an old pit from which white clay had been dug. The water was deeper than any the cubs had swum in. Round the edge grew reed-maces; it was early June and the wind-shaken anthers were dropping the yellow pollen on the juicy heads which would pass, with autumn, into the drab hues of decay. Ten duck-lings were hiding in the reeds, while their mother circled in the starry sky, telling them, with soft cries of *quaz-qua-a-a-az-quaz*, not to move. She had flown up when the dog-otter had caught and eaten the drake, swimming up underneath it. At the time of capture the drake had been trying to swallow a frog, by quapping with its bill, which held one of the legs. When the otter's teeth had gripped the drake, the frog had es-caped; but it commenced to swell on the water and so it could not swim down to the pit's floor. Tarka saw it above him as he pushed about eagerly underwater; the frog showed darkly in the dim surface mirror which reflected the grey sludge of the pond's bed. Tarka caught it, and ate it under a thorn bush planted by a thrush beside the pond.

Mother and cubs roved about in the water for awhile, and the dog joined them. The frogs and eels, having seen them, were hiding, and so the bitch climbed out through grey-lichened whitethorn bushes and ran among rushclumps to the next pit. They hunted through four ponds before they had caught enough to be ready for romping. The fourth pond was larger than the others, and so deep that Tarka had not breath enough to follow the grown otters down in the gloomy water, although he tried many times. He knew they were playing, and mewed to them to come up. Sometimes a string of luminous bubbles shook up and past him, but that was all he saw of the fun; he could see above him, but all was obscure beneath, although he could sometimes hear them.

The old dog-otter was happy, because he had another otter to play with him. His wander years were past; he had killed salmon in the Severn, eaten pollack on the rocks of Portland Bill, and lampreys in the Exe. Now he dwelled among the reeds and rushes of the White Clay Pits, and whenever otters journeyed to the ponds, which formed an irregular chain in a wide flat valley drained by the stream, the old dog, who was rather deaf, would join them; and in the deep pond, he would lure one or another down to a rusted, weed-grown engine that had lain for years half-buried in the clayey ooze. A great joy it was to him to hide in the funnel, and to swim out upon the otter seeking him. Again and again after taking in air he would swim down to his engine, but if any otter except himself tried to hide in the funnel, he would bite it furiously with the few worn teeth that remained in his jaws.

For three years he had lived on the frogs and eels and wild-fowl of the ponds. The clay-diggers often saw him as they went home in the trucks; they called him Marland Jimmy.

The pollen-holding anthers of the reed-maces withered and dropped into the water, but still the bitch and cubs stayed on the land of ponds. Here Tarka tasted his first pheasant, caught by the bitch in the woods where game was preserved. It was a cock-bird, and, had only one wing, the other having dropped off in the winter, after a shot-gun wound. The bird was a swift runner, and nearly pecked out the eye of the otter before it died.

By day they slept in the reeds. From his couch of bitten and pressed-down hollow stems, Tarka watched the dragonflies which flew glittering over the water. On a reed beside him was fixed the brittle greyish mask of a nymph which had crept out of the pond the day before, having done with the years of preying on pollywiggle, minnow, and water-flea. The sun looked upon it; it dried; it heaved at its mask, which split down the back. Legs and head of a colourless insect crept out with short and flaccid wings. It clung limply to the reed, while its wings uncreased and hardened in the heat. It took the dragonish breath of noon and changed it into gleams of scarlet; its eyes grew lustrous with summer fire. The pond glittered. Its wings, held low near its body, glittered a little; they spread wide and were tremulous for flight. It was gone among the whirring dragonflies, whose bodies were banded with yellow and black, and bright with emerald and red and blue.

Cuckoos were calling, and sedge-warblers chattering among the green pennons of the reeds. Sometimes one flew over the pond with a mild and hawk-like flight, calling *wuck-oo*, *wuck-wuck-oo*, and the little agitated warblers flew after it. The hen cuckoos did not sing their name, but made a low gobbling cry as they answered their mates. They were noisy about the pond, as they sought warblers' nests wherein to drop their small, thick-shelled, greyish-brown eggs. Once a cuckoo was flying over with an egg in its beak when a sparrowhawk dashed at the bird and the egg dropped into the water. *Splap!* Tarka awakened, saw the egg, dived, brought it to the couch, and ate it before the shadow of a grass-stalk had moved its own width on the bank.

CHAPTER 4

*T*arka was rolling on his back in the beams of the sun one morning, when he heard the distant note of the hunting horn and soon afterwards the tongues of hounds. The bitch listened, and when the baying became louder, she pressed through the reeds with the cubs and took to the bramble undergrowth beyond the north bank of the pond. A south wind was blowing. She ran down the wind, the cubs following just behind her. When she stopped to listen, she also licked her neck; and a human observer might have thought that this act showed her to have no fear of being hunted.

The heart of the otter was beating quickly; and

whenever she stopped to listen, her aroused nervous force was as a burden, only to be eased by movement.

Now the hounds were hunting Marland Jimmy, who was swimming about the pond and looking at them from among the reeds. When he was tired of swimming backwards and forwards under water, he crept out through brambles and ran across a few acres of boggy moorland to the stream. He was fat and, for an otter, slow on his broad pads. Hounds were after him when he was halfway across the rushy tract, where lichens and mosses held a distinct scent of him. The old otter reached the stream and went down with the water until he came to a drainpipe, where he had often sheltered. Soon the tongue of Deadlock boomed up the pipe, but he lodged there in safety. Then a terrier named Bite'm crept to within a foot of him and yapped in his face. His hearing having dulled with the years, the otter was not disturbed by these noises; nor was he alarmed by the thuds of an iron bar over his head. Bite'm was called back and another terrier yapped away at him until it, too, was recalled. Voices of men quietened; and after a few minutes the sounds came down the length of pipe behind him, followed by a disgusting smell. Marland Jimmy endured the smell and more thumpings above him; and when, an hour later, he crept out into bright light, the water passed away from him with a coloured smear on its surface. The old otter licked the greyish-yellow fur of his belly, and nibbled the smarting skin between his toes, all the rest of the afternoon, but the smell of paraffin stayed on him.

The bitch and cubs were safe, for although hounds drew down the brook, finding and carrying their line to a wood, the hunt was stopped by a keeper. Young pheasants were in the wood, and gins were tilled for their enemies. Hanging from the branch of a tree in this preserve were the corpses of many vairs and fitches, some green, others hairless and dry, some with brown blood clotting broken paws and noses. All showed their teeth in death, as in life. With them were bundles of claws and beaks and feathers, which once had been dwarf owls, kestrels, magpies, sparrowhawks, and buzzards. The hues and sheens of plumage were gone, and their eyes' light; soon they would drop to the earth, and flowers dream out of their dust.

The brook was a haunt of dippers, whose cries were sudden as the cries of water-and-stones; speedy little brown birds, white-breasted, who in flight were like drab kingfishers. A tawny owl perching against the trunk of a larch tree also saw the otters coming up the stream, and its eyes, soft with light as the dark blue sloe is soft with bloom, watched them until they crept into a rocky cleft below a fall, where royal ferns cast their great shadows and water-violets were cooled by dripping mosses.

After sunset a swarm of cockchafers whirred and flipped about the top of the larch, and the owl, hungry after huddling still for fifteen hours, flapped up through the maze of cone-knotted twigs and caught two in its feet. It ate them in the air, bending to take them in its beak; and when it had caught and swallowed a dozen,

it let out a quavering hoot to its mate – for the tawny
owls liked to be near each other in their hunting – and,
perched on a low branch of another tree, listened and
watched for a young rabbit. After a few moments, its
head was tilted sharply downward: the otter and cubs
were going through the wood.

At midnight the western sky was pale blue and
hollow like a mussel-shell on the seashore. The light
lingered on the hill-line, where trees were dark. Under
the summer stars a hundred swifts were screaming as
they played away the night, two miles above the earth;
in fine weather they kept on the wing for many days
and nights together, never roosting. Their puny screams
were heard by Tarka as he rubbed his neck against the
grassy mound of an ants' nest.

While he was enjoying the feeling a loud chakkering
noise came down from the wood. The otters swung
round. Four heads pointed towards the trees. The bitch
ceased to nibble her fur; the other cubs forgot their
play with the head of a corncrake. The noise, distinct in
the dewfall, was met by other cries as harsh and angry.

When the curious otters reached the wood, other
noises were mingled with the chakkering. Green points
of light glinted in the undergrowth about them, like
moonlight in dewdrops, for many vairs were watching
a fight of the two dog-fitches on the woodland path.
Running along the bank of a ditch beside the path, the
fitches had met at the mouth of a drainpipe, out of
which strayed a hunger-making smell. The pipe, covered with grass sods, lay beside an oak-log felled for a

path across the ditch. Both ways had been made by the keeper; one for himself and the other for fitches and vairs, whose liking for pipes and covered ways he knew. There were many such ways in the wood, and to make them more attractive, the keeper had placed the flesh and entrails of dead rabbits inside the pipes.

Each dog-fitch was trying to break the other's neck by a bite behind the ear. They rolled and snapped and scratched with their long claws, their black-tipped tails twitching with rage.

Every stoat and weasel which heard them ran to watch the fight on the pathway made by the hobnailed boots of the keeper. Tawny and dwarf owls peered down from branches of oak trees, while from afar a fox listened, and prowled on again. A crow awoke in an ivy-thick holly, muttered *aa-aa*, and laid its beak among its neck-feathers once more. Tarka circled round the stoats with the other cubs, mewing and yikkering with excitement; and then he smelled the rabbit flesh inside the drainpipe. The youngest cub also smelled it. She was quicker than Tarka, and her head and shoulders were inside one end when he ran in at the other. He had bared his teeth to snatch the flesh when there was a hard snap, a knock of iron on the pipe, a blow on the side of his head, and a loud whimpering and tissing from the cub.

Immediately the bitch was by her, running round outside the pipe in her anguish. She panted and blew as she had in the hollow tree when her mate was being worried by hounds, she ran up the ditch and mewed to the cub to follow, she returned and licked its rudder. The green points of light flicked out together.

Disturbed by the clatter in the drainpipe, a pheasant crew in the covert, and a cock defied the pheasant from its roost among hens in an apple tree by the keeper's cottage below the wood. The bitch scraped at the sods covering the pipe, blowing and gasping anew when a retriever started to bark. She ran away, whistling the cubs to follow her, but returned to the cry of the cub, who had fallen out of the pipe and was dangling by its rudder.

The barking changed to an eager whine when a door of the cottage opened and a man's voice spoke. Sounds came up distinctly from the combe below. While the otter tore with her teeth at the chain, the spring, and the closed jaws of the gin, Tarka and the other cub ran among the oak saplings, rustling the buff leaves of an old year and breaking the stalks of seeded bluebells whose caps dropped round black seeds on the earth. There were faggots of hazel wands just inside the wood, cut and drying for a thatcher, who would split them and make spears for binding the reed of cottage roofs. They burrowed under the faggot, driving out a vair that had been sucking the blood of an aerymouse, or pipistrelle bat. The small weasel made a loud *kak-kak-kak* of rage at them and vanished with the limp aerymouse in its mouth. A loud barking was coming from the field, with the yikkering of the otter. Tarka heard the yelp of the retriever, but the sound that followed made him tiss, for it was the shout of a man.

When the keeper, hurrying up the field, was within twenty yards of the wood's edge, the otter left the chain she had been breaking her teeth on and ran away. The retriever rushed at the cub to worry it, but the ferocity of the unfamiliar beast made it hesitate. The otter remained standing by her cub even when the keeper was pushing through the undergrowth. Thinking that a fox or badger was in the gin, he went forward to kill it with a blow of the holly staff he carried. He was peering forward when the retriever, a young animal, ran to him snarling; something flung itself violently against his legs – the otter weighed fifteen pounds – and nearly bit through the leather of his boot at the ankle. He struck at it, but hit only earth. He hurried back to the cottage for his gun, calling the retriever to heel, lest it be injured.

The struggles of the cub pulled the iron peg out of the ground, and it was able to drag itself out of the ditch and slowly away among the saplings. The bitch whistled to Tarka and the other cub, who ran out from under the faggot and followed her. The mother ran on with them a little way, then returned to the cub that followed so slowly with the gin ripping brambles and clanking against stones and roots. Pheasants in the covert crew from their roosting branches; blackbirds flew from the hollies with wild alarms; wrens and robins complained in the brambles. Hedgehogs rolled themselves into spiny balls, and voles crouched by the withered mosses under the oaks.

Behind the otters came the noise of the keeper

crashing through undergrowth, and the retriever's feet pattering near them, *Wough-wough-wough* to its master. Blood ran down the face of the otter where the wounded cub had bitten her as she was trying to free the gin which gripped her rudder. The cub threw itself up and down, writhing and blowing, and not knowing what had happened; it snapped at its mother's paws, at her ears, at her nose, at her neck. The otter left it to fight the pestering retriever, her eyes yellow and gem-like.

When the keeper came up the cub was gasping with the weight of the iron it had dragged over a hundred yards. He fired at the noise in front of him and the noise ceased. Into the darkness of the wood he fired the second barrel; and listened. He heard stray pellets rattling in the distance and the dragging of the gin as the retriever tried to lift it.

At dawn the crow that slept in the ivy-grown holly saw a new corpse hanging among the fitches and vairs which had run into one end of a drainpipe, but never run out again. The crow said *aa-aa*, and flying to the gallows tree, picked out its eyes.

When daylight came the otter and her cubs were far from the wood, having arrived at new water, deep and dark and slow moving. They swam to an islet, where rose sallows and ash-poles, and swaying at the trees' tops were rafts of twigs roughly pleached, being the nests of wild pigeons. The male birds were awake, and cooing to their mates, when the otter walked out of the water. Green sedges grew by the upper end of the islet, where sticks and roots of winter floods were lodged, and through them the otters crept. The mother trod down a place in the middle and bit off sedges for a couch, and afterwards, hearing a watery croak near her, she sank silently into the pool. Her head emerged by the nest of a moorhen which flew clumsily away from off six eggs, brown like the curling tips of sedge and speckled with dark blotches. These were carried back, one by one, to the cubs, who cracked them and sucked the yolks, afterwards playing with the shells. Sometimes Tarka whimpered and stopped play, for the bruise on his head was aching. Then the mother licked it, and washed him all over, and he fell asleep; and the sun had risen when she had cleaned herself and nibbled the lead pellets out of her coat.

Time flowed with the sunlight of the still green place. The summer drakeflies, whose wings were as the most delicate transparent leaves, hatched from their cases on the water and danced over the shadowed surface. Scarlet and blue and emerald dragonflies caught them with rustle and click of bright whirring wings. It was peaceful for the otters in the back-water, ring-rippled with the rises of fish, a waving mirror of trees and the sky, of grey doves among green ash-sprays, of voles nibbling sweet roots on the banks. The moorhen paddling with her first brood croaked from under an arch of stream-side hawthorn, where the sun-shafts slanting into the pool lit the old year's leafdust drifting like smoke underwater. The otter heard every wild sound as she lay unsleeping, thinking of her lost one.

The cubs breathed softly, but sometimes their nostrils worked and their legs moved, as though they were running.

CHAPTER 5

When Tarka awoke he saw a small eye quizzing
him from among the ash-sprays. He stretched
up his head and sniffed, and at that moment the eye
disappeared. Ticking cries sounded from the middle of
the tangle.

Hearing them, an ackymal that had been searching
the streamside hawthorn boughs for green caterpillars
flittered to the islet and chittered beside the crackey.
The ackymal had a mate in a stump hole, brooding
over a family of thirteen in a nest of moss and feathers,
and the crackey had a mate and a family of eight in a
ball of grasses hidden in the side of a haystack. Both

nests were hundreds of wing-flutters away; yet when the hens, both shorter than a man's finger is long, heard the cries of their songfolk, they left their young and hastened to join them. Their scolding was a summons to all small birds. Blackbirds flew in from the fields and let out shrill ringing cries which jerked their tails as they perched above the otters. Soon many small birds were gathered in the trees of the islet, and their mingled cries brought six larger birds, who sloped up one behind the other. They were among birds what the Irish are among men, always ready in a merry and audacious life to go where there is trouble and not infrequently to be the cause of it. Raising their crests and contracting their light blue eyes, the six jays screamed with the noises of tearing linen.

The cubs lay still, but the otter lifted up her head. She had met jays before, and knew that men sometimes go where the pretty crows are nagging. For half an hour she was anxious, ready to take her cubs into the friendly water immediately the jays' cries became shorter; which would mean the coming of the greatest enemy, man.

The birds became hungry. The crackeys and acky-mals and ruddocks – Devon names for wrens and tomtits and robins – flew away when the otters neither heeded nor harmed them. The jays remained; but when a sparrowhawk dashed into the trees in search of a pigeon, they departed and mobbed the hawk, helped by a pair of carrion-crows.

Again the spirit of the green place was tranquil, with

peaceful doves cooing in the noonday's rest. All the long day the sun swung over the islet until the hilltops were fiery. Shadows lifted from the waters and moved up the trunks of trees. They faded in evelight. The pool darkened. Over the fields flew a white owl, one of hundreds which like great blunt-headed moths were quartering the pastures and tilth of all the lands served by the Two Rivers. It fanned above the vole-runs, where the craneflies rose in flight from flower and bent. The reeling song of a nightjar on a gatepost ran through the ground mist not high enough to hide the flowers of ragged robin and the hardening seeds of the flowering rush. The pigeons settled at the tops of the ashpoles, and ceased their clapping and flapping of wings.

A drop of water splashed, another and another. The otter had withdrawn her head from the river, wherein she had been hearkening for stir of fin or wave of tail. Filling her lungs with new air, she slipped into the water and swam to the other end of the islet, where a scour had been formed by the flood-rains of the last south-westerly wind. Here the grown family of the moorhen was paddling. When almost under them, the otter saw the legs and the images of legs joined to them, black in silhouette against the less dark surface. She seized one of the moorhens and drew it under, releasing it to bite it in her jaws, and carried it back to her cubs, swimming with her nose, whiskers, eyes, and part of the dead fowl out of the water. The cubs were waiting, and seeing that she had food, they ran to her and pulled it out of her mouth, tearing away feathers and mewing with their pads on the dead bird. When the otter returned to the scour the moorhens were gone, so she dived and sought fish.

Late at night she returned with the cubs to the wood, and whistled for the lost one. She did not know it was dead; she knew only her longing for it. Her whistles went far in the still night, as she ran with nose to the ground, stopping to whine when her grief became acute. The cock on the apple bough heard her and crew to the dog in the kennel, who barked to its master. Hearing the bark, the otter took her cubs away; and at the end of the night, when they reached the big river, the lost cub was forgotten.

They hunted and ragrowstered for many days under the high wooded hills, below which the river wound and coiled like a serpent. When the moon hung thin and bright in the dusk – the fourth he had seen – Tarka could swim thirty yards under water before he needed to put out his nose to breathe. In one of their haunts, the smaller cub caught a big trout driven upwater by the bitch, and as she dragged the flapping fish on the stones, Tarka seized it above the tail. She snapped at his head, dropping her bite to do so, and he dragged it away. She bit it through the red-spotted back, and they tugged, wrenching the fish into pieces which they ate held in pads and munching with their heads on one side, whereas before they had usually swallowed without chewing. At any threat of piracy one whipped round to eat facing another direction; very soon all the trout was gone except a scruddick, or fragment, of the tail.

There was no more yinny-yikkering when they had fed, for then was the time for play. When Tarka had drunk some water, he snapped playfully at the cub's head, and inviting her by his manner to catch him, romped through the shallow into the pool. Sometimes he swam with only his hindlegs, as his mother did when she was not close upon a fish, but when his sister was so near to his rudder that she could touch the tip of it, he used all four webs and swerved by a swish of his rudder which swung him round in his own length. In one of his turns she caught him and they rolled in the water, pretending to bite each other, and kicking as kittens do. And so it was that Old Nog, the wisest heron of the Two Rivers, heard the noise of bubbles breaking on the water as he alighted by the pool side. He watched, prepared to jump-and-flap if there were danger. He saw a swirl on the water, and the roll of two dark sleek bodies. He waited. They rolled nearer. With neck and beak held low – a two-pointed horn spear on a shaft hidden by long narrow feathers – he waded into water over his knee joints. While he paused for a plunge of the spear, which had pierced and held many a rat and eel, the bitch's head arose a yard from him, and at her sharp cry the cubs fell apart and swam under. The heron, with a harsh squawk of anger and alarm, jumped into the air and beat away slowly, the legs stretched out behind him and neck tucked between his lean shoulders. *Krack* cried Old Nog, as he flew to his next fishing place.

For several nights after feeding, the cubs went down to a mill-pool to ragrowster, always with the mother, who delighted in playing tricks upon them. Once she whistled the food-cry, and they ran in excitement to her, only to find a large leaf laid on a stone. It was fun, and they chased her. The pool, placid after a dry month, was made turbid by the fragments of leaf, stick, and stone stirred from the weedy bottom. She let them catch her, and enjoyed the rage of her little cubs who snarled so fierce and bit so hard, but could not hurt her.

Early one morning the south-westerly wind arose from off the Atlantic, and brought fast low clouds over the land. A blown grey rain hid the trees on the slopes of the valley. At night the young moon was like a luminous grub spinning a cocoon around itself in the sky. The river pushed to the sea with the fresh, or brown flood-water, and at nightfall their holt, rising three feet under a waterside alder, was filled. The otters rode down on the fresh, over the spillway of the Dark weir, where branches were fixed amid long claws of water. They spread their legs and floated. The noise of the great waters filled Tarka with joy. A log rolled in front of him, and he scrambled on it, to jump off again with happy cries. He pretended that froth was fish, and turned over on his back, trying to clutch it. The river swilled him along, while he whistled in happiness. A memory of big fish was moved in the otter's mind by the smell of the fresh, and she was taking her cubs down to river-bend above Canal Bridge, where she and her mate had killed salmon and peal before the cubs were born.

During the journey the clouds were blown to the north-east, over the high and cold moorland, and when the otters had drifted under Rothern Bridge the moon was shining bright in a dark blue sky. Bubbles glinted around Tarka's head, where the water, hurrying too fast over shoals, tumbled back upon itself. Round a bend the river began to slow and deepen – it was dammed half a mile below by a concrete weir built diagonally from bank to bank. This was the head of the weir-pool. The otters drifted on, round another bend until they came to where the smooth and thundering fall-over of the bubble-whitened water slanted across the river, broken near the left bank by the plunge of breakers down the fish-pass. A mist hung over the river. An icicle stood in the moonlight below the fish-pass, a silver spark for an eye.

Below the fish-pass the water rushed in a foamy spate. Above, it slid black and polished. Presently out of the lower whiteness a silvery flicker shook and vanished. The silver spark vanished and glinted lower. Old Nog, peering below the pass, was so excited that he nearly fell over the three long green toes of each foot, in his haste to overlook more of the water. A second fish tried to leap the weir: with sideways flaps of tail it struggled up the spillway, but the claws of the water pulled it back. The moon in its first bright quarter was smitten into a myriad shimmerings by the lower turmoil. Suddenly, it seemed, the shimmerings were drawn together into a silvery curve, and fell into the pool above, soundlessly in the immense roar of the fall.

The otters were lying in an uvver, or hover, near the right bank, away from the tug of the cascade plunging down the fish-pass. The water in the uvver turned quietly. On its surface revolved a wheel of sticks, riveted by bubbles. The otters turned with it, hanging rudders down in the current. When the salmon leapt the weir, the bitch became rigid and her nostrils widened; but before the burst of the splash had dropped back, she had become supple again. The back of her sleek head gleamed and was gone. The cubs followed her, naturally so swift that a human observer might have wondered what cry or signal had been made by the otter.

They swam by the bank until the pull of the water grew less, when the mother turned into midstream and sought the salmon by working upwater from bank to bank through the gloomy and tumultuous spate. The current forced them to swim with the webs of four feet. Tarka swam on her left flank and the other cub on her right. Sometimes he was flung sideways, or spun in another whirling wheel. He was swimming out of one when the bitch either scented the fish or saw the swift ream of its dorsal fin, for she turned and swam with the current, leaving them behind. Tarka turned after her, and was pursuing with all his strength when a narrow fish, larger than any he had ever seen, swished past him. A few moments afterwards the otter followed, but Tarka had to rise to breathe, and when he swam down again he was alone. He knew that hunted fish usually went upwater, so he swam against the current, swinging from side to side as he had learned by imitating his mother.

When, after several minutes, he could find neither mother nor sister, he climbed on the bank, where wet vegetation and sticks loading the lower branches of nut trees showed how quickly the fresh had risen, and was falling. Plashes of water covered the grassy depressions of the meadow, where moorhens were feeding; and Tarka was returning from an unsuccessful pattering after the birds when he heard his mother's whistle. She had been swept down the fish-pass and hurled against the concrete rim of the middle trough, where the water had pounded her until she had been flung out on the straight rush and left, gasping and coughing, on rocky shillets heaped against the lower bank by old floods. She was savage in failure, and took her cubs over the plashy meadow to a wood to find rabbits. In this wood she had never heard the *iclack* of a sprung gin, so she had no fear. But the rabbits told their fear by thumping their hindlegs, and those which did not bolt into the open ran to their buries and sat there quivering, with ears laid back over shoulders. The otters followed them to where they crouched, inert in terror, their faces pressed into the earth where the tunnels stopped. Twelve were dragged out squealing, and killed, three being skinned by the bitch. While they were feeding a harsh chattering came from one of the holes, with two

pricks of greenish light. Here stood Stikkersee the
weasel, who was in a rage because the water-fitches
were in his wood. Stikkersee was about half as long
as the otter's rudder, but he was not afraid of her.
He came within a yard of her nose and raved so
persistently at the smell of so much blood that she
turned away from the little beast's racket and went
back to the river.

When the moon had come to its full round shine,
Tarka was hunting his own food in the pools and necks
of the clear water running round the bend above Canal
Bridge, which rod-and-line men declare to be the best
salmon beat of the Two Rivers. One August night,
after play under the oaken fender that took the heat
away from the pool, he had left his mother but a short
while and was running along the bank, when a raucous
cry in the darkness made him halt. His paw was raised.
His nostrils twitched. The cry had come from the
meadow, where tufts of rush-grass and sedge were left
uncropped by cattle. It was followed by others – slurred
and throaty notes which rose slowly into the air and
ended in a sweet and liquid cry. The curlews, which
were feeding with their young flown from the moors
where they were born, were disturbed by something,
and had cried the alarm. Tarka had heard curlews
crying during many nights, but never before in such a
way. He heard thuds in the ground; and from the river
the warning whistle of his mother.

Remembering what had come with the ground thuds
before, when the air of the hollow tree had shaken to

the baying of hounds, Tarka ran swiftly to water. The bitch had left the river and was standing on the bank, sniffing the night wind. A cloud like the seal of an otter drifted across the moon. Tarka slipped into the river, but returned to his mother, being curious. The alarm cries of the curlews had ceased, and other notes fell from the sky. In the riverside sedges two warblers began to speak to one another. They mixed hastily the notes of song and alarm, with the gentle under-song voice used only to their mates when brooding in the cradles woven to the green flags.

The ominous sound of a human voice came to Tarka, and a houndlike taint which raised the hair of his neck. Immediately the mother yikkered a threat, and with her cubs ran down the bank and hid among the sedges. Clouds hid the shine of the moon.

On the bank, dark against the sky, appeared the figures of men, and a long-legged lurcher dog. The men scrambled down to the river's verge. There was a moment of quiet, when the trilling cries of the flying curlews rose above the water murmurs and the wind in the trees.

A scratching noise and the flickering of a small light. It went out. Another match was struck and shielded by a hand, until spread into a lurid flame, over-casting with ruddy glow the dim shades of trees across the water. The flare lit the faces of two men. One held a pitchfork with gleaming prongs. They stood still and watchful. Then a youthful voice ten yards higher up the river said: 'Fine li'l brown dog going through the daggers, Shiner! Wish I'd took hold of'n.'

Neither of the men answered. They were staring intently at the water. Slowly the torch-bearer raised an arm and pointed. The spear was poised, to quiver over the man's head, while a ream, or little arrowy wave, skated over the pool.

A hoarse voice whispered 'Now!' and the fork was plunged into the water. A curved flash of fire scattered its ripple. The torch-bearer threw down his torch and waded into the water followed by the young man, who had run down the bank when he had seen the jumping salmon. They were groping for the fish, guided by the agitated spear-shaft, when the man yelled that one of the prongs had gone through his hand. He held it up, dripping blood, and cursing that the top of one of his fingers was knocked off.

The man on the bank picked up the torch – oily rags tied to a stick – and held it as far out as he could over the water without filling his boots. The youth cried out that he had got a grip on the sow's gills and that he couldn't hold it much longer. Before the man could get to him, he had dropped the fish, yelling that he had been bitten in the leg by the little brown dog.

On the moonlight bank, beside the black-and-red smoking rags, they tried to bind their wounds; and the uninjured man was bending down to pick up his empty sack when the lurcher dog began to growl. Its snarls increased; it ran forward; it yelped with pain and ran back past them, followed by two yellow, glowing eyes.

'Fine li'l brown dog you zee'd in the daggers,'

growled the poacher called Shiner, who had lost a finger-joint. 'Us may as well keep whoam when they sort o' dogs be about!'

CHAPTER 6

Yellow from ash and elm and willow, buff from oak, rusty brown from the chestnut, scarlet from bramble – the waters bore away the first coloured leaves of the year. Beeches preserved their tawny form in rain and hail, but yielded more and more to the winds. Sandmartins and warblers deserted their old haunts; kingfishers and herons remained. The reeds sighed in the songless days, the flags curled as they withered, and their brittle tops were broken by the rains.

Eels began to pass down to the sea. They were the females, travelling from ponds and lakes, from dykes and ditches and drains, from the hill streams of Dartmoor where the Two Rivers had their ancient source. The eyes of the eels grew larger as they were swept down in the turbid waters, as they writhed over wet grass, along cart ruts and drains. These eels were urged seawards by a common desire – to journey onwards from where the shallow bed of ocean broke off and dropped deep into its grave below Ireland. To reach their spawning bed across the Atlantic these fish would swim against the warm Gulf Stream, coming at last to a great eddy, or stagnancy, where, below ancient oak timbers rotting in seaweed, strange fish carrying lights moved in heaviest darkness far under the floating weed of the Sargasso Sea, whence as transparent, flat, ribbon-shaped elvers they had set out for the fresh waters of Europe. After their immense journey the elvers had reached the mouths of rivers and passed up to ponds and ditches, where those that were not killed by man, otter, heron, gull, water-fowl, cormorant, king-fisher, dwarf owl, and pike, lived and grew until desire and instinct moved them to seek their ancestral birthplace off the Gulf of Mexico.

The eels of the Two Rivers were devourers of the spawn and fry of salmon and trout, and the otters were devourers of eels. Tarka stood on the shillets of the shallow stream while they twisted and moved past his legs. At first he ate a small portion of each capture near the tail, but when his hunger was gone he picked them up, bit them, and dropped them again. The more he killed the more he wanted to kill, and he chopped them until his jaws were tired. It was a slimy sport, and afterwards he washed for nearly half an hour, squatting on a mossy rock.

While the eels were migrating the otters found their food easily, as there was no hunting to be done. They followed the eels down the river, eating them tail-first as far as the vent, and leaving the head and paired fins. They played away most of the night. The mother took her cubs to a steep, sloping bank of clay which had been worn in past winters by many otters sliding down it. Nine feet below was a pot-hole with seven bubbles turning in the centre with a stick, and as Tarka slid down head-first he meant to seize the stick and play with it. When he looked up through the water it was gone, and many other bubbles rode there, a silver cluster about the blurred image of another otter. Hearing the strokes of an otter's rudder he looked in the direction of the sound, and saw a strange cub, with the stick in its mouth, travelling under the foamy current. Tarka followed the dim form until he reached a barrier made by an uprooted pollard willow and broken branches lodged in the stream. He climbed on the trunk, shaking water from his ears and eyes, and ran back with jubilant whistles to the sides. There he saw the cub, the stick in its mouth, standing with a grown otter. Tarka yikkered, and ran back to the water. The grown otter mewed to him, ran after him, licked his face, and purred in his ear. He tissed at her, and whistled to his mother, who came to him, but did not drive the stranger or the cub away.

The stranger had been the mother of many litters

long before Tarka's mother had been born. Her fur was grizzled on pate and shoulders, and her muzzle was grey. Her canine teeth were long and yellow and she had lost three of her incisors. She knew every river and stream that flowed north into the Severn Sea. She had roamed the high cold moors of three counties, and had been hunted by four packs of otter-hounds. Her name was Greymuzzle.

She played with the otters at the slide, and remained with them when the low clouds became rosy in the east. That day all five hovered on Leaning Willow Island, and she curled beside Tarka, and washed his fur, treating him as though he were her own cub. Then she washed the other cub, who had a white-tipped rudder. Greymuzzle had met White-tip wandering alone three weeks before, and had remained with her ever since. There was friendship and sympathy between the two grown otters, for they never yikkered or tissed at each other. Indeed, although Tarka's mother did not remember Greymuzzle, the old otter played with her and her cub brothers all one night in one of the duckponds near the estuary.

The rain was blown in grey drifts down the valley, and the river flooded the martin holes that riddled the sandy banks. Trees and branches and dead animals bumped towards the sea. So heavy was the autumnal fresh that the otters could not see to hunt in the river. They travelled up the valley on land, feeding on little voles turned out of their drowned homes, and on rabbits which they caught in a warren in a wood where the corpses of herons, kingfishers, red-throated divers, cormorants, and shags were nailed to an oak tree. Some had been shot, others trapped. The cormorants and shags were beheaded, for the Two Rivers Board of Conservancy paid one shilling for every head. The wings of the kingfishers were cut off their tiny bodies, for some women in towns were willing to pay money for the bright feathers, which they wore as ornaments on their hats.

After another gale the birds' nests of old summer began to show in the woods above the winding river. Very beautiful were the wild cherry trees at the fall of their vermilion leaves. The gales of the October equinox stripped them off the branches and whirled them away. The otters went down again on another fresh, sometimes leaving the water to cross bends of marshy ground and fields, following trackless paths which otters had run along before fields were ploughed; before wild men hunted them for their skins with spears of fire-hardened wood. These paths were older than the fields, for the fields were once the river's wider bed, in the mud of which the heavy rudders had whilom dragged. They floated under Halfpenny Bridge, and lay by day in the reeds of the old canal bed. A dog disturbed them, and the next night they travelled inland, and sought a resting-place in the hillside earth of badgers. The white-arrowed faces of the Brocks only peered and sniffed at them. A few dawns previously a fox had crept into the same earth among the hillside pines, but the badgers had turned him out as he stank, and his habits were displeasing to their tidy ways. Had the fox crept there during the day, and his wheezing told them that he was being hunted by hounds, he would not have been bitten and driven out, but given shelter, for man was their common enemy.

The Brocks allowed the otters to sleep in one of their ovens – as countrymen call the chambers connecting the tunnels, for they were the size and shape of the cloam ovens wherein some Devon farm-wives still bake bread. The otters were clean, and washed themselves before sleeping and so the badgers were agreeable. At fall of night they left the earth together, Tarka keeping close to his mother, for the size and appearance of the old boar who had been snoring during the day on his bed of bitten grass and moss in the next oven made him uneasy. The badgers waddled down their paths trodden through the spindleberry shrubs and blackthorns, but the otters made their own way among the brambles to the sloping top of the hill. They ran along a row of sheep-nibbled rape to the skyline, crossed a road, and pushed through the hedgebanks of many small fields. Travelling down a pasture, and through a wood of oak and holly, they came to a pill, or creek, whose banks were fissured by guts and broken by tidal waters. White-tip suddenly galloped away over the mud, for she recognized the Lancarse pill which carried the stream coming down the valley from the Twin-Ash Holt, where she had been born. It was low tide, and the water ran below glidders, or steep muddy slopes. They spread their legs and the water took them under a road-bridge to the river, which ran through a wide and shallow pool crossed by black round iron pillars of the Railway Bridge – the Pool of the Six Herons. Whenever Tarka crawled out to catch one of the little birds feeding by the water-line, his feet sank into mud and his belly dragged. Alarmed by the otters the birds arose with cries which seemed to awake echoes far down the river. These were the cries of ring plover and golden plover, or curlew, whimbrel, snipe, and redshank, and all the way down into a dim starlit distance the cries were borne and repeated.

The brown water rocked them down, and as they were drifting in a wide curve Tarka saw something which filled him with fear. The constellation of the Plough, which had been before them, was now on their left, with its starry share touching the tops of the trees far away. The stars were friendly, being of the night, and the water, but these strange lights were many times the size of the morning star. They stretched in a twinkling line across the river, throwing a haze above them, like the dawn which the otters of the Two Rivers know as a warning.

Neither of the older otters was afraid, so Tarka swam without diving. The lights made the three cubs uneasy. As they drifted nearer, rumbling sounds came on the night breeze which had arisen two hours since with the flowing of the tide over the estuary bar.

Soon the sweep of the fresh lessened, for the tide was pressing against the river. A wavelet lifted Tarka and passed behind him, another curled like a long razor-fish shell and broke over him. He shook the water from his whiskers, and licked his lips, liking the strange taste. He lapped and drank. The fore-running press of the young tide lifted him up and down, and chopped with playful foam at his pate. On every ribbed shoal and mudbank the wavelets were lapping the stones and stocks, lapsing with faint trickling sounds, and leaving the domes of froth which trembled and broke in the wind. As the otters swam down with stronger strokes the mudbanks changed to sandy shoals, and air bubbles out of rag-worms' holes shook up in the shallow water through which they paddled. Long dark shapes rode on the water, swinging slowly in the tide, and the wavelets went flip flup against them. Tarka was afraid of the salmon boats, but the old otters ignored them. The lamplights on the bridge were now very large and bright, and had ceased to twinkle. They passed more boats at their moorings. The rumbling noises of traffic on the bridge were loud, and figures were seen. In front, twenty-four arches, of different shapes and sizes, bore the long bridge. Greymuzzle dived, and the four followed her.

She had caught the scent of men and dogs blowing from the bridge, two hundred yards in front. Underwater Tarka swam until he could swim no more, and rising quietly to vent, he turned his head to see if any danger were near, and swam on. He rose to breathe nine times before reaching the bridge, and the eighth rising brought him under one of the arches. He swam hard against the tide pouring between two piers.

This was the first time Tarka passed under the ancient Long Bridge, which the monks built across their ford two centuries before the galleons were laid down in the ship-yards below to fight the Spanish Armada. When the otters had passed under the bridge they had to swim hard, keeping near the right bank of the river to avoid the main flow of the tide. Flukes were caught in the estuary that night by the otters diving to deep water; they were not easy to find, for the dabs and plaice lay flat on the sand when they saw the dark shapes above them, and their sand-speckled backs hid them. The otters raked the bottom with their paws, driving up the fish which they seized and took on the bank to eat.

In the nights that followed Tarka learned to eat crabs, cracking them with his teeth. With the other otters he sought the shelfish among the rocks below the stone quay of a fishing village at the meeting-place of the Two Rivers, where often at night they were disturbed by the pailfuls of rubbish flung over by the natives. Once a pailful of hot ashes came down, burning both Tarka and White-tip.

By day the otters slept in the reeds of a duckpond which they reached by drifting with the tide up the other horn of the estuary, and turning into the Branton pill, where ketches and gravel barges were moored. At dawn, they left the salt water and rang over the eastern sea-wall to the duckpond shaped like a ram's horns. In the brackish waters of the duckpond the otters took mullet which had been washed in when the sea-wall had broken years before, and rainbow trout put there by the owner. Old Nog fished these waters, and at night many kinds of wildfowl flapped and quacked beside the reeds: mallard, wigeon, teal, coot, dabchick, and strays of the duck family – shoveller, pochard, and golden eye.

On the fourth night of the otters' arrival at Ram's-horn duckpond, the swallows which settled among the reed-maces at sunset did not sleep. They twittered among themselves when the first stars gleamed in the water, for they had received a sign to leave the green meadows they loved so well. They talked in the under-song voices – which men seldom hear, they are so soft and sweet – while clinging to the unburst heads of the reed-maces. They talked of white-and-grey seas, of winds that fling away the stroke of wings, of great thunder-shocks in the sun-whitened clouds under, of wild rains and hunger and fatigue to come before they saw again the sparkles in the foam of the African strand. But none talked of the friends who would fall in the sea, or be slain in France and Spain and Italy, or break their necks against the glass of lighthouses, for the forktailed birds of summer had no thought of these things, or of death. They were joyous and pure in spirit, and alien to the ways of man.

During the day Tarka had been watching them, being curious. He had watched them sweeping above him with a windy rush of wings that darkened the sky, and had listened to their sharp cries as they dipped and splashed in the wind-ruffled water. As he was stretching himself before leaving his couch at sunset they flew like a great sigh up to the stars. *Krark! Krark! Krark!* cried Old Nog, standing grave and still in the shallow water at the pond's edge. It was the last English voice many of them would hear, the blue-winged ones of summer, who had begun the weary migration from the land of thatched-homesteads and old cob linhays.

Some days after the swallows had gone, Tarka heard a strange, soft curlew-like whistle while playing in the Ram's-horn duckpond. The five otters ceased their play and listened. The whistle came again, and Tarka's mother answered. The answering whistle was keen and loud. The bitch swam towards it, followed by Greymuzzle and White-tip. The whistle made Tarka cry in rage, *Ic-yang*, and when a dog-cub has cried thus he is no more a cub, but a dog-otter.

The night before, the otters had fished in the estuary by the seaweedy hurdles and posts of a silted-up salmon weir, where in former times salmon were left penned by the tide. They had returned to the duckpond across fields and dykes, along an otter route, and on their trail an old dog-otter had followed.

Now he had trailed them to the duckpond, a big, flat-headed, full-thighed dog and with great whiskers, more than double the weight of Tarka. He frightened the crier of *Ic-yang*, who crouched tissing with his sister when the stranger sniffed at her nose and then licked it. This action caused Tarka's mother to behave in a curious manner. Turning fiercely on the cub, she rolled her over, bit her, and chased her underwater. Many bubbles were blown up. Tarka dived to see why this strange thing had happened, but the dog turned in a swirl of water to snap at his head. Tarka was so scared that he swam to the bank and crawled out among the dry thistles. Here, while the water ran from his fur, he whistled to his mother. He saw her swimming with her head out of water, with the strange dog behind pretending to bite her. She was heedless of her cub's cries, and dived with the dog in play. For hours Tarka ran on the grassy bank of the duckpond, following his mother as she played in the water. Once the dog rose to the surface with a mullet in his mouth, which he did not trouble to kill before leaving it to float on its side. Tarka whistled again and again, and at last the big dog left the water and chased the small dog for whistling to his mate.

Tarka ran away. He crossed over the sea-wall, and worked up the stony bed of the pill, catching the flukes and green crabs which were feeding at the mouth of an open sewer. He met White-top and Greymuzzle, and together they returned to the duckpond when the wildfowl flighted over. He was swimming round one bend of the Ram's-horn when the big dog heard the strokes of his hindlegs and swam after him again. Tarka dived and twisted, and although he was bitten twice in the neck and once through the paw, he was not caught. His mother's training had made him swift and strong. He quitted the water and was pursued through grassy tufts and thistles and bunches of frayed flags to the sea-wall, where the big dog turned and whistled to his mate. Hearing another whistle – it was really an echo of his own – he galloped in rage back to the duckpond. Then Tarka whistled, and the dog returned to kill him. Tarka went up and over the sea-wall at his greatest speed, across the mud and stones of the pill and to the western sea-wall, where he stopped. He cried *Ic-yang!* several times, but if the dog had returned in answer to the challenge, it is doubtful whether Tarka would have waited to drink the blood of his enemy.

Already his mother had forgotten, and perhaps would never again remember, that she had loved a cub called Tarka.

CHAPTER 7

*T*arka was alone, a young male of a ferocious and persecuted tribe whose only friends, except the Spirit that made it, were its enemies – the otter-hunters. His cubhood was ended, and now indeed did his name fit his life, for he was a wanderer, and homeless, with nearly every man and dog against him.

He fished the pools and guts of the Branton pill, eating what he caught among the feathery and aromatic leaves of the sea-wormwood plants which grew in the mudded cracks of the sloping stone wall with the sea-beet, the scentless sea-lavender, and the glasswort. One night a restlessness came over him, and he rode on the flood-tide to the head of the pill, which was not much wider than the gravel barges made fast to rusty anchors half-hidden in the grass, and to bollards of rotting wood. The only living thing that saw him arrive at the pill-head was a rat which was swarming down one of the mooring ropes, and when it smelled otter it let out a squeak and rapidly climbed over the sprig of furze tied to the rope to stop rats, and ran back into the ship. Tarka padded out of the mud, and along the footpath on the top of the sea-wall, often pausing with raised head and twitching nostrils, until he came to where the stream, passing through a culvert under the road, fell into a concrete basin and rushed thence down the fish-pass. He swam under the culvert, following the stream round bends and past a farmyard, through another culvert under a cart-road, and on till he came to a stone bridge near a railway station. A horse and butt, or narrow farm cart, was crossing the bridge, and he spread himself out beside a stone, so that three inches of water covered his head and back and rudder. When the butt had gone, he saw a hole and crept up it. It was the mouth of an earthenware drain, broken at the joint. He found a dry place within. When it was quiet again, he went under the bridge and fished up the stream, returning at dawn to the drain.

He was awakened by the noise of pounding hooves; but the noises grew remote and he curled up again, using his thick rudder as a pillow on which to rest his throat. Throughout the day the noises of hooves recurred, for below the bridge was a ford where farm horses were taken to water. Twice he crept down the drain, but each time there was a bright light at the break in the pipe, and so he went back. At dusk he slipped out and went upstream again. Just above the bridge was a chestnut tree, and under it a shed, where ducks were softly quacking. He climbed on the bank, standing with his feet in sprays of ivy, his nose upheld, his head peering. The scents of the ducks were thick and luring as vivid colour is to a child. Juices flowed into his mouth, his heart beat fast. He moved forward, he thought of warm flesh, and his eyes glowed amber with the rays of a lamp in the farmhouse kitchen across the yard. The chestnut rustled its last few rusty leaves above him. Then across the vivid smear of duck scent strayed the taint of man; an ivy leaf trembled, a spider's web was broken, the river murmured and the twin amber dots were gone.

Beside the stream was a public footpath and an illuminated building wherein wheels spun and polished connecting-rods moved to regular pulses which thudded in the air like the feet of men running on a bank. Tarka dived. He could not swim far, for by the electric power station the river slid over a fall. He swam to the right bank, but it was a steep wall of concrete. Again he dived, swimming upstream and crawling out on the bank. For many minutes he was afraid to cross the railway line, but at last he ran swiftly over the double track, and onwards until he reached the stream flowing deep under a footbridge.

He had been travelling for an hour, searching the

uvvers of the banks for fish as he had learned in cubhood, when on a sandy scour he found the pleasing scent of otter. He whistled and hurried upstream, following the scent lying wherever the seals had been pressed. Soon he heard a whistle, and a feeling of joy warmed his being.

A small otter was waiting for him, sitting on a boulder, licking her coat with her tongue, the white tip of her rudder in the water. As Tarka approached, she looked at him, but she did not move from the boulder, nor did she cease to lick her neck when he placed his fore-pads on the stone and looked up into her face. He mewed to her and crawled out of the water to stand on hindlegs beside her and touch her nose. He licked her face, while his joy grew to a powerful feeling, so that when she continued to disregard him, he whimpered and struck her with one of his pads. White-tip yikkered and bit him in the neck. Then she slid into the water, and with a playful sweep of her rudder swam away from him.

He followed and caught her, and they rolled in play; and to Tarka returned a feeling he had not felt since the early days in the hollow tree, when he was hungry and cold and needing his mother. He mewed like a cub to White-tip but she ran away. He followed her into a meadow. It was strange play, it was miserable play, it was not play at all, for Tarka was an animal dis-spirited. He pressed her, but she yikkered at him, and snapped at his neck whenever he tried to lick her face, until his mewing ceased altogether and he rolled her over, standing on her as though she were a salmon just lugged to land. With a yinny of anger she threw him off, and faced him with swishing rudder, hissing through her teeth.

Afterwards she ignored him, and returned to the river as though she were alone, to search under stones for mullyheads, or loach. He searched near her. He caught a black and yellow eel-like fish, whose round sucker-mouth was fastened to the side of a trout, but she would not take it. It was a lamprey. He dropped it before her again and again, pretending to have caught it anew each time. She swung away from his offering as though she had caught the lamprey and Tarka would seize it from her. The sickly trout, which had been dying for days with the lamprey fastened to it, floated down the stream; it had been a cannibal trout and had eaten more than fifty times it own weight of smaller trout. Tar from the road, after rain, had poisoned it. A rat ate the body the next day, and Old Nog speared and swallowed the rat three nights later. The rat had lived a jolly and murderous life, and died before it could fear.

The lamprey escaped alive, for Tarka dropped it and left White-tip in dejection. He had gone a few yards when he turned to see if she were following him. Her head was turned, she was watching. He was so thrilled that his whistle – a throat sound, like the curlew's – was low and flute-like. She answered. He was in love with White-tip, and as in all wild birds and animals, his emotions were as intense as they were quick. He felt neither hunger nor fatigue, and he would have fought for her until he was weak now that she had whistled to him. They galloped into the water-meadow, where in his growing desire he rushed at her, rolling her over and recoiling from her snapping of teeth. She sprang after him and they romped among the clumps of flowering rush, startling the rabbits at feed and sending up the woodcock which had just flown from the long low island seventeen miles off the estuary bar.

White-tip was younger than Tarka, and had been alone for three weeks before the old, grey-muzzled otter had met and taken care of her. Her mother had been killed by the otter-hounds, during the last meet of the otter-hunting season at the end of September.

Tarka and White-tip returned to the stream, where among the dry stalks of angelica and hemlock they played hide-and-seek. But whenever his playfulness would change into a caress, she yinny-yikkered at him. She softened after a while, and allowed him to lick her head, once even licking his nose before running away. She was frightened of him, and yet was glad to be with him, for she had been lonely since she had lost Greymuzzle, when a marshman's dog had chased them out of a clump of rushes, where they had been lying rough. Tarka caught her, and was prancing round her on a bank of gravel when down the stream came a dog-otter with three white ticks on his brow, a heavy, slow-moving coarse-haired otter who had travelled down from the moor to find just such a mate as the one before him. Tarka cried *Ic-yang!* and ran at him, but the dog-otter, who weighed thirty pounds, bit him in the neck and shoulder. Tarka ran back, tissing, swinging and swaying his head before he ran forward and attacked. The older dog rolled over him, and bit him several times. Tarka was so mauled that he ran away. The dog followed him, but Tarka did not turn to fight. He was torn about the head and neck, and bitten thrice through the tongue and narrow lower jaw.

He stopped at the boulder where White-tip had been sitting when first she had seen him, and listened to the whistles of his enemy. The water sang its stone-song in the dark as it flowed its course to the sea. He waited, but White-tip never came, so he sank into the water and allowed himself to be carried down past bends and under stone arches of the little bridges which carried the lanes. He floated with hardly a paddle, listening to the song of the water and sometimes lapping to cool his tongue. The wheels and rods of the power station turned and gleamed behind glass windows like the wings of dragonflies; over the fall he slid, smooth as oil. Slowly and unseen he drifted, under the chestnut tree, under the bridge, past the quiet railway station, the orchards, the meadows, and so to the pill-head. The current dropped him into the basin of the fish-pass, and carried him down the slide to salt water. With the ebb he floated by ketches and gravel barges, while ring plover and little stints running at the line of lapse cried their sweet cries of comradeship. The mooring keg bobbed and turned in the ebb, the perches, tattered with seaweed, leaned out of the trickling mud of the fairway, where curlew walked, sucking up worms in their long curved bills. Tarka rode on with the tide. It took him into the estuary, where the real sea was fretting the sandbanks. He heard a whistle, and answered it gladly. Greymuzzle was fishing in the estuary, and calling to White-tip.

The old otter, patient in life after many sorrows and fears, caressed his bitten face and neck and licked his hurts. They hunted together, and slept during the day in a drain in one of the dykes of the marsh, which was watered by a fresh stream from the hills lying northwards. Night after night they hunted in the sea, and often when the tide was low they played in the pool opposite the fishing-village that was built around the base of a hill. The north-east wind blew cold over the pans and sandy hillocks near the sea, but Greymuzzle knew a warm sleeping-place in a clump of round-headed club-rush, near the day-hide of a bittern. She became dear to Tarka, and gave him fish as though he were her cub, and in the course of time she took him for her mate.

CHAPTER 8

*T*he trees of the riverside wept their last dry tears, and the mud in the tidehead pool made them heavy and black; and after a fresh, when salmon came over the bar, beginning their long journey to spawn in the gravel where the rivers ran young and bright, broken black fragments were strewn on the banks and ridges of the wide estuary. in November the poplars were like bedraggled gull-feathers stuck in the ground, except for one or two or three leaves which fluttered on their tops throughout the gales of November.

One evening, when the ebb-tide was leaning the channel buoys to the west and the gulls were flying silent and low over the sea to the darkening cliffs of the head-land, Tarka and Greymuzzle set out on a journey. They had followed the salmon up the river, and Greymuzzle had returned for a purpose. The bright eye of the lighthouse, standing like a bleached bone at the edge of the sandhills, blinked in the clear air. The otters were carried down amidst swirls and topplings of waves in the wake of a ketch, while the mumble of the bar grew in their ears. Beyond the ragged horizon of grey breakers the day had gone, clouded and dull, leaving a purplish pallor on the cold sea.

The waves slid and rose under the masted ship, pushing the white surge of the bar from her bows. A crest rolled under her keel and she pitched into a trough. On the left a mist arose off a bank of grey boulders, on which a destroyer lay broken and sea-scattered. It had lain there for years, in bits like beetle fragments in a gorse-spider's grey web-tunnel. One of the great seas that drive the flying spume over the potwallopers' grazing marsh had thrown it up on the Pebble Ridge. During the day Tarka and Greymuzzle had slept under the rusty plates, curled warm on the wave-worn boulders rolled there by the seas along Hercules Promontory.

Two hours after midnight the otters had swum five miles along the shallow coast and had reached the cave of the headland, which Greymuzzle had remembered when she had felt her young kick inside her. The tide left deep pools among the rocks, which the otters searched for blennies and gobies, and other little fish which lurked under the seaweed. They caught prawns, which were eaten tail first, but the heads were never swallowed. With their teeth they tore mussels off the rocks, and holding them in their paws, they cracked them and licked out the fish. While Greymuzzle was digging out a sand-eel, Tarka explored a deep pool where dwelt a one-clawed lobster. It was hiding two yards under a rock, at the end of a cleft too narrow to swim up. Four times he tried to hook it out with his fore-pad, the claws of which were worn down with sand-scratching, and in his eagerness to get at it he tore seaweed with his teeth. The lobster had been disturbed many times in its life, for nearly every man of the villages of Cryde and Ham had tried to dislodge it with long sticks to which they had lashed hooks. The lobster had lost so many claws that, after nine had been wrenched off, its brain refused to grow any more. Its chief enemy was an old man named Muggy, who went to the pool every Sunday morning at low spring-tide with a rabbit-skin and entrails, which he threw into the water to lure it forth from the cleft. The lobster was too cunning, and so it lived.

The otters rested by day on a ledge in the cave under the headland. Here dwelt Jarrk the seal, who climbed a slab below them by shuffles and flapping jumps. Sometimes Tarka swam in the pools of the cave, rolling on his back to bite the drops of ironwater which dripped from the rocky roof, but only when Jarrk was away in the sea, hunting the conger where the rocks of Bag Leap ripped foam out of the tide.

The greatest conger of Bag Leap, who was Garbargee, had never been caught, for whenever it saw Jarrk the seal, its enemy, it hid far down in the crab-green water, in a hole in the rocks of the deepest pool, where lay shellcrusted cannon and gear of H.M. sloop *Weazel* wrecked there a century before. When no seal was about, Garbargee hung out of the hole and stared, unblinkingly, for fish, which it pursued and swallowed. One morning as Tarka, hungry after a stormy night, was searching in the thong-weed five fathoms under the glimmering surface, something flashed above him, and looking up, he saw a narrow head with a long hooked preying beak and two large webs ready to thrust in chase of fish. This was Oylegrin the shag, whose oily greenish-black feathers reflected light. The smooth narrow head flickered as Oylegrin shifted his gaze, and a pollack below mistook the flicker for a smaller surface-swimming fish. The pollack turned to rise and take it, and the shag saw the gleam of its side at the same time as Tarka saw it. Oylegrin tipped up and kicked rapidly downwards faster than an otter could swim. His tight feathers glinted and gleamed as he pursued the pollack. Garbargee also saw the pollack and uncurled a muscular tail from its hold on a jut of rock. The conger was longer than a man is tall, and thicker through the body than Tarka. It weighed ninety pounds. It waved about the weedy timbers, and as it passed over, crabs hid in the mouths of cannon.

Bird, animal, and fish made a chasing arrow-head whose tip was the glinting pollack; conger the flexible shaft, otter and shag the barbs. Oylegrin swam with long neck stretched out, hooked beak ready to grip, while he thrust with webbed feet farther from the bubbles which ran out of his gullet. The pollack turned near Tarka, who swung up and followed it. Oylegrin braked and swerved with fourteen short stiff tail-feathers and one upturned web. The pollack turned down a sheer rock hung with thong-weed, but, meeting Tarka, turned up again and was caught by Oylegrin.

The chasing arrow-head buckled against the rock, in a tangle of thongs and ribbons and bubbles shaking upwards. The giant conger had bitten the shag through the neck. Wings flapped, a grating, muffled cry broke out of a bottle of air. Tarka's mouth opened wide, but his teeth could not pierce the conger's skin. The gloom darkened, for an opaqueness was spreading where there had been movement.

Now Jarrk the seal, who had been searching round the base of the rock, saw an otter rising to the surface, and was swinging up towards him when he saw a conger eel wave out of the opaqueness, which was Oylegrin's blood staining the green gloom. Garbargee held the shag in its jaws. The undersea cloud was scattered by the swirls of flippers as the seal chased the conger. Garbargee dropped the shag, and the cleft of rock received its grey tenant. Jarrk swung up with a bend of his smooth body, and lay under the surface with only his head out, drinking fresh air, and looking at Tarka six yards away. *Wuff, wuff,* said Jarrk, playfully. *Iss, Iss,* cried Tarka in alarm. The pollack escaped, and soon afterwards was feeding with other fish on the crab-nibbled corpse of the shag.

It was not often that the otters went fishing in daylight; usually they lay in the warm noonday sun on the sand of a cove behind the Long Rock – a spur of which was the plucking perch of Chakchek the One-eyed, the peregrine falcon. One morning Chakchek half-closed his wings and cut down at Tarka, crying *Aik-aik-aik!* and swishing past his head. It was the cream-breasted tiercel's cry of anger. He was a swift flyer and soon mounted to where his mate waited at her pitch in the sky above the precipice, scanning the lower airs for rock-dove, oyster-catcher, finch, or guille-mot. When they had swept away down the north side of the landhead, Kronk the raven croaked thrice, deeply, and took the air to twirl with his mate in the windy up-trends.

Near Sandy Cove was the Cormorants' Rock, where five cormorants squatted during most of the daylit hours, digesting their cropfuls of fishes. Each cormo-rant, as it arrived with steady black flight, would pass the rock about fifty yards, swing round and fly back into the wind, alighting uneasily among its brethren, some of whom had the tails of fishes sticking out of their gullets. They held out their wings and worked their shoulders to ease the fish down into their crops. The top of Cormorants' Rock, where they sat, was above the highest wave.

Bag Leap was a sunken reef stretching about half a mile from the point over which the tides raced. Here the currents brought many seals, which had followed salmon up the Severn Sea, on their return home to Lundy Island. With them was a grey seal, a stranger, who had come down from the north. For several days the seals fished off the Leap, while Jarrk roared among them and joined in their favourite game of chasing the smallest seal, who was not black and yellowish-brown like themselves, but a rare silvery-white. They would swim round the rocks looking for her, sometimes remaining under water for nearly a quarter of an hour. Once when Tarka was searching for a bass in four fathoms he met Jarrk face to face, and the shock made him blow a big bubble. He turned and kicked up to the light, while Jarrk swum round him in a spiral. Jarrk was always gentle, for he had never an enemy to shock him into fear, and when Tarka tissed and yikkered at him, the scimitar-shaped lip-bristles of his broad muzzle twitched, his upper lip lifted off his lower jaw, he showed his yellow teeth, and barked. *Wuff, wuff*, said Jarrk, jovially. *Ic-yang*, yikkered Tarka. The seal snorted; then his back, stretched and gleaming, rolled under like a barrel.

When the seals left Bag Leap for the seventeen-mile swim to their island home, one remained with Jarrk. She was the stranger grey seal, and often while the other seals had been romping, she had been exploring the far dark end of the cave behind the Long Rock, where was a beach of boulders. Greymuzzle explored the beach for the same purpose, and sometimes otter and seal passed by each other in the pools. On one high-tide the seal swam into the cave, and did not return with the ebb. For three days she hid herself, and then she flapped down the sand and splashed into the sea, very hungry.

Many times during the rise and fall of tides the bitch-otter ran into the cave, and on the morning of the grey seal's return to the sea she swam round the Long Rock and crawled out of the surge among the limpet-studded rocks of Bag Hole. Three hundred and ten feet above her, perched on the swarded lip of a sand-coloured cliff, Kronk the raven watched her running round and over boulders. She reached the base of the precipice, and scrambled up a slide of scree, which had clattered down during the rains of autumn. Gulls wove and interwove in flight below the raven, floating past their roosts in the face of the cliff. The scree had fallen from under the Wreckers' Path, made during centuries by the cautious feet of men and women descending after storms to gather what the sea had thrown on the boulders of the Hole. It was not much wider than one of the sheep-paths on the headland. Greymuzzle ran along it, and turning a corner by a lichened boulder, disappeared from the sight of Kronk. She had climbed here alone several times during the previous night.

Less than a minute afterwards the raven jumped leisurely over the edge, and opening his wings, rose on the wind, and turning swept back over his perching place, over snares pegged by rabbit-runs in the grass, and to a shillet wall a hundred yards from the precipice.

One of the brass snares Kronk was watching. It had been drawn tight about the neck of a rabbit since early morning; the rabbit had died after two hours of jumping and wheezing. It was cold; its fleas were swarming in agitation over its longer hairs. Kronk was waiting for a meal off the rabbit, but he did not like to go near it until he knew for certain that the trapper, whom he had watched setting the snare the afternoon before, had not tilled a gin beside it specially for Kronk. The raven knew all about the methods of trappers, and the gins and snares they tilled. Several times Kronk had sailed with the wind over the snared rabbit; he sailed without checking by tail or wing lest the trapper be spying upon him. In every other act of his life he was as cautious, having learned many things about man in more than a hundred years of flying.

The raven was waiting for Mewliboy, the cowardly soaring buzzard hawk, to espy the rabbit; and when Mewliboy had ripped it open with one stroke of his hooked beak, the raven intended to call *krok-krok-krok* rapidly, and so summon his mate to help him deal with the buzzard, if he were not trapped. And if he had sprung a hidden gin, then it would be safe for Kronk. So the raven reasoned.

Greymuzzle came to the end of Wreckers' Path, and climbed up springy clumps of sea-thrift, among gull-feathers and mussel-shells and fish-bones, and ran along another path to the top of the precipice. She looked left and right, often pausing to sniff the air. She picked up a feather, ran with it a few yards, and dropped it again. She cast round over the sward, peering into rabbit-holes, and pulling out dry stalks of thrift that the wind had blown there. Kronk watched her running, swift and low, along the narrow wandering lines pressed in the sward by the feet of rabbits; he saw her stop by the snared rabbit, bite on to its neck, and watched her tugging at it. *Crr-crr!* said Kronk to himself.

He jumped off the wall, which was covered with dry lichens dissolving the stones with acids, and circling above Greymuzzle, croaked a long, harsh note, meant to call the gulls. He dived at Greymuzzle, repeating the harsh cry, and very soon nearly fifty herring gulls were screaming about her. Alarmed by the noise, she ran back the way she had come; the gulls followed, and Kronk had the rabbit to himself. Seeing him, the gulls returned, screaming and flying as near to him as they dared. Kronk pecked and pulled at his ease, knowing that the gulls would give the alarm should a man come round either the south or the north side of the wall, which hid approach.

Greymuzzle was slipping down the scree at the end of Wreckers' Path, carrying a brown dry tussock of sea-thrift in her mouth, when the remote crying of gulls became loud above the cliff. *Quoc-quoc-quoac!* many were muttering in anger. Several hundred wheeled and floated above the otter. She heard a soughing of wings, and looking up, saw the beak and eyes of the raven growing larger as he plunged towards her. He had taken nine long hops away from the rabbit, and the tenth had taken him over the precipice edge as a man, walking fast, had taken his ninth stride round the northern wall, three hundred yards off. Kronk opened his wings when half-way down the cliff and sailed without a wing-beat round the Point.

Mewing and scolding, the gulls floated higher in the wind, and hearing them, the grey seal, who had been lolling beyond the break of rollers, swam out twenty yards and turned to watch the top of the cliff. She knew that the tossing flight and the cries of *quoc-quoc-quoac!* meant the presence of man. And, some years before, the seal had been fired at by a man with a rifle.

Greymuzzle swam round the Long Rock with the mat of roots in her mouth, and crawled out of the sandy surge. Tarka was lying on his back, playing with a smooth green flat pebble of glass that he had carried from the bed of a pool. When he saw her, he turned on his pads – neither bone nor muscle showed in action – and ran to see what she carried. Greymuzzle lifted her burden out of his playful way, but he jostled her, wanting to take it and knowing nothing of her purpose. He bit off three rootlets, and at the mouth of the cave he ran back to his glass pebble.

The seal watched with bleary eyes the man climbing down, and his spaniel dog sitting three-quarters of the way down the path, frightened to follow its master farther. Tarka played with his pebble, hidden behind the orange-lichened and towering wall of the Long Rock. In a scattered and unled flock the gulls drifted above the cliff. Over them Kronk the raven, most powerful and black, cleaved the air on outspread wings; sometimes he twirled on his back, recovering immediately. He was practising the upward or impaling lunge of beak that he had learned from his father a hundred and thirteen years before. High above the raven a small dark star twinkled and swept in its orbit, twinkled and poised on its pitch. Chakchek the One-eyed, slate-blue pinioned and cream-breasted, was aloft. *Crr-crr*, said Kronk, as sea and greensward turned up and over and upright again. *Crr-crr-crr*, as the man disappeared round the Long Rock, and Kronk sailed downwind to be over him.

A thousand feet below the raven, Tarka tapped his pebble of glass, green and dim as the light seen through the hollow waves rearing for their fall on the sand. The noise of waves, continuous and roaring on the rocks at low tide, was swelled by the echo beaten back by the cliff, and Tarka saw the man climbing round the Long Rock before he heard him. The man, jumping from boulder to boulder, did not see Tarka; but when he reached the sand he saw the trails of two otters. One trail led into the cave straitly, with regular five-toed prints, except where the track swerved from the impetuous and uneven trail of a galloping otter. Three rootlets of sea-thrift were dropped on the spurred sand. The strait trail led on; the other turned back to the wetted grey pebble, where lay crab-shells, corks, fishtails, and a piece of glass.

The man followed the strait tracks into the cave, into twilight, clambering over ice-cold rocks, and shining a light on the pools wherein drops glistened and struck loud in the stillness. He moved slowly, with glances over his shoulder at the diminishing circle of daylight. The roof of the cave was red and brown with the iron in the rock. Sometimes his foothold wobbled on a stone that in the motion of tides had worn a cup for itself. A hundred yards from its mouth the cave turned to the left, shutting darkness and sea-whispers together. The man went on, bending down to find his way by the light he carried. The pools became shallower, without life or weed; the roof lower and dry. A wailing cry ran along the walls. Holding the electric torch before him, he saw four pricks of light that moved, vanished, and appeared again, one pair above the other. The wail went past him again, like the cry of a hungry infant. On the grey boulder at his feet the wan light showed a black mark, as of tar on bitten fish-bones – the spraints of an otter.

In five minutes he had walked another fifty yards into the cave. The pale yellow eyes shifted noiselessly in front of him. The toe of his boot kicked something that clattered on the stones, and looking down, he saw a bone; and near it, other bones, skulls, and shrunken hides. He picked up a jawbone, with grinder teeth, cuspless and oblique, set along it. Many seals had died in the cavern.

Again the wailing, not far away. The boulders sloped upwards, and pressed one against another by his feet, made a noise of pob-pobble that rang solidly and echoed down the cave and up again. Before them something white was stirring. Picking it up, he stroked the soft, warm hair of a baby seal, putting his finger in its mouth to stop the wailing. While he was nursing it, he heard the hollow echo of a plunging splash, a grumbling noise like *uch, uch!* and slapping as of the palms of great hands on flat rocks. Turning his torch down into the gloom, he saw two dull red orbs, and heard the angry bleat of a mother seal.

He carried the white calf to the inner wall of the cave and laid it down; then hurried to the other wall, where ledges formed natural steps. On the top ledge an otter was crouching. By the shape of the head he knew it was a bitch-otter; an old otter, with grey and grizzled hairs on its muzzle. He climbed as high as he dared, and saw that it had made a couch of dry seaweed and grasses and thrift. He peered into the couch. The otter moved to and fro on the narrow ledge, tissing. He could see no cubs; nor did she appear to be in whelp.

Uch, uch! gasped the seal, exhausted and aching after her anguished journey over the boulders of the cavern. She had hurried by pressing the palms of her flippers on the ground and lifting her body forward by short jumps, moving fast as a walking man. She reached her cub and caressed it with her tongue, making sounds over it between sobbing and bleating. Then she turned her back to the man, and flung sand and pebbles at him with quick scooping strokes of her flippers. The man took from his pocket a wooden whistle made from an elderberry stick and played several soft tunes upon it. The seal looked at him, as though calmed by the rude music. She lay still with her calf, whose head was turned on one side as it sucked through the side of its mouth. The man played on, moving away from the seal.

CHAPTER 9

The otters were alarmed by the coming of the man, and that night they left the headland, returning to the Burrows, and hunting rabbits in the great warren of the sandhiils. A cold mist lay on the plains and in the hollows, riming the marram grasses and the withered stems of thistle and mullein, so that in the morning mildew and fungi in strange plant forms seemed to have grown out of the sand. On the coarser hairs of the otters' coats the hoar remained white, but on the shorter and softer hairs it melted into little balls of water. Everything except the otters and birds and bullocks was white. The sedges and reeds of the duckponds were white, so was the rigging of the ketches in the pill. The hoof-holes of cattle were filmed with brittle ice. In the cold windless air came distinct the quacking of ducks and the whistling of drakes as the wild-fowl flighted from the ponds and saltings in the sea, where they slept by day.

The otters lay up near a cattle shippen, among reeds with white feathery tops. A dull red sun, without heat or rays, moved over them, sinking slowly down the sky. For two days and two nights the frosty vapour lay over the Burrows, and then came a north wind which poured like liquid glass from Exmoor and made all things distinct. The wind made whips of the dwarf willows, and hissed through clumps of the great sea-rushes. The spines of the marram grasses scratched wildly at the rushing air, which passed over the hollows where larks and linnets crouched with puffed feathers. Like a spirit freed by the sun's ruin and levelling all things before a new creation, the wind drove grains of sand against the legs and ruffled feathers of the little birds, as though it would breathe annihilation upon them, strip their frail bones of skin and flesh, and grind them until they became again that which was before the earth's old travail. Vainly the sharp and hard points of the marram grasses drew their circles on the sand: the Icicle Spirit was coming, and no terrestrial power could exorcize it.

The north wind carried a strange thickset bird which drifted without feather sound over the dry bracken of Ferny Hill, where Tarka and Greymuzzle had gone for warmth. Its plumage was white-barred and spotted with dark brown. Its fierce eyes were ringed with yellow, the colour of the lichens on the stone shippens. Mile after mile its soft and silent wings had carried it, from a frozen land where the Northern Lights stared in stark perpetuity upon the ice-fields. The thickset bird was an Arctic Owl, and its name was Bubu, which means Terrible. It quartered the mires and the burrows, and the grip of its feathered feet was death to many ducks and rabbits.

Clouds moved over land and sea with the heavy grey drifting silence of the ice-owl's flight; night came starless, loud with the wind's rue in the telegraph wires on the sea-wall. As Tarka and his mate were running down to meet the flood-tide in the pill, a baying broke out in the sky; whiskered heads lifted fixed to hearken. For a minute the otters did not move, while the hound-like baying passed over. The long skein of south-wending geese swung round into the wind, flying with slow flaps and forming a chevron that glided on downheld, hollow wings beyond the pill-mouth. Cries of golden plover, twined in the liquid bubble-link of the curlews' chain-songs, rose up from the saltings.

The white-fronted geese, eaters of grass and clover, had come before the blizzard howling its way from the North Star. A fine powdery snow whirled out of the sky at night, that lay nowhere, but raced over the mossy plains and hillocks, and in the burrows, faster than the grains of sand. Tree, dune, shippen, and dyke – all were hid in whirling white chaos at daylight. The next day thicker snowflakes fell, and out of the storm dropped a bird with white wings, immensely swift in flight, whose talon-stroke knocked off the head of a goose. It stood on the slain, holding by the black sickle-claws of its yellow feet; its hooked beak tore breast-bone and flesh together. Its plumage was brown-spotted like the plumage of Bubu – the hue of snow and fog. Every feather was taut and cut for the swiftest stoop in the thin airs of its polar ranging. Its full brown eyes glanced proudly as any Chakchek, for it was a Green-land falcon.

Beyond the shaped and ever-shifting heaps of sand, beyond the ragged horizon of the purple-grey sea, the sun sank as though it were spent in space, a dwarf red star quenching in its own steam of decay. The snow fled in the wind, over the empty shells of snails and rabbit skeletons lying bare and scattered, past the white, sand-stripped branches of dead elderberry trees, and the dust of them aided an older dust to wear away the living tissue of the Burrows. Night was like day, for neither moon nor sun nor star was seen. Then the blizzard passed, and the snow lay in its pallor under the sky.

And the sky was to the stars again – by day six black stars and one greater whitish star, hanging aloft the Burrows, flickering at their pitches; six peregrines and one Greenland falcon. A dark speck falling, the *whish* of the grand stoop from two thousand feet, heard half a mile away; red drops on a drift of snow. By night the great stars flickered as with falcon wings, the watchful and glittering hosts of creation. The moon arose in its orbit, white and cold, awaiting through the ages the swoop of a new sun, the shock of starry talons to shatter the Icicle Spirit in a rain of fire. In the south strode Orion the Hunter, with Sirius the Dogstar baying green fire at his heels. At midnight Hunter and Hound were rushing bright in a glacial wind, hunting the false star-dwarfs of burnt-out suns, who had turned back into Darkness again.

Old Nog the heron, flying over the Ram's-horn Pond, saw Greymuzzle among the reeds, for she was the only dark thing in the white wilderness below. She was hiding a solitary cub by curling herself round it, so that her chin rested on her flank. During the storm she had not left the couch of bitten reed and floss; the heat of her body melted the snowflakes. For two days and a night she had kept the snow from the blind cub; and when the air was clear, a black frost gripped the waters of the ponds, bound the drifts, and hung icicles from drain and culvert. Then Greymuzzle arose, and called to Tarka over the ice. He answered from the northern horn of the pond.

He had kept a fishing hole in the ice, which he bit free as it froze. Fish were hard to see, for the top of the water under the ice was a bad reflector of light to the lower water. As it grew colder, the fish buried themselves in the mud, and when Greymuzzle roved in the brown dim water, she saw only her own vague image

following her above. More wild-fowl flighted to the
estuary, and the cries of birds when the tide was
flowing and covering the sandbanks were myriad as
the gold flickerings in the night sky. The otters crossed
the swift waters to the sandbanks where they were
feeding, swimming under the waves and rising to
breathe with only their wide nostrils above. Greymuzzle swam up under a duck and seized it, and the change
of note in quacking was heard by the birds, who threw
the alarm over the estuary. Thousands of wings
whipped jets on the water. The wild-fowler creeping
up in his narrow boat pulled the trigger of his gun too
late – a long red flame sent a blast of shot swishing
over the head of Greymuzzle as she dived. She swam to
the mouth of the pill with the duck in her jaws, and
ate it on an icy litter of twigs and seaweed left by the
last high tide.

The next night the fishing hole was sealed, and no
longer marked by a ring of scales and bones, for the
rats and crows had eaten them. Greymuzzle was scraping at a fish frozen in the ice when the sheet whanged
and whined and creaked, then *boom!* a crack ran across
it, and water spurted in the fissure. When it was still,
Orion was reflected there, with the red and green
flashes of Sirius; but as Greymuzzle peered the starshine
glazed, and mock-trees of the Icicle Spirit grew on the
water.

The cold sharpened. To the estuary came sanderlings
in white winter dress, who ran at the tide-line like
blown sea-foam. Snow-buntings followed, and went

south with them. The flat-fish swam to warmer water beyond the bar, and often when the otters dived in the estuary they rose empty-mouthed to the surface, except perhaps for a green crab. Old Nog the heron grew so thin that he looked like a bundle of grey flags stripped by wind and clinging to two reeds. His inland fishing-ponds were frozen, most of the streams ran under plates of ice, and the only food he could spear was to be found at low tide in the pools of the Sharshook Ridge, where gravel had been dug.

The pans and plains of the Burrows were crossed by a thousand tracks, the prints of larks, finches, wagtails, crows, and gulls; the presses of weasels, rabbits, and stoats; the pads of badgers and foxes; the triple toes of herons and bitterns, like the veining of leaves. Many of the smaller birds were so weak that they could not fly, and their bodies were eaten by rats and weasels, which were eaten by the larger owls and hawks.

Other otters from the Two Rivers came down to the estuary, some of them cubs of ten to twelve pounds in weight, who had kept together with their mothers. Families of three and four and one of five — a bitch and four cubs from the boggy moorland hill where the Two Rivers began in the peat — came to the duckpond along the otter-path from the saltings, and finding it frozen, went down the pill and out to the coast. Tarka met White-tip with her mate by an overturned hulk one night; she was scratching at the web-mark of a wigeon, frozen in the mud with its scent. One look, and they had passed in the darkness.

Many of the dog-otters wandered solitary. Last of all, slow and fatigued, after weeks of hunger, came Marland Jimmy, the old dog with his split ear who had played the funnel-game with Tarka's mother in the deep clay pit. He limped along the otterpath, which many pads had pressed into ice; the cysts between his toes, inflamed by paraffin, were raw and frostbitten. The tide was ebbing when he crawled over the white sea-wall, and down the dark and hard mud to the water, crackling the brittle ice-forms of the glasswort. Hearing a whistle across the pill, Marland Jimmy walked into the water and swam. He kicked slowly, and the current carried him aslant, amid plates of ice broken off by the last tide. The trickles in the mud channers and salting guts had already ceased. So black and bitter the night that not even the whippering cries of golden plover were heard in the pill. The water ebbed in a blank silence of fixed star-points. Marland Jimmy swam across the pill and crawled out steaming. His breath froze on his muzzle, and his rudder was pointed with an icicle when he reached Tarka, a hundred yards along the bank. Tarka was rubbing his head and the side of his neck against a fish longer than himself, with gaps in its dull-shining length. A week before, Jarrk the seal had chased it over the bar, and as it turned past his head, he had taken a bit out of its belly. The dying salmon drifted with the tides until Greymuzzle and Tarka caught it in the pill. What a feast they had had! As soon as they had carried it streaming out of the sea, ice crystals had glittered on the scales.

Tarka rolled on the crisp snow while the aged otter tore at the fish, breaking off bone and frozen pink flesh. He moved from gills to tail, from tail to gills again, gulping icy mouthfuls, wheezing with hard swallowing, and when he had breath, yikkering at Tarka to keep away. Tarka, warmed by his fullness, rolled and rolled, until he rolled into the water. *Hu-ee-ee-ic!* whistled Tarka.

The split-eared dog had gorged himself when Greymuzzle returned for another meal. He quaddled down the hard mud to where Tarka was sliding into the water. With a heavy rippling of his body, he ran to the top of the slide, and holding his legs rigid, slipped down on his ruined feet into the water. Greymuzzle heard the happy whistles of the playing dogs, and slid with them until she heard the squeals of rats fighting by the broken carcass of the salmon. The noise made her remember her cub, for rats had squealed among the scrikkits of bones and scales around Tarka's fishing hole during the snowstorm. Tarka played on until he was hungry, when he went back to the salmon. Marland Jimmy played alone at the slide.

The ebb-tide moved along the seaweedy perches stuck in the mud to mark the fairway. A mist was rising like steam from the top of the water, which moved slower with its weight of surface slush. The slush became clotted, and hardened, and suddenly ceased to move. The star-points dulled. Orion was stripped of his flashing, the green tongue of Sirius was mute, the Swan lost her lustre, the glare of the Bull faded.

Kack! croaked Old Nog, flapping up from the fish carcass as a fox slunk down to it. The tips of his open beak were red with the frozen blood of a speared rat, which was sticking in his gullet. In swaying flight, reed-like legs hanging with weakness, the heron set off for the gravel pools of the Sharshook. *Kack!* he called to his mate, who was standing in the ebb to her knees fifty yards beyond the slide. She did not move; nor did the tide.

Krark! called Old Nog at dawn, flying over the pill, and calling his mate again. *Hu-ee-ee-ic!* whistled Tarka to Marland Jimmy, who had not answered since the star-points had suddenly dimmed and vanished off the water. *Hu-ee-ee-ic!* – a thin, hard cry which Greymuzzle heard among the reeds of the duckpond. *Hu-ee-ee-ic!* travelling through the ice-blink in the pill, and out across the estuary.

Bubu stared down at Tarka walking over to the eastern sea-wall, fanned above him before beating away. The Arctic Owl perched fifty yards below Tarka's slide on something that swayed and creaked to its weight, but bore it upright. Staring around with several complete turns of his head, Bubu fixed orange-rimmed eyes on a mask set stiff before and below it. There was no movement; there was no life. The owl stared round again, and flew away, as though nodding to the head of Marland Jimmy gazing film-eyed out of the ice.

CHAPTER 10

The little thin cub, on its couch among the reeds frozen and bent like the legs of dead spiders, greeted Greymuzzle with husky mewing whenever it heard her coming, and would not be comforted by tongue caresses. Frost had stricken its eyes. Greymuzzle prowled all day and all night when she was not warming and suckling her cub; and although she was so hungry, she still played with Tarka, sliding head-first down a snowy hillock. They had to travel to the estuary for food, for every incoming tide pulled up its floating floes at the pill-mouth, with grinding shrieks and shuddering booms that sounded far over the Burrows. At low tide the frost welded them in a high and solid barrier.

Both otters had blistered their tongues by licking ice, and to ease their thirst, they rasped them against snow on the sea-wall in the middle of the day. Greymuzzle went into the village one night searching the.gardens for food. She found the duckhouse under the chestnut tree in the farmyard above the bridge, and although she sought an entrance for more than an hour, she found none. The smell of the ducks was painful.

A fox slunk near her, passing with drooping brush and ears laid back, pad, pad, pad, in the snow.

Unable to get the ducks, she walked down the frozen pill to the estuary, meeting Tarka at the pillmouth, near the salmon-fishers' hut built on the shillet slope of the sea-wall. The fox followed her, hoping to get another meal of salmon. He followed her until the dawn, and was near her at sunrise, when she returned to the couch in the reeds of the duckpond. She winded him and ran him, and although he was chased by the marshman's dog when she had left off pursuit, the fox returned, knowing that she had young somewhere in the reeds. His name was Fang-over-lip, and he had wandered far in his hunger.

While the pallor of the day was fading off the snow a skein of great white birds, flying with arched wings and long stretched necks, appeared with a measured beat of pinions from the north and west. *Hompa, hompa, hompa,* high in the cold air. Greymuzzle and Tarka were eating seaweed and shellfish on the Shar-shook, but when the swans splashed into the estuary, they slipped into the tideway and drifted with the flow to where the wild swans were floating. Fang-over-lip licked out some of the mussel-shells they had dived for, and cracked up a crab's claws, before following along the beach.

The beams of the lighthouse spread like the wings of a starfly above the level and sombre sands. Across the dark ridge of the Sharshook a crooked line of lamps winked below the hill. In one of the taverns a sailor was singing a shanty, the tune of which came distinctly over the Pool. The swans moved up with the tide, the otters after them. They were thin and weak; for mussels, winkles, and sometimes a sour green crab were poor nourishment for an otter who, in careless times, had eaten a three-pound sea-trout at a sitting and been hungry two hours afterwards.

The tide beyond the tail of the Sharshook was divided by a string of froth made by the leap and chop of waters beginning to move north and south, along the arms of the sea stretching to the Two Rivers. The swans turned north, borne by the tide racing past Crow Island. They paddled out of the main flow and turning head to tide, began to feed in the shallow over a sandbank. The otters drifted nearer, only their wide nostrils above water. When they were ten yards away from the nearest swan the nostrils sank, and chains of bubbles rose unseen above them. A swan saw a dark form under the water, but before it could lift out its head, Tarka had bitten on to its neck. Heavily its wings beat the water. Every curlew on the sandbank cried in a long uprising whistle, *cu-u-urleek, cur-r-r-leek*, and the alarm flew up and down the estuary as fast as sound travelled. The treble whistle of the redshank was piped from shore to shore, the ring plover sped over the water, turning and wheeling as one bird. Old Nog cried *Kra-r-rk!* Wind from the swan's wings scalloped the water and scattered the spray, and one struck Tarka a blow that made him float slowly away. But Greymuzzle hung to the swan's foot, even when her rudder was nearly out of the water as she was dragged along. The swan trumpeted afar its anger and fear. Bubu the Terrible flew towards the sound.

Before the Arctic Owl arrived Tarka was un-dazed and swimming to help his mate. Seeing and hearing the struggle, Bubu stretched his toes, opened his beak, and gave a loud and terrifying hoot; but when he reached the conflict, fanning above like a shade of chaos, there was nothing to see save only feathers and bubbles. Silent as snow and fog, staring like the Northern Lights, taloned like black frost, the Arctic Owl flew over the Sharshook and dropped upon Fang-over-lip, but the snarl and the snap of teeth drove him up again.

Across the pull of the tide, among the grating ice-floes, the otters took the swan, whose flappings were getting feeble as the death-fear grew less. Tarka had bitten the artery in the neck. When the otters rested, the bird lay quiet on the water. It heard the wings of its brethren beating out the flying song of swans, *Hompa, hompa, hompa,* high and remote in the night. It flapped thrice and died.

Tarka and Greymuzzle swam with the swan to the shore, where. they bit into the throat and closed their eyes as they drank its hot blood. Soon mouthfuls of feathers were being torn away, but before they could eat its flesh Fang-over-lip crept upon them. He, too, was famished, having eaten only a mouse that night – and that small biter of willow bark was but fur and bone. With the boldness of starvation the fox rushed upon them. The snarling brought a boar badger, who had been digging for the roots of sea-beet in the crevices of the stones of the sea-wall. The boar lumbered down the slope, over the seaweed, and across the shingle to where Fang-over-lip, with fluffed-out brush and humped back, was threatening the otters. The badger, who was called Bloody Bill Brock, by certain badger-digging publicans, had never before been so hungry. For two days the walls of his belly had been flat. He had no fear of any animal. The otters bit his hide, but could not hurt him, as under the long grey tapered hairs his skin was nearly half an inch thick. Pushing them away and grunting he seized the swan in his paws and dragged it away. He dropped it again to bite Greymuzzle; and then he stood absolutely still, except for his nose. Fang-over-lip did not move, nor did Greymuzzle, nor Tarka. Their heads were turned towards the cottage looming white on the sea-wall. A door had opened and closed.

The marshman had with him two bob-tailed cattle dogs, which rushed on to the shingle. They found a circle of feathers. Downwind the wave-worn shells tinkled as though a wind had risen off the sea and was running over the beach towards the tarred wooden hospital ship. This was the sound of the fox's departure. Bloody Bill Brock was slower and clumsier, and his black bear-claws slipped on the boulders of the sea-wall's apron. Tarka and Greymuzzle were lying in three feet of water, with only their ears and nostrils showing. They heard the pursuit of the badger, and some moments later the hoarse voice of a man. One dog yelped, two dogs yelped, and both returned to their master on three legs, while the thick-skinned badger continued his way with the swan on four sound legs.

Some hours later all of the swan, except the larger bones, feet, wings, and bill, was inside Bloody Bill Brock, who was snoring inside a sandy rabbit-bury where he slept for three days and nights.

Greymuzzle returned to the duck pond with only seaweed and shellfish to nourish herself and her cub. Unsteadily it dragged its little body towards her, and opened its mouth to greet her. No sound came from its mouth. Its legs trembled and could not carry its head, which hung over the couch of reeds. Its paws were frost-bitten, its eye-sockets empty. Greymuzzle stared at it, before lying down and giving the shelter of her body. She spoke to it and took it in her paws and licked its face, which was her only way of telling her love. The cub tottered away, and sought the milk which it could not find. Afterwards it slept, until she left again to seek food in the wide daylight, following the slot of deer across the snow. The hind, which had come down from the high ground with a herd and wandered away with her calf that had been with her since its birth the previous May, caught the scent 'of the otter and ran away, the calf beside her. The otter followed, but turned away when she saw a small bird crouching on the snow, unable to fly further. She ate the fire-crested wren – a thimbleful of skin, bone, and feather. After a vain prowl round the garden of the marshman, she returned to the duckpond, crossing the pill three hundred yards below the place where men were breaking up, for firewood, the hulk of an old dismantled ketch. In the field she picked up the skull of a sheep and carried it a few yards before dropping it. She had picked it up and dropped it many times already.

The ice-talons set harder in the land. No twitter of finch or linnet was heard on the Burrows, for those which remained were dead. Vainly the linnets had sought the seeds locked in the plants of the glasswort. Even crows died of starvation. The only noises in the frore air were of saws and axes and hammers, men's voices, the glassy sweep of wind in the blackened thistles, the cries of lambs and ewes, ravens' croaking, and the dull mumble of breakers on the bar.

Every day on the Burrows was a period of silence under a vapour-ringed sun that slid into night glowing and quivering with the zones and pillars of the Northern Lights. More wild red deer from Exmoor strayed to the Great Field, which even the rats had quitted. The deer walked into the gardens of the village, some to be shot stealthily, others to sleep into death. The shepherd of the marsh-grazing stumped at night round his fire, clad in the skins of sheep, and swinging his arms. Beyond the straw-and-sack-stuffed hurdles, foxes, badgers, and stoats slunk and prowled and fought for each other's bodies. Over the lambs in the fold flew Kronk the raven, black and croaking in the moonlight. *Ck!* cried Old Nog, tottering to the Sharshook from the sandhills, where he hid shivering during the time of high-tides. The wind whined in the skeleton of his mate broken at the knees, near the skull of Marland Jimmy gaping at the crown, eyeless and showing its teeth in ice.

When two foxes and a badger had been shot, Greymuzzle went no more where ewes pared hollow the frozen turnips and suckled peacefully their tail-wriggling lambs. One night, raving with hunger, she returned to the wooden duckshed in the farmyard by the railway station. High over the shed rose the chestnut tree, black and bare and suffering, with one of its boughs splitten by frost. Other creatures had been to the duckhouse before her.

Fang-over-lip had started to dig a hole under the rotten floorboards, but returning the night after, he had smelt that during the day the hole had been deepened and a gin tilled there to catch him by the paw. When he had gone, Bloody Bill Brock had grunted to the duckshed and, putting head between paws, had rolled on the metal tongue holding the jaws apart. The gin had clacked harmlessly against his grey hairs. The badger had scratched farther down and up again, reaching the floorboards by daylight; and departed, to return in the next darkness and to see a gin lying there with jaws as wide as his back – a gin unhidden and daring him, as it were, to roll across it. The gin's rusty jaws were open in an iron leer, its tongue sweated the scent of man's hand. Bloody Bill Brock, who had sprung many gins in his life, grunted and went away.

There were no stars that night, for clouds lowered in the sky. As Greymuzzle walked on the ice upstream, snow began to fall in flakes like the breast-feathers of swans. From the estuary the scrambling cries of thousands of gulls, which had returned with the south-west wind, came indistinctly through the thick and misty air. The South was invading the North, and a gentle wind was its herald. The dreadful hoot of Bubu was heard no more, for the Arctic Owl had already left the Burrows.

Greymuzzle walked under the bridge, and smelling the ducks, climbed up the bank. As she was walking past the beehives, she heard a sound that made her stop and gasp – the *ic-clack!* of a sprung gin. Tarka was rolling and twisting and jerking the heavy gin and chain off the ground. It held him. He lay still, his heart throbbing, blowing and tissing and slavering. The sight closed Greymuzzle's nostrils, so that she breathed through her open mouth. She called to him. The gin clanked, the chain clicked. She ran round him until

Tarka's leaps, that wrenched the sinews of his leg, ceased in weakness, and he sank across the long rusty spring, blowing bubbles of blood out of his nostrils. A duck quacked loudly, and when its strident alarm was finished, the air held only the slight sounds of snow-flakes sinking on the roof of the shed. They floated to rest on Tarka's fur, gently, and shrunk into drops of water. The chestnut tree suddenly groaned, and the corpse of a sparrow frozen for weeks to one of its twigs fell to earth. It dropped beside Greymuzzle and was flicked against the duckshed by a swish of her rudder as she stood over Tarka, gnawing in a fury the iron jaws of the gin.

Far away in the estuary gulls were running on the sandbanks through the yellow froth of wavelet-lap. Their jubilant and sustained cries told the winter's end. Under the tree Greymuzzle rasped the bone of the trapped paw with the sharp stumps of her broken teeth. A rat passed near, brought by the smell of blood; it fled when it saw whose blood was wasting. Grey-muzzle's face was torn, but Tarka did not know that he had bitten her.

She bit through the sinews, which were strong and thick, and Tarka was free. He rushed to the river. Greymuzzle remained, remembering her cub.

When the ducks heard the gnawing of wood, they began to run round inside the shed, quacking continu-ously. In the farmyard a dog in its kennel was barking loudly. There was an answering shout in the house that set the animal jumping against its chain. Both Greymuzzle and Tarka knew the sequence of barking dog and the shout of a man in a house! Greymuzzle stayed until the farm door opened, and then she ran away, splinters of wood in her bleeding mouth.

When the farmer came to the shed with his gun and lantern, he found his gin sprung and three toes of a paw lying in a red spatter about it. Seeing dots of blood leading away over the snow, he hurried to the cottage of one of his labourers and knocked on the door. He shouted, 'I've got'n,' as his father had shouted in the church door during a sermon half a century before, calling the men to leave and pursue the tracks of a fox through the snow.

The labourer and his two sons put on their boots warming on the slate hearth, and went out to the farmer. Armed with a dung-fork, the handle of a pick-axe, a ferreting crowbar, and the gun, they set out on the trail of the wounded otter. The lantern showed the red dots leading over the railway crossing, and on the snow by the station yard. 'Come on, you,' cried the farmer to three men going home after the closing of the inn. It was ten o'clock. One had a staff, and the others kicked up what stones they could see.

The collie dog found the otters for them, in a shed where Tarka had crawled for a refuge. Tarka stood back in a corner on a heap of artificial manure sacks, while Greymuzzle ran at the dog, tissing, and snapping her broken teeth. The lantern light made of her eyes two tawny orbs of menace. Tarka found a hole in the wall, while Greymuzzle fought the collie. Weakened by starvation, she was not able to fight for long, and as the farmer said afterwards, it was not even necessary to waste a cartridge, when a dung-fork could pin her down and a ferreting bar break her head.

They carried the body back to the farm, where the farmer drew a pint of ale for each of his helpers from the XXXX barrel in the cellar. While they were drinking 'Best respects, Varmer,' the collie dog began to bark, and as it would not stop after several cries of 'Shut that rattle, you,' the farmer went out and gave it a kick in the ribs. The collie yelped and went to kennel, but hardly had the farmer gone into his kitchen again when it set up a furious barking. It was banged on the head with the stag's horn handle of a hunting whip, but even this did not check its desire to tell its master that an enemy was in the yard. It kept up an intermittent barking until the dawn, when it was flogged with its head wedged in the door. The farmer was a poor man and not very strong and a sleepless night made him irritable. When he felt better he gave the dog the skinned carcass of the otter, and praised its courage and virtue in the Railway Inn, telling how it had warned him and how it had tracked the 'girt mousey-coloured fitches' to the shed, where one escaped through a hole behind the sacks. He forbore to say how noisy his dog had been afterwards, deeming this a point not in its favour, for how was he, his natural senses dulled by civilization, to have known that an otter had remained all night in the farmyard, waiting for the mate that never came?

Tarka was gone in the mist and rain of the day, to

hide among the reeds of the marsh pond – the sere and icicled reeds, which now could sink to their ancestral ooze and sleep, perchance to dream of sun-stored summers raising the green stems, of wind-shaken anthers dropping gold pollen over June's young maces, of seeds shaped and clasped and taught by the brown autumn mother. The south wind was breaking from the great roots the talons of the Icicle Spirit, and freeing ten thousand flying seeds in each brown head.

Water covered the pond ice, deep enough to sail a feather, and at night every hoof-hole held its star.

After seven sunrisings the mosses were green on the hillocks, lapwings tumbled and dived and cried their sweet mating cries, the first flower bloomed in the Burrows – the lowly vernal whitlow grass, with its tiny white petals on a single leafless stalk. Under the noon sun sheep grazing in the marsh had silver outlines. Linnets sat on the lighthouse telegraph wire, wing to wing, and talking to the sky. Out of the auburn breasts fell ravishing notes, like glowing strokes of colour in the warm south wind.

And when the shining twitter ceased, I walked to the pond, and again I sought among the reeds, in vain; and to the pill I went, over the guts in the salt grey turf, to the trickling mud where the linnets were fluttering at the seeds of the glasswort. There I spurred an otter, but the tracks were old with tides, and worm castings sat in many. Every fourth seal was marred, with two toes set deeper in the mud. They led down to the lap of the low water, where the sea washed them away.

The Last Year

*B*ogs and hummocks of the Great Kneeset were dimmed and occluded; the hill was higher than the clouds. In drifts and hollows of silence the vapour passed, moving with the muffled wind over water plashes colourless in reflection. Sometimes a colder waft brought the sound of slow trickling; here in the fen five rivers* began, in peat darker than the otter which had followed the Torridge to its source.

Broken humps, rounded with grey moss and standing out of a maze of channers, made the southern crest of

*Taw, Tavy, Teign, Torridge, Dart.

the hill. In the main channer, below banks of crumbling peat, lay water dark-stained and almost stagnant. The otter walked out and lifted his head, sniffing and looking around him. Drops from his rudder dripped into the water and the stirred fragments of peat drifted slowly as they settled. The river's life began without sound, in darkness of peat that was heather grown in ancient sunlight; but on the slope of the hill, among the green rushes, the river ran bright in spirit, finding the granite that made its first song.

Tarka climbed up one of the humps of grey club moss and trod in its centre a bed soft and warm, yet cool for the paw thrust among the long, tight-growing fronds. The moss grew on and over a bush of heather, whose springy stems yielded to his curled body. He had travelled from the estuary, sleeping by day in riverside holts and marches and feeding at night; remembering nothing, because the moor was unfamiliar to his nose and ears and eyes. When his paw ached, he licked it. It had been a happy journey up the river swollen with snow water, hunting fish and playing with sticks and stones, while mating owls called through the darkness of valleys.

He slept curled in the moss until the last sun-whitened wisps of clouds trailed away into space above the northern slope of the hill, and the plashes took light and colour. The sun awoke him and he heard the twit of a bird – a little drab pipit alone in the fen with the otter. It watched anxiously as the otter warmed the dingy, yellow-white fur of his belly in the sun and rolled to scratch his ears with a sprig of heather. The pipit had seen no enemy like Tarka before, and when the rolling otter fell off his bed and splashed into the water below, the bird flew out of the heather in straight upward flight, twittering as it dropped, fluttering wings that seemed too feeble to carry it higher than its first weak ascent. Up it mounted, to fall back again, until it turned with the wind and slanted down quickly into the heather. Again the wilderness was left to wandering air and water, until webbed feet began to patter in the black soft peat, past wan yellow tussocks of withered grasses, and clumps of rushes dying downwards from their brown tips.

Running in the plashes, treading the spider-like tufts of red-rusty cotton grass, he came to a deeper and wider channer fringed with rushes. Down a crumbling sog of peat and into the still brown-clear water. He swam its winding length, seeking eels under the ooze which arose behind him in a swirl of heath fragments, dark and up-scattered by the kicks of his hindlegs. A minute's swimming and the channer widened into a shallow pit above whose broken banks the heather grew, on sprigs dispread and blasted under the sky. Some still bore the bells of old summer, that made a fine sibilance in the wry wind-music of the moor.

Tarka ran past a heap of turves, set around the base of a post marking Cranmere tarn, now empty, whither his ancestors had wandered for thousands of years. A fox had been walking there during the night, seeking the oval black beetles which, with the moths, pipits, wheatears, and sometimes a snipe, were the only food in and around the fen. As Tarka ran out of the tarn a bird passed swiftly over his head gliding on down-curving dark wings and crying *go-beck, go-beck, go-beck!* when it saw him – one of the few grouse which lived and bred on the lower slopes under the wind. The bird had flown from a hut circle to the south, where seeds of gromwell were to be found. The gromwell had grown from a single seed carried from the lower tilled slopes of the moor on the fleece of a sheep, to which it had hooked itself. Gromwell seeds were the favourite food of the grouse around the source of the Two Rivers.

Tarka watched the bird until it glided below the hill, when he ran on again, finding nothing in the plashes moving only with images of sky and clouds and birds of solitude. Then the sun took the water, breaking brilliant and hot in every plash; the otter galloped with instant joy and sank in a bog to his belly. He dragged himself on to a tussock of grass, rolled, shook himself, and set off again, roaming around the fen until he heard again the cry of running water. The cry came out of a hollow, whose sides were scarred by the sliding of broken hummocks – the faint cry of a river new-born. Through a winding channel in the turf, no wider than the otter and hidden by grasses growing over it, the little thread hastened, seeking its valley to the sea.

It fell over its first cascade and cast its first bubbles; and through a groove between hills it found a marsh where a green moss grew with rushes. Beyond the marsh it ran strong and bright over its bed of granite gravel, everywhere glinting and singing. Over and under and past boulders of granite, splashing upon mosses, whose browny-red seeds on the tall stalks were like bitterns standing with beaks upheld. Lichens grew on other boulders: silver with black undersides, and curled like strange pelts curing: grey-green in the shapes of trees and plants: bones with scarlet knuckles: horns of moose: shells and seaweeds. The lichens fastened to the granite were as the fantastic and brittle miniatures of strange and forgotten things of the moor.

By pools and waterfalls and rillets the river Taw grew, flowing under steep hills that towered high above. It washed the roots of its first tree, a willow thin and sparse of bloom, a soft tree wildered in that place of rocks and rain and harsh grey harrying winds. A black-faced sheep stood by the tree, cropping the sweet grass; and when a strange, small, flashing, frightening head looked out just below its feet, the sheep stamped, bounded away up the hill to its lamb asleep by a sun-hot boulder. Tarka had caught a trout, the first in a mile of river; he ate it, drank, and slipped away with the water.

He caught sixteen fish in an hour, the biggest being three ounces in weight; and then he climbed upon a slab of granite and dozed in the sunlight. High above him a small bird was flying in sharp, irregular flight, mounting high to swoop towards the marsh. Every time it swooped it opened its tail against the rush of air, so that the feathers made a sound between the bleat of a kid and a dove's cooing. Its mate was flying near it. They were snipes, who had chosen for nesting-place a rush-clump in the marsh, and Tarka had disturbed them. He lay still in sleep, and they forgot that he was there, and flew down to find worms by pushing their long bills into the juggymire. When the sun sank behind the high tors, Tarka awoke and went down with the river. A small bullock, with long, black, shaggy hair, was drinking by a gravelly ford, and smelling the otter, it snorted and plunged away, alarming the grazing herd.

At night the stars were shorn of their flashes and burning dully through the cold vapour which drifted down from the hills. Everything was moistened – sprigs and faded bells of heather, young ruddy shoots of whortleberry, mosses, lichens, grasses, rushes, boulders, trees. The day rose grey and silent. When the sun, like an immense dandelion, looked over the light-smitten height of Cosdon Beacon, Tarka was returning along a lynch, or rough trackway, to the river. The grasses, the heather, the lichens, the whortleberry bushes, the mosses, the boulders – everything in front of the otter vanished as though drowned or dissolved in a luminous strange sea. The icy casings of leaves and grasses and blades and sprigs were glowing and hid in a mist of sun-fire. Moor-folk call this morning glory the Ammil.

The brimming light gladdened Tarka, and he rolled for several minutes, playing with a shining ball he found in the grass – the old dropping of a wild pony. Afterwards, running down to the water, he found a holt under a rock. It was cold and wet inside, and Tarka always slept dry when he could. He ran out again, liking the sun, and settled on a flat rock in the warming rays.

The rock was embedded below a fall, its lower part green with mosses hanging in the splashes. The mosses dropped and glistened. Tarka washed himself, the water-sounds unheard; he would have heard silence if the river had dried suddenly. The green weeds waved in the clear water with a calmer motion than the tail-fanning of idle fish. And then a sturdy, dark brown bird, with white throat and breast, lit on a stone down the stream, and pausing a moment, jumped down into the water. The dipper walked on the river-bed, seeking beetles and shrimps and caddisgrubs. When its beak was crammed, it walked out of a shallow, flew up in a coloured rain of drops, and following the turns of the river, checked fluttering by the rock whereon Tarka lay. It thrust its beak into the moss, six inches above the tumbling water. Rapid notes, as of water-and-stones sharpened to music in a singing bird's throat-strings, came out of the moss, a greeting by the dipper's mate, who was brooding on five white eggs in her wet nest. When she had swallowed the food, the water-ouzel flew away upstream, low over the water, following the bends of the river. As he flew he sang, sipping his song from the stones and the water.

The shadows moved, and the bright green weeds of

morning waved darkly in the river. Many times the water-ouzels flew to and from the nest; they did not see the otter which slept so still in the rocky cup above them.

Tarka gave chase to a rabbit during the next night, bolting it from a hillside clitter of rocks in a hollow at the head of a cleave. Near the clitter a tall stone reared head, shoulders, and body above the rocks embedded there, in the outline of a sea-lion, smooth and curved. The rabbit ran as far as a hole in the north-western base of the stone sea-lion, but turned back in terror as it smelt the dreaded smell of a fitch, or stoat. The rabbit's wits went from it in a thin squealing; its will to run away was gripped in the base of its spine by a feeling of sickly fascination. Its squeals caused an excited chakker-ing near it, and almost immediately the fitch had it by the side of the neck, and was dragging it into the hole. The fitch, whose name was Swagdagger, was about to kill it when Tarka ran through the opening. Swag-dagger loosened his bite to threaten the strange big invader, flicking his black-tipped tail and glaring at Tarka. One kick of the rabbit's hindlegs, so powerful for running, would have broken Swagdagger's neck; but it crouched still, its nervous force oozing away. Tarka ran at it. Swagdagger faced him with an angry chakker, and was nipped in the shoulder. The fitch ran out through the opening, but turned outside and gibbered in fury. Tarka looked once at the green points that were the fitch's eyes, and went on with his work. Swagdagger went away, to climb a granite stone, and chakker into the night. The moon was rising, dim in the mist, and the harsh notes echoed about the grey stillness of the granite clitter. *Kah-h' kak-kak*, he rattled, throwing his call one way, then another. He was summoning the stoats of Belstone Cleave.

Tarka had eaten half the rabbit when a strong scent made him look round again. He saw in the low opening several greenish dots, that stared and swung about and stared again. He went on eating. Delicate sniffs, sudden rustles and paddings, scratchings, a quick sneeze – he peered for another way out, wanting to be alone. He found a crack and explored it with his nose, before beginning to scrape. He sucked in the scent of fitch, for Swagdagger's mate had her nest of young beyond the crack.

She had been hunting a rabbit three hundred yards away when Swagdagger had climbed the stone, and as soon as she heard the call, she galloped back. Other fitches had run to the summons of Swagdagger. Sharp-toothed, bloodthirsty, and without fear they ran up and down by the opening, sniffing the delicious scent of fresh-slain rabbit, weaving quick bodies and lifting their small heads to sniff, sniff, sniff. The noises of teeth at work made a furious stir in the assembling tribe. The older dog-fitch yakkered with rage, as he wove in and out of the swift and impatient throng.

The little angry fitches in the cranny, beyond the nose of Tarka, heard the cry of their mother and spat at the enemy – all moving things unknown were enemies to the little fitches. She ran through the fitches outside in the moonlight and into the cave, jumping in her twisty way for a bite behind the otter's ear. Tarka shook her and tried to kill her, but she ran at him again, and with her ran Swagdagger and all the fitches who had come at his alarm. Tarka trod on stoats; he was pricked all over by the teeth of stoats; he chopped one through the ribs and back, but its biting did not cease; he chopped it again, trying to hold it by his fore-paws, but though broken, it was alive and angry, and bit through the skin of his throat and hung there, as long as his rudder. He pushed through fitches into the moonlight, and the fitches followed him, including the four young ones who were excited and eager for play. The pack chased him, throwing their sharp tongues, all the rugged way down to the river, into which Tarka jumped with a splash. Three of them fell in after him, but they did not like the water and crawled out spitting and sneezing, tough and lithe and sinuous as bines of honeysuckle. Unable to find the otter, the dog-fitches started a fight among themselves.

As Swagdagger's mate went up the hill again with her young running behind her, she met a badger, who was going to drink in the river. The grey waddler, animate granite, whose head was heavier than her whole body, lumbered out of the way. He sought no unnecessary trouble with fitches, and he had eaten up the rabbit under the Seal Stone.

The river hurried round the base of the cleave, on whose slopes stunted trees grew, amid rocks, and scree that in falling had smashed the trunks and torn out the roots of willows, thorns, and hollies. It wandered away from the moor, a proper river, with bridges, brooks, islands, and mills.

Soon the oaks above the river would break into leaf. Magpies had topped their nests with thorns, and buzzards were soaring long after owl-light. Kingfishers and dippers had hatched their eggs – there was a dipper's nest, hanging dishevelled like a beard of moss, under nearly every stone bridge spanning the river. The innocent white flowers of the savage blackthorn had withered brown and shaken into the wind. Lent lilies – the wild daffodils of the woods and meads – clasped with their blooms, shrivelled and loving, the seeds of winter's hope. Already the celandines were old thoughts of the spring, their leaves hid by rising docks and nettles and flowering dog's-foot mercury. Badger cubs had been taught to use the latrines outside the tunnels. It was mid-April, swallow-time in the West Country. Otter cubs romped in a big stick-heap resting on the nose of an island above a bridge, eager to play with the moon on the water. Their mother, who was Tarka's sister, attacked him when he looked on them in the stick-heap, and bit him in the shoulder, for she was most anxious, and did not remember her brother cub.

Though the birds scolded, the foxes snarled, and his own kind drove him away, Tarka had many friends, whom he played with and forgot – sticks, stones, water-weeds, slain fish, and once an empty cocoa-tin, a bright and curious thing that talked strangely as it moved over the shallows, but sank into the pool beyond, sent up three bubbles, and would play no more.

CHAPTER 12

*A*t sunset, as he was crossing a shoal to deep water under an old ash tree, he stopped at the taint of hounds lying on the scour pitted by their feet. Quietly he turned back to the water to swim sunken in the current, rising only to take in air. Round two bends he drifted, then landed and hearkened. Ran up the bank, uncertain. Rose on hindfeet, dripping and anxious. A dwarf owl making a peacock-like yowling in the woods beyond the meadow, the squeak of mice, the dry cough of an ewe. He ran back to the river, after eating fish, he played with a rope of water twisting and untwisting out of a drain, trying to catch it between his paws and bite it as it plattered on his face and chest.

An otter-path lay across the next bend, and he followed it to the middle of the field, where he hesitated. Strange smells lay in the dew. He scraped at a place in the grass where paper had been rammed by a pole, near orange peel covered by a loose tuft. He walked on, nose to ground, and smelt man, where hob-nailed boots had pressed the turf and crushed cigarette-ends. He turned back, and would have gone straight to water if he had not heard the cry of a bitch otter at the far end of the path. *Hu-ee-ee-ic!* he answered, and ran along to find her. Near the middle of the meadow he stopped as though he had trod on a gin. The taint of hounds lay thick with the scent of otter. Grasses were smeared with blood and spittle. His hair rose on his back. He blew through open mouth, swung his head about as though looking for hounds, and was gone, silent as his low moon shadow.

The river flowed darkly to the bend, where it broke shallow over shillets that scattered the moonlight. Tarka saw a movement at the tail of the shoal, where an otter was listening. She ran to him and licked his face, then she mewed, and ran on alone by the riverside. Tarka followed her. She was draggled and miserable. She caught a trout and called him, but when he reached her she yikkered and started to eat it herself. She mewed again, and ran into the water. And following her, Tarka returned to the scour opposite the ash-tree holt where that morning the hounds had plunged and bayed. All the way upstream she had been calling, and searching under banks, and on the beds of pools. At length she crawled on the scour with something in her mouth, and dropped it on the stones. She licked it from head to tail, and mewing again, sank back into the water and returned with another, which she laid with the first-found. Perhaps she could not count beyond two; perhaps White-tip had not known in her terror how many cubs she had dropped in the water, when the terrier had driven her out of her holt. The Master had seen them, sinking in the pool, lit by a sun-shaft; and hounds were whipped off. They drew on up the river, and found the dog-otter, her mate, and killed him three hours later as he tried to cross a meadow to the wooded hillside.

The old dog and White-tip had wandered together since Tarka had been driven from her in the autumn. Her first litter had been born in January, when the river had frozen, and one day White-tip, returning to the holt, had found them gone. She had called them, seeking everywhere, and in pain, but she had found none to suckle, for a badger walking on the ice had dug them out with his long black claws and eaten them. White-tip's grief had been so keen that soon it had grown less; and she had lain with her mate in the bracken of Ferny Hill.

And now White-tip was grieving again. For two nights, as she travelled down the river with Tarka, she would cease hunting, and run aimlessly on the banks, whining and searching. During the third night she left him and returned to the ash-tree holt, wherein she had been making ready a couch of reeds and grasses. Into the holt she carried a stone, laying it on the couch, and licking it, until a sudden cry called her outside again. She traced the cry to a stone on the shallow, and brought it in her mouth to the holt; soon the couch was filled with wet stones.

Tarka travelled on alone. As the river grew older, so the meadows and cornfields beyond its banks stretched a wider green over the age-long silt filling the valley's groin. Foxgloves claimed the hillsides wherever the oakwoods were felled, storing in their leaves the green power to raise red-purple spires to the midsummer sky. Seen by day from the hilltops, the river lay in its course like a viper broken by a buzzard's beak and claws, marked with brown on its twisted and bluish-white coils. Twin burnished lines were set by the river, touching its banks, straitly leaving it to its windings, and crossing it on stone bridges topped by tarred iron girders. Under the girders jackdaws were building their nests of sticks and sheep's wool and paper picked up in the early morning from cottage gardens. The rolling thunder over their heads did not disturb them, for, like the otters, they had grown to the noise of trains in the valley.

Below one bridge the river slowed into a wide pool, where the waters of a smaller south-flowing river meditated before turning north with big brother Taw. Tarka was cruising over the bed of the Junction Pool when the moon, shaking and distorted by eddies above, was cut by dark and narrow slips. A down-strike of his strong rudder and a push off a rock by his hindlegs swung him up for the chase of shoaling fish. They darted away in a zigzag, turning together, up and down and across the pool. Tarka pursued one until he caught it, but as he was swimming to the bank he saw another, and followed it with the fish in his mouth. He snicked it as it darted back past his shoulder. Strokes of the heavy tapering rudder over two inches wide at its base and thirteen inches long, that could stun a fish by its blow, enabled him to turn his body in water almost as quickly as on land.

He shook the fish out of his mouth as soon as he had killed them, for now he was hunting for sport. The dace glinted about the water, the slayer often leaping after a fish that threw itself into the air and jumped as it hit water again. A stain began to move in the water, and a plaice flapped off the bottom and swam in what it thought was the beginning of a flood, when worms came swirling into the Junction Pool. This sea-fish had lived a strange and lonely life in fresh water ever since it had been swallowed in the estuary by a heron and ejected alive from the crop a quarter of an hour afterwards when the bird, flying up the valley, had been shot by a water-bailiff.

The shape of an otter loomed in the water, and the plaice swam down again in a rapid, waving slant, perceived by a one-eyed eel that was lying with its tail inside a bullock's skull wedged in a cleft of rock. Thrust through the eel's blank eye-socket was the rusty barbed point of a hook, the shank of which stuck out of its mouth – a hook almost straightened before the line had broken. Tarka swam up behind the eel on his blind side, and opened his mouth side to bite across the back.

The eel was longer than Tarka. It lashed its tail round his neck and bit on to his nose, then gripped below the paired fins. Bubbles were blown in two strings, one of them fine as charlock seeds, for the hook-shank was rammed up the otter's left nostril. Then the strings ceased, and stray bubbles arose, for the eel was throttling the otter. Tarka clawed it with his paws, but the small claws were worn by many weeks' scratching for trout in granite hides, and the eel's skin was slippery. Flattened on the pool's bed, the plaice watched the struggle of its two enemies.

Tarka knocked it with his paws, and scraped himself against stones and rocks, so that he could be free to swim up and eat it. For three minutes until his breath was gone, he tried to shake off the eel. Then he kicked heavily and slowly up to the surface and tried to climb out by the nearest land – a sheer bank. Its head in the air, the eel lifted its bite on the otter's bleeding nose and sank away down. Immediately Tarka sprang half out of the water and with a *plop!* like a round stone went after it, catching it below the vent. The eel lashed again, and Tarka unbit. He swam under and bit it at the back of the neck, and again released it. The eel tried to wobble down to the bullock's skull, but Tarka dragged it back; and so he played with it, always avoiding the bite of its big jaws. At length it grew feeble, and he took it to a shallow, where, after walking round it, and pretending it was not there, he ate what he wanted of the tail-end.

When he had washed his face he went back into the pool, harrying the dace until many score of the silvery fishes floated away on their sides. He harried them until the moon sank under the hill and he grew tired of his sport. Then spreading his legs, he drifted away out of the pool, past an island that divided the river – a narrow island, shaped like an otter, with a rudder of mud carved at its lower end by the swift waters. Alders and willows grew on the island, many broken by uprooted trees lugged down by floods.

Two hours later Tarka was hungry again, and eating a two-pound trout, fat with easy feeding on mully-heads, taken under the third railway bridge after the Junction Pool. Below the bridge, on the right bank, the river passed part of its old course, now dry save for green-scummed pools, left by March risings, among the shillets. The law of life was also the law of water – everlasting change. It had carved this deserted bed through the centuries, raised it with shillets, and turned away to a newer course. Brambles, thorns, elderberry bushes, nettles, and briars grew entangled along the silent waterway. It was the haunt of grass snakes, frogs, mice, and a wild sandy ram-cat without front paws. For the first three years of his life the cat had been lean, feeding on rats in and around a corn-mill and answering to the name of Shaggery. During its fourth year it had gone wild in the woods and grown fat on rabbits, until caught in a gin. It limped back to the mill and became tame again, but when the pad had rotted away and the stump had healed, it had lain rough in the woods. It was caught a second time, losing its other paw. For two years it had lived in the old river-bed, prowling forth at night and living on frogs, mice, beetles, and carrion fish left by otters on the banks and shoals. It moved by bounding hops from its hindlegs, like a rabbit. Its claws had drawn up above the ends of the short stumps, useful for a hugging hold on its prey, but a hindrance in washing its face. Sometimes otter-hounds, tearing their way through the undergrowth, had owned the scent of this cat, whose hiding-place was in a deep rabbit-bury under a thorn brake.

Tarka ran over its scent, and followed it along the old river-bed. The cat was sitting on a boulder, from which it had been watching a vole-run below. Tarka stopped, surprised as the cat. Shaggery's ears flattened, its body increased into a loop of agitated fur, and it let out such a waul that Tarka's back began to twitch. The cry was loud, and slowly champed through teeth. It sank to a low grinding threat when Tarka stood up to sniff what was wauling at him. He steadied himself by touching the stone on which it stood and the ram-cat made a noise like one Tarka had heard before, when a pailful of hot embers had been shot over the village quay by the estuary. He fled remembering a burn. Alone again, the ram-cat lowered body on stumps, and lifted ears to listen for voles.

When the next night White-tip followed Tarka's

trail along the dry bed, Shaggery was sitting above the bury, in an old mossy-damp magpie's nest. Again the waul and the grinding of teeth, again the spitting hiss, and again an otter hurrying back to water.

Tarka had gone under the last bridge above the tide, and the sun was rising when he crept out by a mud glidder and curled himself in a bed of green flags. Water ran clear and shallow on its rocky bed below the mud. Swallows flew to and fro over the river channel, winding deeper and broader through the meadows. All things were warmed in the sun. The grass and dock-leaves under the tide-wall were greenish grey with salt and silt dried on blade and stalk and leaf, after the sluggard tide's lapse. Seaweed, black and brittle, lay below the wall with scriddicks of old rush-tops and sticks among white flowers of scurvy-grass. The sun moved above the oakwood that sloped from the rocky bank across the river; the leaves of lower branches were blenched, and weed-hung. A hot, broken glitter, like a flight of silver birds, played lightly on the green flags where Tarka was lying. One brilliant beak of light slipped round a flag and pecked at his eye until he awoke, and yawned, and turned on his back. His nostrils lazily tested the wind that sometimes trembled the tips of the flags. It was a clean wind, and he lay content.

Three buzzards sailed over the river, one above the other, like the stars in Orion's Belt; the top bird moving with steady wings, the lower bird circling, and the lowest veering on broad vanes, cleavershaped, heavily with rolling sweeps into the lingering wind that eddied about the top of oak trees. The tree-trunks were dark; only from the high young branches had the sun struck colour, yellow and pale green.

A lustrous blue line was drawn against the dark forest of trunks as a kingfisher sped down-river. The buzzards drifted away south, their wings narrowing with a gold glister, and shrank into the sun.

Peet! The short, shrill cry came from a silver point drawing a ruddy line over the mud. With a fish in its beak the kingfisher sped up-river to its young in a sandy bank above the Mouse Hole Pool. Martins twittered along the river-bank, and hovered about the heads of bullocks, taking crisp-winged flies from their muzzles and between their horns. Tarka yawned, and dozed again.

A dark cloud arose over the crest of the oakwood, and the greenery of young leaves faded. Rain beat on the flags. A million million drops in the river leapt to meet the drops fresh-risen from the Atlantic. The cloud passed, and again the meadow was hot and bright. The swallows flew up the river, quitting at the coils its glitter and yellow kingcups, and fleeing on across the green meadow to the road by the bridge. Here, in the hollows of the broken road surface, was to be found after rain a greyish mud that set harder than the browny mud of the salty scourings in the river. Only by the bridge was this mud to be found, for the road sloped up and down over the river, and the slopes were not tarred, lest the feet of horses slip. The aerial masons were about to build their nests on the rafters of shippen and barn; they flew in pairs, singing their sun-songs.

Beside the bridge grew an elderberry tree, straight and sturdy as a young oak in a park; one of the few soft-cored elderberry trees in the country of the Two Rivers that had not grown up a cripple of the winds. Its leaves partly hid a motor-car, in whose closed body, shut away from the wind and the sun of the English spring, sat some men and women. They were awaiting hounds before moving to the parapet of the bridge, and perhaps, if a kill seemed certain and early, to the meadow over the low wooden fence. Other motor-cars stopped on the bridge. The swallows swooping over the stonework saw the sunlight browned by the smoke of engines, and dived back again over the grass. The baying of hounds above the bridge became louder, for the otter had swum through the lower stickle, and was travelling downstream.

The hunted otter was White-tip. She had been chased for nearly three hours. Always the cries and tongues and legs had followed her, up the pools and down the pools, from holt to holding, from holding to shallow.

Tally Ho!

She saw faces and waving arms above the bridge, but she did not turn back.

Light-laden drops rolled down the green flags as their points drew down the sky. Tarka lay still, watching. They rustled and broke with soft sappy noises. White-tip was pressing the bed of flags. Her mouth was open. Tarka, who had been listening for half an hour to the distant cries of men and hounds, stared at the movement. A sudden clamour ran down the river loud and startling, for Deadlock had found White-tip's deep seàls in the mud, where she had crept out of the water.

The two otters ran through the flags and slid down the mud to the river again. Tarka spread himself in the shallow flow, moving with light touches of claws just over the rocks and stones of the bed. He moved slowly, as an eel moves, as smooth as the water, and with sinuous ease. Sometimes he crept out at the edge of the mud, walked a few yards, and slipped back into the water again. Hounds were crushing the flags around his bed, and throwing their tongues along his line.

He swam through a long pool at his fastest pace, putting up his nostrils every fifty yards to breathe, and down again immediately. He left the oakwood behind him, and came to a narrow gut draining the water of a small marshy valley, where bullocks were grazing. The gut lay under trees above a rocky bank. Its other bank was mud. Seaweed hung on the roots of trees six feet above his head. Tarka walked up the gut, as far as the first channer in its glidder, partly hid by the broad strongly-keeled leaves of river sedge. He followed it into the marsh, and climbing out, ran along a path trodden by cattle, through a gate and down to a lower marsh, hidden from the opposite bank by a tide-wall. The tongue of Deadlock spoke across the river, and Tarka slipped into another gut. He trod through brown mud to a black ooze, in which he moved like an eel. The drain led under the tide-wall to the glidder above the river. It led into darkness, with light coming through the chinks of a circular wooden trap, that kept the tides back from the land. He sniffed at a chink, and waited in the ooze.

For two hours Tarka lay behind the wooden trap, while the noises of hunting moved away into remoteness. Slowly the sound of the low running river was stilled into slack water. Tricklings, the lap and slanting wash of ripple-ends, a turning drift of froth and sticks below the mud – the sea was moving up again. A heron alighted at the bottom of the muddy glidder, and stalked gravely into water to his knees. Flukes were rising off the silt, seeking food. The heron bent down and peered. He stepped forward on one foot, and speared with a swift plunge. Then he stared up the river. A thin-drawn thread of sound in the air, looped to another and another and another; loosed as four gossamers floating by in the wind. It was the recall to hounds. In the after-quiet the heron stalked to his spearing again. The murky water twirled by the knee-joints of his thin green legs. Splash, flicker, and shaken drops – he swallowed fluke after fluke; but when twenty yards beyond the trap he straightened up his neck, stood on his toes, jumped hurriedly out of the water, and flapped away, pulling up his shanks after him, and tucking his long neck and head between his shoulders. He had seen the heads of men.

Smells of the lower river, riding up with the young

tide into the Mouse Hole Pit, had overspread the wishy washy otter-scent, and the pack was being taken back to kennels. The horn-like voice of the huntsman, as he talked to hounds by name, came to the otter through the chinks of the sodden elmwood trap. They trotted on the opposite bank happy at the huntsman's heels, led home by aged Harper who had taught them all to mark an otter. Flews to flews with him was Deadlock, and at his stern, Bluemaid, old before her time, worn-out by swimming. Then came Pitiful, who worked hard and alone; whenever it was possible to go wrong, Pitiful went wrong; it was Pitiful who, when-ever they passed by the dry river-bed, led them on the trail of Shaggery the ram-cat; if a hound were missing it was always Pitiful. Near her was Captain, a black-and-tan rough dog, who looked like a lurcher; the huntsman did not take Captain to important meets, for Captain's voice was like a knife whose edge is turned. He did not throw his tongue, he screamed; and some-times in his excitement he babbled, flinging water-lies about. Bite'm the terrier hurried among them, some-times sniffing in tufts, hoping to find a rat to shake; and following Bite'm, like an easy-going, big, heavy boy led by a sharp little quick-eyed tacker, came Rufus, who cared more for a nest of field-mice than for a joint or rib of rank otter. After Rufus on the tide-wall ran Dewdrop, whose long fawn-coloured hair was curly with wet. Her ears hung long and loose.

Often while the trophies were being taken by the huntsman those ears would flap between blue-stock-

ing'd legs, and teeth would slyly nip through wool, as
though it were brown fur of the worry. By the Whar-
fedale bitch – for Dewdrop was the only true otter-
hound in the pack – ran Playboy and Actor, whose
dingy-white shapes were so alike that only the huntsman could name them truly. Behind them came
Render and Fencer, who always tore at roots of a holt
with their teeth; Hemlock, with one eye blind, the dark
pupil grey-veined with the scar of a blackthorn prick;
Hurricane, the ancient Irish staghound with the filed
canines; Barbrook and Bellman, Boisterous and Chorister, Coraline, Sailoress, Waterwitch, and Armlet, who
always stood apart from the pack during holt-marking
and bayed moodily like a lighthouse siren. Then came
Sandboy, who fought other hounds at the worry, and
Grinder and Darnell – hounds who had chased the fox.
They trotted on the side-wall between the short, quick-
stepping huntsman and the long-legged whip and
kennel-boy, whose long loose striding had been formed
in early years by crossing ploughlands on his way to
school.

Twenty paces behind the pack walked the Master
with two members of the Hunt. He was saying that it
had been a great day, only lacking a kill to complete it,
when old Harper stopped and lifted his muzzle. The air
on the water, colder than the land air, was brimming
over the sea-wall, and Harper had smelled an otter.
Deadlock moved into the air-stream, threw up his
head, whispered, and ran down the grassy bank to the
broken turf above the glidder. Sterns were waved like

feathers. Deadlock leapt into the river, followed by half the pack. Pitiful started patiently to work the waterline of the mud and Captain babbled in excitement as he lapped and swam.

The water was three feet deep. Hounds scrambled up the glidder, some slipping down, drawing long clawlines on the harder clay beneath. They whimpered and scratched before the round wooden trap, and Armlet bayed them on from the bank above. Terrier Bite'm pushed his small eager body between their flanks, under their legs, whining and yelping. Five men waded the river, testing a footway with taps of iron-shod poles before them. Thinking that the otter they had hunted for more than five hours was hiding inside, and that the tired hounds would have no chance to kill even an exhausted otter in the rising water, the pack was not withdrawn when Bite'm was taken to the open end of the drain, where Tarka's deep seals in the lower ooze showed like big blackberries crushed in the mud. Bite'm was given a pat on his ribs and gently shoved into the dark hole. He crept in, quick and shivering.

The ooze sucked at Tarka's webs as he turned away from the light-stripped lid of the drain. His heart beat as fast as waterdrops drip without dribbling. The hanging sodden door went *sug-plog-sug* as paws struck it. He looked up and down, round and up again, for a way of escape. He crawled in the ooze, away from the immense din, and saw an enemy coming towards him an instant before he smelled it. *Is-is-iz!*

They met and joined and twisted into shapes

smoothed by ooze. The terrier got a grip on the otter's rudder and hung on to it. Tarka bit and bit and bit, quick as a striking viper, in cheek, shoulder, flank, nose, and ear. Noises of bumping and squelching and snarling and tissing became louder when the trap was lifted and light showed the red and black shaking shapes. The otter's rudder near the opening was seized and pulled by a hand. Another hand gripped the terrier's scruff. The long black smooth shape was lugged out of the drain, the terrier fixed to it. Hounds were leaping and clamouring up at the men. A hand held Bite'm's tail-stump, another hand squeezed, trying to make him unclench. Tarka writhed and contorted as he hung by his rudder; his back became a bow, suddenly bending up, and his teeth made a row of holes in a hand. The jerk made his rudder slip, and he dropped among boots, to squirm between legs and away down the glidder. He pulled Bite'm with him.

Hounds trod on him, snarling and thrusting. Tarka was hidden under their heads, picked up and thrown sideways, then dropped and picked up and shaken. Eight jaws held him at one time in the midst of a deep sullen growling. He was hid in the plunging of white and brown and black bodies. He bit Deadlock through the flews, and again in the nose, as he was lifted on other muzzles, Bite'm still joined to the base of his rudder. The pack bore him down to the tide, where the worry broke up. Heads were lifted again, and tongues thrown. Hounds stooped to water; some swam after Captain, who was cutting the air with his knife-edge voice.

But Tarka was gone, and so was Bite'm. The terrier came to the surface a minute later, forty yards away, and swam inshore, spluttering and gasping, the short hairs of the otter's rudder still between his teeth.

CHAPTER 13

The tide was flooding fast in midstream. It carried
with it sunken branches that sometimes showed a
stick, and turned under again. Tarka passed them as he
swam into a riband of water returning under the steep
and broken rock-face that was the river's left bank. The
riband moved down again, feeling the roots of oak
trees, and reclaiming the seaweed hung there since the
morning ebb. The otter drifted to a root and rested his
paws upon it, breathing through his mouth. Two pink
nicks above his nose welled red immediately; so did his
paws. He bled also from rudder, back, neck, flank, and
shoulder. While he was among the hounds he had felt

neither fear nor hurt for the power of all his senses had been in movement to escape. Now his wounds smarted with the salt in the water, and he listened in a still dread for Deadlock's tongue. He lay still for a quarter of an hour.

No hound spoke. The water rose, and lifted him off the root, and carried him away. He drifted through the Mouse Hole Pit and beyond the oakwood to the deeper winding bed in the meadow, where oarweed hung dry on the lower branches of thorns, with sticks, grasses, sometimes the skeleton of a rabbit or bird. Dead brambles tangled in the thorns were swinging in the water, combing the scum of the tide. Cuckoo flowers grew above the top of the flood, their small pale gentle faces rising on tall stems from the dead stumps of trees, some broken and wilting, trodden into the mud and asleep again.

Through the soft pasture ground the river roamed, coiling and uncertain. The tide-water filling it gleamed dully like a seal's hide, greyish brown and yellow freckled. The mud at its edges streamed with tiny bubbles out of the ragworm's holes. It carried Tarka with its other flotsam to the middle of its last sea-bend, where the tide lay like a dead seal. Already it had started to ebb. Tarka crawled into shallow fresh water singing round stones, and reached two rocks covered with green water-moss. Here he sat and licked his wounds, and lapped the salt from his mouth. Long shadows were on the grass and the faint-screaming swifts were high over the valley, eager for the sunset and their mystic star-games.

Above the tide's head the banks were of brown soil and upright under the broken turf. Seedling plants of balsam were four inches high. Willows were green and waving in the evening wind. Tarka walked under the bank on dry shillets and sandy scours washed loose of mud, until he reached the roots of a big tree based at the tail of an eddying pool. He crept into darkness, to a dry shelf within, and slept.

The high stars of mid-May were shining through the branches when he came out of the holt, slow and stiff and hungry. Below the two rocks the water gushed in many clear rills. Tarka walked across a bend, down a bank, over the shallow, and up the other bank. He made a landloop that took him to the bottom of the railway embankment, and pushing through a low thorn hedge, he climbed the grassy bank to the rails. Over the wooden sleepers he walked so that the stenches of oil and tarred cinder would mingle with his own scent, in case the enemies were trailing him.

At the next bridge, under which a dwarf owl nested, he left the track and went to water again. Working down the river, crossing from side to side and searching for fish under stones and in deep holes, he left the grassy sloping tide-walls behind and passed by boats resting on a ridge of gravel above a long road-bridge. Swimming with a fluke to the riverside, he could find no bank. The water lapped a stone wall. He swam under an arch of the bridge and ate the fish on a ledge of sand raised over an old galvanized iron bath thrown away into the river. Below the bridge was a railway bridge, supported by round iron piers sunk into the gravel. A wave washed against the base of the pier near the right side of the river as he swam round it, hoping to find mussels clinging there. The sea was returning again. It poured over the ridges of sand, making a sound with every stone and shell and shillet tumbling before its eager spread. *Hu-ee-ic!* Tarka chopped at the froth, the new smarting of his wounds unheeded. *Hu-ee-ic!* The salt wave was of the sea, and the sea was the friend of otters.

As he was swimming down in a turbulent pool, Tarka saw a big fish turn before him. He raced after it. His hindlegs pushed forward under his body for the full double-thrust, and the arch of his back opened the big bite of Deadlock that had nearly touched the spine. He bled, but felt no pain in the joy of hunting a big fish. The mullet – one of many that had come up from the estuary, feeding in the muddy collar of the tide's head – nearly dashed into the stone wall of the quay in its terror. It saved itself by a leap that took it a yard into the air, and falling back, it sped swiftly down the river. Tarka followed it to where it had leapt, stood head and shoulders out of the water, while he looked round, before rolling under again. He swam up the base of the wall and turned back by the railway bridge, swimming three double-thrusts to the left, then three to the right, while watching for the glint of scales. He followed the wall until he came to an opening in the quay where the tide was rushing. Another fish turned in the turbid swirling water before him, and darted up the pill. Tarka swam up the narrow way, but seeing nothing, swung back into the wide river. He swam across the tide to the opposite bank by a shipyard, then returned along the piers of the bridge, searching by the stone sterlings.

The tide was pouring fast between the piers when he reached the wall again. Swimming along the wall he turned up the pill, and let the tide take him. With easy strokes he explored the water, swinging in a zigzag course from side to side. At the end of each crossing he threw head and shoulders out of the water, to breathe and survey before pushing off again with a thrust of hindlegs from the stones under the glidders. Many times he swerved off his course to peer round and under things that lay on the bed, broken kettles, cooking-pots, basins, and battered oil-drums thrown away in the mud.

He saw fish-shapes in the water beyond and above him, and headed them again as they would dash back to the estuary. The mullet swam away from him at thrice his speed, but he followed surely. The springtide was now flowing at six knots and the mullet went up with the press of water. Tarka drove them under another bridge, past which, by some steps in the quay, water from a mill-leat was splashing under a culvert. Above this the walls of stone ended, and rows of weed-hung stakes leaned over the mud glidders. Following the westward curve of the pill, Tarka passed by a timber-yard, and after a minute's swimming, swung north again and then east. The creek was like a great hollow slug filling with water.

Above the next bridge the leading fish rushed back and scurried by him, missing his snap by a curve that gleamed all its side, and a flack of its tail that filled Tarka's mouth with air. It escaped with six of its grey brethren, but the last two were headed again. Tarka drove them up the straight and narrowing pill, through the collar of the tide and into still water, which was strange to the mullet, it was so clear and shallow.

Tarka was now a mile from the pillmouth. The image of the bright moon rolled in shaken globules in the hollows of the brook's swift waters, blending as quicksilver. Every ten yards two clusters of small bright beads arose out of the blackness and vanished in a dipping streak. Sometimes a delicate silver arrow pointed up the brook and was tangled in a fishtail swirl. Every ten yards the whiskered head looked up for direction – only the immediate foreground was visible underwater – and smoothly vanished. Tarka swam with all his webs thrusting together against the swift current, just above the bed of the brook, ready to leap up and snap should the fish try to pass him.

He swam under a bridge of the small-gauge railway, whose shadow darkened the water. As he thrust up his head to vent, Tarka saw beyond the shadow-bar the white blur of water sliding over the sill of a weir. Underwater again, he looked from side to side more quickly, for in this dark place the fish might easily slip by him, although the water was not two feet deep.

When midway through the shadow, his rudder

swished up sickle-shaped, slanting his body. His hindlegs touched stones; he sprang. The scales of the two fish coming straight towards him in the darkness reflected only the darkness, but he had seen a hair of faintest light where the ream of a back-fin had cut the surface and glimmered with the moon-frosted slide. His teeth tore the tail of the leading fish, which escaped – his rudder lashed for another turn, his body screwed through the water, and struck upwards with teeth into the mullet's gorge. Tarka swam into moonlight and dragged the five-pound fish (despite its beats and flaps) on to a shillet heap under the spillway of the slide. He gripped it with his paws and stood over it and started to eat it, while its gills opened and closed, and it tried feebly to flap.

The chewing of its bony jaws soon made him impatient, and he fixed his teeth into the shoulder and tore away his bite. For five minutes he ate, then stretched up his head, with its piky neck-hair raised, and excitedly assayed the air . . . *Hu-ee-ic!* His nostrils opened wide. *Hu-ee-ic!* White-tip looked over the weir-sill and slid down with the water. *Yinn-yinn-y-y-ikk-r!* she cried, through her white teeth, and pulled the fish away from Tarka, who rolled on his back and tried to play with her tail. Then he rolled on his pads again and stared down through the rectangular space under the bridge, remembering the other fish.

He slid off the rock. White-tip ate two pounds of the mullet. Then she followed Tarka.

The leat, with its swift clear water and brown weed-like clusters of stoats' tails – ran parallel to the brook, a few yards away and past a limewashed mill with a ruined water-wheel. A fence made of old iron bedsteads was set in the leat's grassy bank, and here White-tip saw the dark shape of Tarka's head against the nobbled lines of framework. He was eating. Seeing her, he whistled. As she ran over the grass, she smelled the scales where he had dragged the fish. *Yinn-yinn!* she cried again, jumping on the fish and clutching its head in her paws. Tarka watched her. Then he licked the blood from his wounds and ran back to the pill. He was going after more big fish.

In the meadow near the limewashed mill was a dump of house-rubbish, tipped there by dust-carts, and spread about. A sow and her growing farrow were routing in the mess of rotten flesh and vegetable food, crunching up egg-shells and bones and cinders with eager delight. Here, while the moon was waning and the low mist was growing white, the otters returned to play a strange game. It was begun by White-tip making a splash before Tarka, to make sure that he would see her leave the water and climb the bank. When he followed, she ran around the meadow and back again, passing close by, but not once looking at him. After a while, they went back to the pill and romped like porpoises. Then they ran up the bank together and wandered off alone, up and down, passing and repassing many times through the squares of the wire fencing, without recognition or purpose, as though they were both mazed. To the water once more, a drink and a search for eels, and again the strange play in the meadow.

Each was pretending not to see the other; so happy were they to be together, that they were trying to recover the keen joy of meeting.

On the seventh round White-tip ran near a young pig that on sniffing her scent jumped and grunted and squealed and then stood still. Every black jowl lifted from the pleasant garbage. Hot ears ceased to flap. White-tip moved, and ten pigs jumped, and squealed, and hurriedly bolted. The sow, a ponderous and careful animal with eyes sunken in fat, that had eaten two rats and a cat besides twenty pounds of other food that night, pointed her ringed snout at the troublesome smell and moved her big shaking body towards it. White-tip threatened her, crying *Is-iss-iss!* If the sow had caught her, White-tip would have been eaten by sunrise, since she weighed only fourteen pounds and the sow weighed seven hundred pounds. She whistled to Tarka, who ran at the sow.

Seven hundred pounds of flesh returned from the fence with pricked ears and a tail-tip gone; and Tarka ate grass blades, although he was not hungry. He wanted to get the taste out of his mouth.

All night the swifts had been racing over the valley, so high that not even the owls had heard their whistling screams. When these birds saw the golden fume of the sun rising out of the east, they poured down in three funnels to the lower airs of the valley. Their narrow wings made a whishing noise as they fell. Tarka and

White-tip in the weir-pool lay on their backs and watched them as they linked into chains and chased away, some up the valley, others to the estuary. Suddenly the otter heads lifted, looked round, and sank together – they had heard the otter-hounds baying in the kennels on Pilton Hill.

In daylight they drifted down the mill-leat that drew out of the pool, passing from grassy banks to concrete, above which were walls and windows of houses and lofts where pigeons sat and croodled. Some of the older pigeons were already cocking red-rimmed eyes at the sky, for it was near the time of year when the peregrine falcons wheeled aloft the town of Barum, coming from the cliff eyries of Bag Hole, Hercules Promontory, and the red cliffs along the Severn Sea.

A stag-bird, or farmyard cock, saw the otters from its perch on a bough over the leat, and cried *Wock-wock-wock-wick*, while its comb became redder. Then it saw nothing but water, and crowed in triumph among the hens. Tarka had not forgotten the time when a cock had crowed before.

The leat flowed under a road, and under a brick cliff that was one wall of the town mills, swirled back from the locked wheel and gushed under a penstock and through a culvert to the pill, from which the sea was ebbing. Tarka and White-tip swam over the drowned white flowers of scurvey-grass to the bend where timber lay, and climbing out, sought a hiding-place among the pile of oaken trunks. As they crept along a rough bole a rat squeaked, another squealed, and soon all the rats of the timber stack were squealing. An old buck saw Tarka and fled away, followed by others, who were either bucks or does without young. Some of the rats dived into the water, others ran to farther wood stacks, where lived families that fought with the invaders. Their squeals came out of the planks all the morning, while the ringing rasp of circular saws was loud in the sunlight. These rats were heard by the sawyers, and during the dinner-hour one went off to fetch his ferrets.

Tarka and White-tip were lying in a hollow trunk, curled side by side, their heads close together. The hollow was damp; its crevices still held skulls and leg-bones of mice and sparrows, that had looked at Tarka when he was very young. There were also fish-bones with a faint smell, but even these were beyond memory. In the autumn, long after the cubs had left its friendly hollow, the tree had been cut off from its roots and dragged by horses across the meadow and taken away, with other trees, to the saw mills.

Hidden in the pile of trunks, the otters heard the grumbling of the grist mill across the creek, with the noises of traffic and the voices of men. During the morning Tarka shook his ears, tickled by the irritant buzzing of a bluebottle-fly caught and fanged in a spider's web outside the hollow. Long after the fly was dead Tarka heard the buzzing, but without twitching his ears; for similar sounds now came from the bridge, where the motor-traffic crossed two roads. The noises were quieter when the sun was on the top of the sky, and the otters heard distinctly the chirping of sparrows. Then the chirping grew less, for the birds had flown to feed in the quieter roadways. Tarka ceased to listen for footfalls, and slept.

White-tip awakened before Tarka, by the time of an eyeblink. Light from a crevice above, between the trunks resting on the old tree, made two eyes to gleam like no eyes the otters had seen before. They were pink as some blossoms of the balsam, a flower that rose tall by the sides of the Two Rivers every summer. The pink eyes blinked and moved nearer, above a white body. The creature's strong smell, blent with the smell of man, its bold silence, its likeness to an otter, yet so curiously small, made him move uneasily. It peered with its pallid eyes, and sniffed at the tip of Tarka's rudder. Tarka followed White-tip who was more nervous than he was. As they were moving along a trunk, a rat jumped upon Tarka's back and clung to his hair, while screwing up its eyes and yinnering through its bared teeth. It was crying aloud its fear, not of the otter, but of the ferret. This tamed animal of the weasel tribe, whose name was Zippy, followed the rat in a quiet fury, and while Tarka was climbing up through a gap between the first and second layer of trunks, it leapt and bit the rat through the neck, dragging it from its clutch on the bark and shaking it as it drank its blood. Hearing another squeal, Zippy left the limp and dying rat and rippled after the squealer.

When White-tip looked from under the pile of

trunks, she saw a dog peering bright-eyed, its head on one side, above her. A man stood beyond with a cudgel. The dog stepped back three paces as she ran out and yapped as the man struck at her with his cudgel. White-tip turned back, meeting the sharp face of the ferret under a log. She ran round the stack.

The broad sky, grey with heat beating down on the dusty peninsula, dazed the eyes of Tarka, who was stiff with wounds and bruises. He ran to the grassy bank above the creek, slower than the man, who struck him a glancing blow. The blow quickened Tarka, and the man, eager to kill him, threw the ground-ash stick at his head. It twirled past Tarka and scored a groove in the hot and hardening mud. Tarka ran over the cracks beginning to vein the glidder, and sank into the water. He was seen from the bridge, moving round the larger stones like a brown shadow, slowly stroking with his hindlegs and never once rippling the waterflow, which was just deep enough to cover an old boot.

At night Tarka whistled in the creek, but heard no answer. He returned twice to the bend by the silent timber yard, where the eyes of rats were pricked in vanishing moonlight, but White-tip was not there. The flood-tide took him two miles up the river again to the railway bridge where a pair of dwarf owls had their eggs in a stolen jackdaw's nest. These owls, scarcely bigger than thrushes, flew both by day and night, feeding on flukes and shrimps, frogs, snipe, oak-webs or cockchafers, worms, rats, mice, butterflies, and anything small they could catch and kill. When they saw Tarka under the bridge they wauled like Shaggery the ram-cat, they barked like foxes, they coughed like sheep, they croaked like bull-frogs. They flew over him as he walked up the gut that emptied a small brook from the east-lying valley beyond, blaking like herring gulls a yard above his head. When he was driven away from their eggs they hooted with soft pleasure, and left him.

Tarka walked under the road and climbed into a mill-pond, where three eels died. Travelling up the brook, under the mazzard orchards growing on the northern slope of the valley, he reached a great hollow in the hill-side, shut in with trees and luminous as the sky. Tarka saw two moons, one above trees, the other level and in front of him, for the hollow was a flooded limestone quarry. *Hu-ee-ic!* The sweet whistle, like the cry of the golden plover, only softer, echoed from the face of rock across the water. He swam down and down, and could not touch bottom. The sides of the quarry dropped sheer down into the still depths, except at the far end, where was a little bay under a knuckle of land.

He found no fish in the pit, and ran past the deserted lime-burners' cottages and kilns to the brook again. Climbing the right bank he ran over grass-grown hillocks of deads, or rejected shillets of slaty rock, to another drowned quarry. Sombre brakes of blackthorns grew in the slag-heaps near the ivy-covered chimney of the ruinous furnace, and willows bound with mosses leaned in the water, which was dark and stagnant. A tree-creeper had her nest in a crack of the tall chimney, which rocked in every gale, for only the ivy, whose roots had made food and dust of nearly all the mortar between the stones, held it upright against the winds. Every April for five years the tree-creepers' young had been reared within the crack, in a nest that always looked like a chance wind-wedging of dry grasses and litte sticks. The crows and magpies never found the nest, so cunningly was it made each year.

Fish, big and slow-swimming, lived in the sombre waters of the pit, and Tarka chased one down to the mud forty feet under the surface, where it escaped. It was a carp, more than fifty years old, and so wise for a fish that it knew the difference between a hook baited with dough-and-aniseed and one baited with dough-and-aniseed and cottonwool. Its habit, when it found a baited hook, was to expel through its mouth a flume of water on the dough until it was washed off and then it would swallow it; but dough stiffened with cottonwool was left alone.

Hu-ee-ic!

The sky was growing grey. Tarka could not catch a carp, and he was hungry. He went back to the brook.

Hu-ee-ic!

Only his echo replied, and he wandered on.

CHAPTER 14

When the bees' feet shake the bells of the heather, and the ruddy strings of the sap-stealing dodder are twined about the green spikes of the furze, it is summertime on the commons. Exmoor is the high country of the winds, which are to the falcons and the hawks: clothed by whortleberry bushes and lichens and ferns and mossed trees in the goyals, which are to the foxes, the badgers, and the red deer: served by rain-clouds and drained by rock-littered streams, which are to the otters.

The moor knew the sun before it was bright, when it rolled red and ragged through the vapours of creation, not blindingly rayed like one of its own dandelions. The soil of the moor is of its own dead, and scanty; the rains return to the lower ground, to the pasture and cornfields of the valleys, which are under the wind, and the haunts of men.

The moor is to the deer, the badgers, the foxes, the otters, the falcons, and the hawks, pitiless despoilers of rooted and blooded things, which man has collected and set apart for himself; so they are killed. Olden war against greater despoilers began to end with the discoveries of iron and gunpowder; the sabre-toothed tigers, the bears, the wolves, all are gone, and the fragments of their bones lie on the rock of the original creation, under the lichens and grasses and mosses, or in the museums of towns. Once hunted himself, then hunting for necessity, man now hunts in the leisure of his time; but in nearly all those who through necessity of life till fields, herd beasts, and keep fowls, these remaining wildlings of the moors have enemies who care nothing for their survival. The farmers would exterminate nearly every wild bird and animal of prey, were it not for the landowners, among whom are some who care for the wildlings because they are sprung from the same land of England, and who would be unhappy if they thought the country would know them no more. For the animal they hunt to kill in its season, or those other animals or birds they cause to be destroyed for the continuance of their pleasure in sport – which they believe to be natural – they have no pity; and since they lack this incipient human instinct, they misunderstand and deride it in others. Pity acts through the imagination, the higher light of the world, and imagination arises from the world of things, as a rainbow from the sun. A rainbow may be beautiful and heavenly, but it will not grow corn for bread.

Within the moor is the Forest, a region high and treeless, where sedge grasses grow on the slopes to the sky. In early summer the wild spirit of the hills is heard in the voices of curlews. The birds fly up from solitary places, above their beloved and little ones, and float the wind in a sweet uprising music. Slowly on spread and hollow wings they sink, and their cries are trilling and cadent, until they touch earth and lift their wings above their heads, and poising, loose the last notes from their throats, like gold bubbles rising into sky again. Tall and solemn, with long hooped beaks, they stalk to their nestlings standing in wonder beside the tussocks. The mother-bird feeds her singer, and his three children cry to him. There are usually but three, because the carrion-crows rob the curlews of the first egg laid in each nest. Only when they find the broken empty shell do the curlews watch the crows, black and slinking, up the hillside.

Soon the curlew lifts his wings and runs from his young, trilling with open beak; his wings flap, and up he flies to fetch song from heaven to the wilderness again.

A tarn lies under two hills, draining water from a tussock-linked tract of bog called The Chains. The tarn is deep and brown and still, reflecting rushes and reeds at its sides, the sedges of the hills, and the sky over them. The northern end of the tarn is morass, trodden by deer and ponies. Water trickles away under its southern bank, and hurries in its narrow course by falls, runnels, pools, and cascades. One afternoon Tarka climbed out of the rillet's bed, scarcely wider than himself, and looked through green hart's-tongue ferns at the combe up which he had travelled. Nothing moved below him except water. He walked up the hill, and saw the tarn below him. He heard the dry croaking of frogs, and ran down the bank that dammed the dark peat-water. A yard down the slope he stopped.

A hen-raven, black from bristled beak to toes, hopped along the edge of the tarn when she saw him. Tarka heard small plopping sounds and saw ripples in the water, where bull-frogs had dived off the bank. The raven took three hops to a pile of dead frogs, then stopped, crouched down, poked out her head with flattened feathers, and gazed at Tarka. Her small eyes flickered with the whitish-grey membranes of the third eyelids. The raven was not afraid of an otter.

She had been fishing for frogs by dapping the water with her beak. Hearing the noises, the bull-frogs swam to the surface and turned with bulging eyes towards the dapping. The raven made a dry and brittle croak. When the frogs heard it, the skin swelled under their necks, and they croaked a challenge, mistaking the noises for the struggle of a choking female. They swam within a few inches of the raven's beak. One, perhaps two, would leap out of the water, and then the raven opened her beak and caught one, perhaps two. She was very quick. She hopped with them to her pile, spiked them through the head, and walked quietly to another fishing-place. She could carry eight or nine frogs in her craw at once to her nest of young in a rocky clitter near the head of the river Exe. When loaded, she flew with gaping beak. Tarka lifted his head and worked his nostrils. The steadfast glance of the small eyes along the black beak pointed at him. He smelled the frogs, took three quaddling steps towards the raven, and stopped again. The raven did not move, and he did not like her eyes. He turned away. She hopped after him, and nipped the tip of his rudder as he slipped into the tarn.

Krok-krok-krok! said the raven, cocking an eye at the sky. Tarka lay in the water and watched her picking up frog after frog and pouching them, before she jumped off the bank and flew over the eastern hill.

When she returned her mate was with her. They soared above the tarn. Sometimes the cock raven shut his wings, rolled sideways, and twirled on open wings again. *Krok-krok!* he said to the hen, seeing below the form of the swimming otter, darker than the dark tarn. The raven opened his beak wide, set his wings for descent, and croaked *kron-n-n-n-nk* during the slow, dipping swoop, in the curve of a scythe, from one green-lined margin to the other. Then he tumbled and twirled, alighting on the slope of the hill, and walked down to the water to catch frogs.

Several times each day the two ravens flew to the

tarn. The cockbird talked to Tarka whenever he saw
him, and pestered him when he was sunning himself on
the bank. He would hop to within a few feet of him
with a frog in his beak, and drop it just to windward
of Tarka's nose. Once, when Tarka was playing with a
frog and had turned his back on it for a moment, the
raven picked it up and threw it to one side, Bird and
otter played together, but they never touched one
another. The raven, who was one of the three hundred
sons of Kronk, would drop a stick into the tarn and
Tarka would swim after it, bringing it to the bank and
rolling with it between his paws. Occasionally the
raven slyly pinched his rudder, and Tarka would run at
him, tissing through his teeth. With flaps and hops the
raven dodged him, flying up out of his way only when
driven to water.

Day after day Tarka slept in the rushes in the morass
at the north end of the tarn. Unless he was tired after
the nightly prowl, the *kron-n-n-k* of the zooming
raven would always wake him, and he would either
run along the bank or swim by the reeds to play with
the bird. One morning five ravens flew over the tarn,
the hen leading three smaller ravens in line and the
father behind them – black constellation of Orion.
They lit on the turf of the dam. The youngsters sat on
the bank and watched their mother dapping for frogs.
Tarka ran along the bank, amid guttural squawks and
cronks, to play with them, but the parents stabbed at
him with their beaks, beating wings in his face and
hustling him back to water. They flew over him when

he bobbed for breath, and worried him so persistently that he never again went near a raven.

When the wind had blown the seeds of the cotton grass and the sedge drooped tawny under the sun, the curlews flew again to the seashore and the rivers. Little jerky flights of pipits crossed over the hollow in the hills, their twittering passed on, and the tarn lay silent as the sky. One afternoon in early September the silence stirred, and along the tawny hillcrest moved something like a leafless top of an oak branch. It became a stag hastening with tongue a-loll to the wooded valleys of the south. Silence settled on the moor until the hill-line was broken by a long and silent file of staghounds running down from The Chains on the line of a deer. Tarka stood on his bed of rushes and watched them until they loped into the sky. When he had settled again a blackcock hurtled down the western hill and flew over the tarn, followed by a grey hen with her two heath poults. Two horsemen in red coats slanted down the side of the hill; and after them came a young farmer riding bare-back a stallion with blown mane and flying tail. Then came a grey hunter, carrying a man with a face nearly as red as his coat. Others followed singly, and at long intervals, on weary horses.

That evening Tarka quitted the tarn, and journeyed over The Chains to water that hastened in a bright thread out of the bog. It entered a narrow goyal, and the moon was hid by the hill before him. After a mile the water turned north, under the hill whose worn grey feet it had broken for its bed. The goyal widened by the Hoar Oak, whose splintered stump, black as its shadow with the moon behind, glistered with the tracks of slugs. Near the Hoar Oak stood a sapling, caged from the teeth and horns of deer, a little tree by the grave of its father.

And Tarka went down the Hoar Oak Water which, under ridge and common, shattered the moon into shards and lost them under the trees which grew together in the lower valley. Its voice passed from leaf to leaf, up through the woods where badgers were seeking mice and black slugs, and to the night over the autumn hills.

Where two waters met, to seek the sea together, Tarka walked over the trail of otters, and recognizing the scent of White-tip, he followed up the water the otter had travelled. Near the end of the night, while he was swimming in a pool scooped in the rock below a fall, he saw an otter-shape before him. It moved slowly with the sway of water, its head lolled on a stone. It had been drowned some hours. The whistles of otters playing at the fall during the previous night had been heard by the water-owner, who had set a gin under the wash of the fall, on a sunken ledge of rock where otters touched after the joyful pounding of the plunge. The otters had come back again.

Iron in the water sinks, and however long cubs call her, a bitch-otter cannot swim with three legs for ever.

Tarka heard the clink of the chain as the swollen body rolled; and his bubbles blown of fear rose behind him.

At sunrise he had crossed two miles of woods and fields – stubble with lines of sheaves, stacked in sixes and tied in fours, fields of mangel and sweet turnip, where partridge crouched, and pasture given over to sheep – and found other water below Beggars' Roost hill. Ducks were paddling by a farm as he walked upstream, passing under a bridge, by which grew a monkey-tree with leaves as sharp as magpies' beaks. Cottages by the waterside and a mill were left behind, and he came to quiet meadows where only robins were singing. He crossed from side to side looking for a place to hide during the sunlight. Half a mile above the mill he found a rock in the left bank of the stream, with a wide opening half under water. Hazels grew on the bank above. Their leaves took on the golden-green of spring in the beams of the low autumn sun as Tarka crept under the rock.

CHAPTER 15

*H*e was awakened by the tremendous baying of hounds. He saw feet splashing in the shallow water, a row of noses, and many flacking tongues. The entrance was too small for any head to enter. He crouched a yard away, against the cold rock. The noise hurt the fine drums of his ears.

Hob-nailed boots scraped on the brown shillets of the waterbed, and iron-tipped hunting-poles tapped the rocks.

Go'r'n leave it! Leave it! Go'r'n leave it! Deadlock! Harper! Go'r'n leave it!

Tarka heard the horn and the low opening became lighter.

Go'r'n leave it! Captain! Deadlock! Go'r'n leave it!

The horn twanged fainter as the pack was taken away. Then a pole was thrust into the holt and prodded about blindly. It slid out again. Tarka saw boots and hands and the face of a terrier. A voice whispered, *Leu in there, Sammy, leu in there!* The small ragged brown animal crept out of the hands. Sammy smelled Tarka, saw him, and began to sidle towards him. *Waugh-waugh-waugh-wa-waugh.* As the otter did not move, the terrier crept nearer to him, yapping with head stretched forward.

After a minute Tarka could bear the irritating noises no more. Tissing, with open mouth, he moved past the terrier, whose snarly yapping changed to a high–pitched yelping. The men on the opposite bank stood silent and still. They saw Tarka's head in sunlight, which came through the trees behind them and turned the brown shillets a warm yellow. The water ran clear and cold. Tarka saw three men in blue coats; they did not move and he slipped into the water. It did not cover his back, and he returned to the bankside roots. He moved in the shadows and under the ferns at his ordinary travelling pace. One of three watching men declared that an otter had no sense of fear.

No hound spoke, but the reason of the silence was not considered by Tarka, who could not reason such things. He had been awakened with a shock, he had been tormented by a noise, he had left a dangerous place, and he was escaping from human enemies. As he walked upstream, with raised head, his senses of smell, sight, and hearing were alert for his greatest enemies, the hounds.

The stream being narrow and shallow, the otter was given four minutes' law. Four minutes after Tarka had left he heard behind him the short and long notes of the horn, and the huntsman crying amidst the tongues of hounds *Ol-ol-ol-ol-ol-ol-over! Get on to'm! Ol-ol-ol-ol-over!* as the pack returned in full cry to the water. Hounds splashed into the water around the rock, wedging themselves at its opening and breaking into couples and half couples, leaping through the water after the wet and shivering terrier, throwing their tongues and dipping their noses to the wash of scent coming down.

Deadlock plunged at the lead, with Caroline, Sailoress, Captain, and Playboy. They passed the terrier, and Deadlock was so eager that he knocked him down. Sammy picked up his shivery body and followed.

Tarka sank all but his nostrils in a pool and waited. He lay in the sunlit water like a brown log slanting to the stones on which his rudder rested. The huntsman saw him. Tarka lifted his whiskered head out of the water, and stared at the huntsman. Hounds were speaking just below. From the pond the stream flowed for six feet down the smooth side up which he had crept. When Deadlock jumped into the pool and lapped the scent lying on the water, Tarka put down his head with hardly a ripple, and like a skin of brown oil moved under the hound's belly. Soundlessly he emerged, and the sun glistened on his water-sleeked coat as he walked down on the algae-smeared rock. He seemed to walk under their muzzles slowly, and to be treading on their feet.

Let hound, hunt him! Don't help hounds or they'll chop him!

The pack was confused. Every hound owned the scent, which was like a tangled line, the end of which was sought for unravelling. But soon Deadlock pushed through the pack and told the way the otter had gone.

As Tarka was running over shillets with water scarcely deep enough to cover his rudder, Deadlock saw him and with stiff stern ran straight at him. Tarka quitted the water. The dead twigs and leaves at the hedge-bottom crackled and rustled as he pushed through to the meadow. While he was running over the grass, he could hear the voice of Deadlock raging as the bigger black-and-white hound struggled through the hazel twigs and brambles and honeysuckle bines. He crossed fifty yards of meadow, climbed the bank, and ran down again on to a tarred road. The surface burned his pads, but he ran on, and even when an immense crimson creature bore down upon him he did not go back into the meadow across which hounds were streaming. With a series of shudders the crimson creature slowed to a standstill, while human figures rose out of it, and pointed. He ran under the motor-coach, and came out into brown sunshine, hearing above the shouts of men the clamour of hounds trying to scramble up the high bank and pulling each other down in their eagerness.

He ran in the shade of the ditch, among bits of newspaper, banana and orange skins, cigarette ends and crushed chocolate boxes. A long yellow creature grew bigger and bigger before him, and so men rose out of it and peered down at him as he passed it. With smarting eyes he ran two hundred yards of the road, which for him was a place of choking stinks and hurtful noises. Pausing in the ditch, he hearkened to the clamour changing its tone as hounds leaped down into the road. He ran on for another two hundred yards, then climbed the bank, pushed through dusty leaves and grasses and briars that would hold him, and down the sloping meadow to the stream. He splashed into the water and swam until rocks and boulders rose before him. He climbed and walked over them. His rudder drawn on mosses and lichens left a strong scent behind him. Deadlock, racing over the green-shadowed grassland, threw his tongue before the pack.

In the water, through shallow and pool, his pace was steady, but not hurried; he moved faster than the stream; he insinuated himself from slide to pool, from pool to boulder, leaving his scent in the wet marks of his pads and rudder.

People were running through the meadow, and in the near distance arose the notes of the horn and hoarse cries. Hounds' tongues broke out united and firm, and Tarka knew that they had reached the stream. The sun-laden water of the pools was spun into eddies by the thrusts of his webbed hindlegs. He passed through shadow and dapple, through runnel and plash. The water sparkled amber in the sunbeams, and his brown sleek pelt glistened whenever his back made ripples. His movements in water were unhurried, like an eel's. The hounds came nearer.

The stream after a bend flowed near the roadway, where more motor-cars were drawn up. Some men and women, holding notched poles, were watching from the cars – sportsmen on wheels.

Beggars' Roost Bridge was below. With hounds so near Tarka was heedless of the man that leaned over the stone parapet, watching for him. They shouted, waved hats, and cheered the hounds. There were ducks above the bridge, quacking loudly as they left the stream and waddled to the yard, and when Tarka came to where they had been, he left the water and ran after them. They beat their wings as they tried to fly from him, but he reached the file and scattered them running through them and disappearing. Nearer and nearer came Deadlock, with Captain and Waterwitch leading the pack. Huntsmen, whippers-in, and field were left behind, struggling through hedges and over banks.

Hounds were bewildered when they reached the yard. They ran with noses to ground in puzzled excitement. Captain's shrill voice told that Tarka had gone under a gate. Waterwitch followed the wet seals in the dust, but turned off along a track of larger webs. The line was tangled again. Deadlock threw his belving tongue. Other hounds followed, but the scent only led to a duck that beat its wings and quacked in terror before them. A man with a rake drove them off, shouting and threatening to strike them. Dewdrop spoke across the yard and the hounds galloped to her, but the line led to a gate which they tried to leap, hurtling themselves up and falling from the top bar. A duck had gone under the gate, but not Tarka.

All scent was gone. Hounds rolled in the dust or trotted up to the men and women, sniffing their pockets for food. Rufus found a rabbit skin and ate it; Render fought with Sandboy – but not seriously, as they feared each other; Deadlock went off alone. And hounds were waiting for a lead when the sweating huntsman, grey pot-hat pushed back from his red brow, ran up with the two whippers-in and called them into a pack again. The thick scent of Muscovy ducks had checked the hunt.

Tarka had run through a drain back to the stream, and now he rested in the water that carried him every moment nearer to the murmurous glooms of the glen below. He saw the coloured blur of a kingfisher perching on a twig as it eyed the water for beetle or loach. The kingfisher saw him moving under the surface, as his shadow broke the net of ripple shadows that drifted in meshes of pale gold on the stony bed beneath him.

While he was walking past the roots of a willow under the bank, he heard the yapping of the terrier. Sammy had crept through the drain, and was looking out at the end, covered with black filth, and eagerly telling his big friends to follow him downstream. As he yapped, Deadlock threw his tongue. The stallion hound was below the drain, and had refound the line where

Tarka had last touched the shillets. Tarka saw him ten yards away, and slipping back into the water, swam with all webs down the current, pushing from his nose a ream whose shadow beneath was an arrow of gold pointing down to the sea.

Again he quitted the water and ran on land to wear away his scent. He had gone twenty yards when Deadlock scrambled up the bank with Render and Sandboy, breathing the scent which was as high as their muzzles. Tarka reached the waterside trees again a length ahead of Deadlock, and fell into the water like a sodden log. Deadlock leapt after him and snapped at his head; but the water was friendly to the otter, who rolled in smooth and graceful movement away from the jaws, a straight bite of which would have crushed his skull.

Here sunlight was shut out by the oaks, and the roar of the first fall was beating back from the leaves. The current ran faster, narrowing into a race with twirls and hollows marking the sunken rocks. The roar grew louder in a drifting spray. Tarka and Deadlock were carried to where a broad sunbeam came down through a break in the foliage and lit the mist above the fall. Tarka went over in the heavy white folds of the torrent and Deadlock was hurled over after him. They were lost in the churn and pressure of the pool until a small brown head appeared and gazed for its enemy in the broken honeycomb of foam. A black-and-white body uprolled beside it, and the head of the hound was thrust up as he tried to tread away from the current that would draw him under. Tarka was master of whirlpools; they were his playthings. He rocked in the surge with delight; then high above he heard the note of the horn. He yielded himself to the water and let it take him away down the gorge into a pool where rocks were piled above. He searched under the dripping ferny clitter for a hiding-place.

Underwater he saw two legs, joined to two wavering and inverted images of legs, and above them the blurred shapes of a man's head and shoulders. He turned away from the fisherman into the current again, and as he breathed he heard the horn again. On the road above the glen the pack was trotting between huntsman and whippers-in, and before them men were running with poles at the trail, hurrying down the hill to the bridge, to make a stickle to stop Tarka reaching the sea.

Tarka left Deadlock far behind. The hound was feeble and bruised and breathing harshly, his head battered and his sight dazed, but still following. Tarka passed another fisherman, and by chance the tiny feathered hook lodged in his ear. The reel spun against the cheek, *re-re-re* continuously, until all the silken line had run through the snake-rings of the rod, which bent into a circle, and whipped back straight again as the gut trace snapped.

Tarka saw the bridge, the figure of a man below it, and a row of faces above. He heard shouts. The man standing on a rock took off his hat, scooped the air, and holla'd to the huntsman, who was running and slipping with the pack on the loose stones of the steep red road. Tarka walked out of the last pool above the bridge, ran over a mossy rock merged with the water again, and pushed through the legs of the man.

Tally-ho!

Tarka had gone under the bridge when Harper splashed into the water. The pack poured through the gap between the end of the parapet and the hillside earth, and their tongues rang under the bridge and down the walls of the houses built on the rock above the river.

Among rotting motor tyres, broken bottles, tins, pails, shoes, and other castaway rubbish lying in the bright water, hounds made their plunging leaps. Once Tarka turned back: often he was splashed and trodden on. The stream was seldom deep enough to cover him, and always shallow enough for the hounds to move at double his speed. Sometimes he was under the pack, and then, while hounds were massing for the worry, his small head would look out beside a rock ten yards below them.

Between boulders and rocks crusted with shellfish and shaggy with seaweed, past worm-channered posts that marked the fairway for fishing boats at high water, the pack hunted the otter. Off each post a gull launched itself, cackling angrily as it looked down at the animals. Tarka reached the sea. He walked slowly into the surge of a wavelet, and sank away from the chop of old Harper's jaws, just as Deadlock ran through the pack. Hounds swam beyond the lines of waves, while people stood at the sea-lap and watched the huntsman wading to his waist. It was said that the otter was dead-beat,

and probably floating stiffly in the shallow water. After
a few minutes the huntsman shook his head, and with-
drew the horn from his waistcoat. He filled his lungs
and stopped his breath and was tightening his lips for
the four long notes of the call-off, when a brown head
with hard eyes was thrust out of the water a yard from
Deadlock. Tarka stared into the hound's face and cried
Ic-yang!

The head sank. Swimming under Deadlock, Tarka
bit on to the loose skin of the flews and pulled the
hound's head under water. Deadlock tried to twist
round and crush the otter's skull in his jaws, but he
struggled vainly. Bubbles blew out of his mouth. Soon
he was choking. The hounds did not know what was
happening. Deadlock's hindlegs kicked the air weakly.
The huntsman waded out and pulled him inshore, but
Tarka loosened his bite only when he needed new air
in his lungs; and then he swam under and gripped
Deadlock again. Only when hounds were upon him
did Tarka let go. He vanished in a wave.

Long after the water had been emptied out of Deadlock's lungs, and the pack had trotted off for the long
uphill climb to the railway station, the gulls were
flying over something in the sea beyond the mouth of
the little estuary. Sometimes one dropped its yellow
webs to alight on the water; always it flew up again
into the restless, wailing throng, startled by the snaps of
white teeth. A cargo steamer was passing up the Severn
Sea, leaving a long smudge of smoke on the horizon,

where a low line of clouds billowed over the coast of Wales. The regular thumps of its screw in the windless blue calm were borne to where Tarka lay, drowsy and content, but watching the pale yellow eyes of the nearest bird. At last the gulls grew tired of seeing only his eyes, and flew back to their post; and turning on his back, Tarka yawned and stretched himself, and floated at his ease.

CHAPTER 16

Swimming towards the sunset Tarka found a cleft in the high curved red cliff, and on the crest of a wave rode into the cavern beyond. The broken wave slapped against the dark end as he climbed to a ledge far above the lipping of the swell, and curled himself on cold stone. He awoke when the gulls and cormorants were flying over the sea, silent as dusk, to their roosts in the cliff.

The straight wavelets of the rising tide were moving across the rock pools below the cleft, where under green and purple laver-weed crabs and prawns were stirring to feed. The weed, so placid before, was kicked and entangled by the searching otter. The crab he climbed out with was bitter, and leaving it, he swam into deep water.

A herring shoal was coming up with the evening tide, followed by a herd of porpoises, which when breathing showed shiny black hides through the waves. Fishermen called them errin-ogs. Once these warm-blooded mammals had ears and hair and paws, but now their ear-holes were small as thorn-pricks, and their five-toed paws were changed into flippers. Their forefathers, who had come from the same family as the forefathers of otters and seals, had taken early to water, shaping themselves for a sealife while yet the seals were running on land. Their young, born under water, needed no mother's back to raise them to the air of life, for ancestral habit had become instinct.

An old boar porpoise flung himself out of a trough near Tarka and fell with a clapping splash on its back, to shake off the barnacle-like parasites boring into its blubber. Near the boar swam a sow porpoise suckling her little one, who, towed along on its back, breathed during every rise and roll of its mother. Tarka caught his first herring and ate it on a rock, liking the taste, but when he swam out for more, the under-seas were vacant.

For a week he slept in the disused lime-kiln on the greensward above the Heddon water, that lost itself in a ridge of boulders above the tide wash. While he was exploring the fresh water a storm broke over the moor, and the roaring coloured spate returned him to the sea.

He went westwards, under the towering cliffs and
waterfalls in whose ferny sides he liked to rest by day.
Once he was awakened by a dreadful mumbling in the
wind far above him. As he lifted his head he heard a
whistling noise, as of falcons in swoop. Flakes of scree
clattered and hurtled past him; then a stag, and three
staghounds. The bodies smashed on the rocks, and
were of silence again. Soon the cries of seabirds and
daws were echoing out of the cliffs. Ravens flew
down, and buzzards, and the air was filled with black
and white and brown wings, with deep croaking,
wailing, and shrill screaming. They jostled and fought
for an hour, when a motor-boat, holding a red-coated
figure, came round the eastern sheer and drove them
into flight. The gulls mobbed Tarka when they saw
him slipping down from his resting ledge, but he found
the sea and sank away from them. That night, squatting
on a rock and eating a conger, the west wind brought
him the scent of White-tip.

At dawn he was swimming under the sea-feet of the
Great Hangman; and he followed the trail until sunrise
was shimmering down the level sea and filling with
aerial gold the clouds over the Welsh hills.

At dusk the shore-rats on Wild Pear Beach, searching
the weed-strewn tide-line, paused and squealed together
when their sharp noses took the musky scent of water-
weasels. They ran off chittering as terrible shapes galloped among them. A rat was picked up and killed in a
swift bite. The cub did not want it for food; he killed it
in fun. He ran into the sea after White-tip, who had

been taking care of the cubs since their mother had been trapped under the waterfall.

Six hours later Tarka ran up Wild Pear Beach and his thin, hard cries pierced the slop and wash of waves on the loose, worn, shaly strand. He followed the trail over the weeds to the otters' sleeping-place under a rock, and down again to the sea. In a pool off Briery Cave he scented otter again, for at the bottom of the pool lay a wicker-pot, holding something that turned slowly as the ribbons of the thong-weed lifted and dropped in the water. The long blue feelers of the lobster were feeling through the wickerwork; it was gorged, and trying to get away from the otter cub it had been eating. The cub had found no way out of the cage it had entered at high tide, intending to eat the lobster.

Hu-ee-ic! Tarka did not know the dead. Nothing answered, and he swam away, among green phosphoric specks that glinted at every wave-lap.

Autumn's little summer, when day and night were equal, and only the woodlark sang his wistful falling song over the bracken, was ruined by the gales that tore wave and leaf, and broke the sea into roar and spray, and hung white ropes over the rocks. Fog hid cliff-tops and stars as Tarka travelled westwards. One night, as he was drinking fresh water from a pool below a cascade, he was startled by immense whooping bellows that bounded from the walls of mist and rebounded afar, to return in duller echoes as though phantom hounds were baying the darkness. Tarka slipped into a pool and hid under lifting seaweed; but the sounds were regular and harmless, and afterwards he did not heed them. On a rock below the white-walled tower of Bull Point lighthouse, whose twin sirens were sending a warning to sailors far out beyond the dreadful rocks, Tarka found again the trail of White-tip, and whistled with joy.

Travelling under the screes, where rusted plates of wrecked ships lay in pools, he came to the end of the land. Day was beginning. The tide, moving northwards across Morte Bay from Bag Leap, was ripped and whitened by rocks which stood out of the billows of the grey sea. One rock was tall above the reef – the Morte Stone – and on the top pinnacle stood a big black bird, with the tails of fish sticking out of its gullet. Its dripping wings were held out to ease its tight crop. The bird was *Phalacrocorax carbo*, called the Isle of Wight Parson by fishermen, and it sat uneasily on the Morte Stone during most of the hours of daylight, swaying with a load of fishes.

Tired and buffeted by the long Atlantic rollers, Tarka turned back under the Morte Stone, and swam to land. He climbed a slope strewn with broken thrift-roots and grey shards of rock, to a path set on its seaward verge by a fence of iron posts and cables. Salt winds had gnawed the iron to rusty splinters. The heather above the path was tougher than the iron, but its sprigs were barer than its own roots.

Over the crest of the Morte, heather grew in low bushes, out of the wind's way. There were green places

where among the grass cropped by sheep grew mush-
rooms mottled like owl's plumage. The sky above the
crest was reddening, and he found a sleeping-place
under a broken cromlech, the burial-place of an ancient
man, whose bones were grass and heather and dust in
the sun.

Tarka slept warm all day. At sunset he ran down to the
sea. He worked south through the currents that scoured
shelly coves and swept round lesser rocks into the wide
Morte Bay. Long waves, breaking near the shallows, left
foam behind them in the shapes of dusky-white seals.
Bass were swimming in the breakers, taking sand-eels
risen in the sandy surge. A high-flying gull saw a fish
flapping in the shallows, with ribbon weed across its
head. The gull glided down, and the ribbon weed arose
on low legs, tugging at the five-pound fish, and dragged
it on to firm, wet sand. *Hak-hak!* cried the gull,
angrily. *Tu-lip, tulip!* the ring plover arose and flickered
away in a flock. Other gulls flew over, and dropped
down. Tarka feasted among the noise of wings and angry
cries. When he was full, he lapped fresh water trickling
over the sand in a broad and shallow bed. *Hu-ee-ic!* He
galloped up the sand, nose between paws. He ran up into
the sandhills, where his passing sowed round orange-red
seeds from the split dry pods of the stinking iris. Over a
lonely road, among old stalks of ragwort and teasel, and
up a steep bank to the incult hill, pushing among
bracken, furze, brambles, following the way of White-
tip. He found the head of a rabbit which she had caught,
and played with it, whistling as he rolled it with his paws.

Already larks were ceasing to sing. When he reached the top of Pickwell down, eastern clouds were ruddy and Hoaroak Hill, seventeen miles away as the falcon glides, was as a shadow lying under the sky. He descended to a gully in the hills, a dry watercourse marked by furze bushes, and thorns, and hollies, growing down to sandhills by the sea. The gully lay southwest; the trees lay over to the north-east, bitter and dwarfed by salt and wind. Under a holly bush, bearer of ruined blossoms and spineless leaves, whose limbs were tortured by ivy thicker in trunk than its own, the otter crawled into a bury widened by many generations of rabbits, and lay down in the darkness.

The wind rushed up the gully, moving stiffly the blackthorns which squeaked as they rubbed against each other. Dry branches of elderberries rattled and scraped as though bemoaning their poverty. Gulls veered from hilltop to hilltop, calling the flock standing far below on the sands that gleamed with the dull sky. The dark base of the headland lying out in the Atlantic was flecked along its length with the white of breaking waves. The sea's roar came with blown spray up the gully. Tarka slept.

He awoke before noon, hearing voices of men. Mist was drifting between the hills. He lay still until a man spoke at the day-dim opening of the bury. An animal moved down the tunnel, whose smell immediately disturbed him. He remembered it. The animal's eyes glowed pink, and a bell tinkled round its neck. Tarka crawled into the bury and ran out of another hole, that was watched by a spaniel sitting shivering and wet, behind a man with a gun on the bank above. The spaniel jumped back when it saw Tarka, who ran down the gully, hastening when he heard a bark, a shout, and two bangs of the gun. Twigs showered upon him, and he ran on, hidden by the thorny brake. Two men clambered down the banks, but only the spaniel followed him, barking with excitement, but not daring to go near him. It returned to its master's whistle. Tarka hid under a blackberry bush lower down, and slept among the brambles until darkness, when he left the shelter and climbed up the hillside.

He ran under a gate to a field beyond, but crossing a rabbit's line, he followed it through hawthorns wind-bent over the stone bank, to the waste land again. The rabbit was crouching under the wind in a tussock, and one bite killed it. After the meal Tarka drank rain-water in a sheep's skull, which lay among rusty plough-shares, old iron pots, tins, and skeletons of sheep – some broken up by cattle dogs, and all picked clean by crows and ravens. Tarka played with a shoulder-blade because White-tip had touched it in passing. He ran at it and bit the cold bone as though it were White-tip. He played with many things that night as he ran across field and bank.

Following the trail he came to a pond in a boggy field below a hill. Moorhens hid in terror when he swam among them. He caught and played with an eel, which was found dead next morning on the bank, beside the seals pressed in the mud by his clawed feet, and the hair-marks of his rolling back. *Hu-ee-ic!* Tarka ran under a culvert that carried a trickle to a smaller pond in the garden of a rectory. *Hu-ee-ic!* while clouds broke the light of the moon.

He climbed round the hatch of the pond, sniffing the tarred wood, and crept under a gap in the wall which ended the garden. The stream flowed below a church-yard wall and by a thatched cottage, where a man, a dog, and a cat were sitting before a fire of elm brands on the open hearth. The wind blew the scent of the otter under the door, and the cat fumed and growled, standing with fluffed back and twitching tail beside her basket of kittens. The otter was scraping shillets by a flat stone under a fall by the road, where farmers' daughters crouch to wash chitterlings for the making of hog's-pudding. An eel lived under the kneeling stone, fat with pig-scrap. Its tail was just beyond the otter's teeth. White-tip had tried to catch it the night before.

Hu-ee-ic!

The cottage door was pulled open, the spaniel rushed out barking. A white owl lifted itself off the lopped bough of one of the churchyard elms, crying *skirr-rr*. An otter's tiss of anger came from out of the culvert under the road. Striking a match the man saw, on the scour of red mud, the twy-toed seal, identical with the seal that led down to the sea after the Ice Winter.

Tarka was gone down the narrow covered way of the culvert, amid darkness and the babble of water. The stream ran under a farmhouse, and through an orchard, under another culvert and past a cottage garden to the watermeadow below. Wood owls hunting far down in the valley heard the keen cries of Tarka.

Hu-ee-ic!

Often the trail was lost, for the otters which had gone ahead of Tarka had left their seals on bank and scour before the rain had pitted and blurred them.

Tarka followed the stream. At the beginning of Cryde village the water was penned above the curve of the road, the pond being kept back by a grassy bank where stood a hawthorn clipped like a toad-stool. Swimming round the edge among flags and the roots of thorns and sycamores, he saw a head looking at him from the water, and from the head strayed a joyous breath. He swam to it – a snag of elm-branch stuck in the mud. White-tip had rubbed against it when swimming by. Tarka bit it before swimming round the pond again to sniff the wood of the penstock. He climbed out and ran along the bank, by the still mossy wooden wheel of the mill. They heard his shrill cry in the inn below. A cattle dog barked, and Tarka ran up a narrow lane which led to the top of a hill. In hoof-mudded patches he found the trail again, for the otters had run the same way when alarmed by the same dog. The trail took him under a gate and into a field, over a bank where straight stalks of mulleins were black in moonlight, to land that had forgotten the plough, a prickly place for an otter's webs. Sea-wind had broken all the bracken stalks. Suddenly he heard the mumbling

roar of surf and saw the lighthouse across the Burrows.
He galloped joyfully down a field of arrish, or stubble.
He travelled so swiftly that soon he stood on the edge
of sandy cliffs, where spray blew as wind. He found a
way down to the pools by a ledge where grew plants
of great sea stock, whose leaves were crumbling in
autumn sleep.

The trail led over the sandhills with their thin stab-
bing marram grasses, and to the mossy pans behind
them, where grew privet bushes and blunt-head club-
rushes. The way was strewn with rabbit skulls and
empty snail shells. Tarka crossed the marsh of Horsey
Island – where grew Russian thistles, sprung from a
single seed blown from the estuary off a Baltic timber
ship years before – until he came to the sea-wall, and
below the wall, to the mouth of the Branton pill. The
tide took him slowly in a patch of froth which the
meeting waters had beaten up, the gossip of the Two
Rivers. He ran over the eastern seawall, and along the
otter-path to the Ram's-horn pond.

Hu-ee-ic!

He swam to the wooden bridge by the boat-house,
and to the withies on the islet.

Hu-ee-ic!

He hunted the brackish waters until the stars were
dimmed by dawn, when he pressed through the reeds
by a way he had trodden before, but forgotten, and
slept on an old couch where lay bones, and a little
skull.

CHAPTER 17

*A*ll day the wind shook the rusty reed-daggers at
the sky, and the mace-heads were never still.
Before sunset the couch was empty. The purple-ruddy
beams stained the grass and the thistles of the meadow,
and the tiles of the cattle-shippen under the sea-wall
were the hue of the sky. Westward the marshman's
cottage, the linhays, the trees, the hedges, the low
ragged line of the Burrows, were vanishing in a mist of
fire.

The tide was ebbing, the mud slopes grey, with
ruddy tricklings. In the salt turf below the sea-wall
great cracks wandered with the fire of the sky. Ring

plover and little stints ran by the guts, and their slender peering images quenched the flame in the water. Bunches of oar-weed on each sodden perch dripped their last drops among the froth and spinning holes of the gliding tide. The mooring buoys rolled and re-turned, each keg gathering froth that the current sucked away under its lowest stave. By an old broken wicker crab-pot, only its rib-tops up, a small head showed without a ripple, moving with the water. Men were walking on the deck of a ketch below; other men were sitting at oars in a boat under the black hull waiting for their mates. A dog began to bark, then it whimpered, until it was pushed over the gunwale. It met the water in a reddish splash.

Men climbed down to the boat, oars were dipped, and the dog swam astern, breathing gruffly and whin-ing. The otter head, drifting nearer, sank when a man pointed with his pipe-stem. Fifty yards below, by the chain sagging and lifting from the bows of the riding ship, the head looked up again beside the broken wicker-work. 'Artter,' said the man who had pointed, and forgot it. They were going to drink beer in the Plough Inn.

Their voices became faint as they walked on the wall. Flocks of ring plover and little stint flickered and twisted over the mud and the water. A late crow left the saltings, as a sedge-owl swept on long wings over the drooping yellow grass of the wall, and slunk away across the water.

Where the pill emerged into the estuary the mud

was scoured, leaving sand and gravel. Below the stone setts and pobbles of the wall's apron, whose cracks held the little ruddy winter leaves of the sea-beet, was an islet of flat stones, apart from the wall by a narrowing channel where water rushed. On the stones stood Old Nog, watching for shapes of fish. The broken crab-pot bumped and lurched along the channel, and the heron straightened his neck when he saw a fish jump out of its crown. He peered in the dusky water, where weeds moved darkly, and saw the fish darting before a tapered shadow. It was green and yellow, with a streamer flying from its back. Old Nog snicked the gemmeous dragonet from before the otter's nose, shook it free of his beak, caught it in a jerk that pushed it into his gullet, and swallowed it while the otter was still searching.

Tarka saw a blur of movement above, and swam on underwater to the wide sea.

Colour faded; the waves broke grey. Across the marsh a shining fly had lit on the white bone of the lighthouse. A bird flew in hooped flight up the estuary, wheeled below the islet, and began feeding. It saw Tarka, and out of its beak, hooped as its wings in downward gliding, fell a croak, which slurred upwards to a whistle, and broke in a sweet trill as it flew away. Other curlews on the sandbanks heard the warning, and to the far shore the wan air was beautiful with their cries.

Rows of hurdles, black and weed-hung, stood out of the water farther down the estuary. They were staked on three sides of a pool, while every rising tide flooded over the tops of the fences. It was an old salmon weir. The hurdles had been torn away so many times by the dredging anchors of gravel barges and ketches, whose crews were friendly with poor net fishermen, that the owner had let the weir fall ruinous. Herons fished from the hurdles, and at low tide crows picked shellfish off the stakes, and flying with them to the islet, dropped them on the stones.

At half tide Old Nog flew to the seventh hurdle up from the western row, where, unless gorged or in love or disturbed by man, he perched awhile during every ebb-tide. He stood swaying and sinuating his neck; the grip of his toes was not so strong as it had been in his early tree-top life. While he was trying to stand still, before jumping to the rim of the sandbank awash below him, a salmon leapt in the lagoon, gleaming and curved, and fell back with a thwack on the water. Old Nog screamed, and fell off the hurdle. Three heads looked up, and dipped again. Old Nog walked along under the hurdles, watching the water. The salmon was many times Old Nog's own weight, but it was a fish, and Old Nog was a fisher.

Tarka was drifting past the weir when he heard the whistle of White-tip beyond the hurdles. His head and shoulder rose out of the water; he listened.

Hu-ee-ic!

White-tip answered him. Her cry was like wet fingers drawn over a pane of glass. Tarka's cry was deeper, more rounded, and musical. He ran across the strip of wet sand, clambered over the hurdles, and down to the lagoon. He touched water, and a ripple spread out from where he had disappeared. His seals in the sand crumpled as they welled water.

Ka-ak! Old Nog ejected the living dragonet in his excitement, for the salmon had leapt again, a glimmering curve. The teeth of White-tip clicked at its tail. Three otter heads bobbed, flat as corks of a salmon net. They vanished before the double splash fell.

The salmon passed through the cubs, cutting the water. They turned together. Tarka drove between them and slowed to their pace, keeping line. Then White-tip, who was faster than Tarka, overhauled them, and the old otters took the wings. The line swung out and in as each otter swam in zigzag. The eager cubs swam in each other's way. Once more the salmon rushed back against the current, Straining through the top hurdles, where the water was deeper and safer. Tarka met it; and the thresh of its turning tail beat up splinters of water. The line of otters forced it into the shallow by the lower hurdles. They swam upon it, resting in two feet of water, but it escaped past one of the cubs.

Soon the tide dropped back from the top row of hurdles and the water was cleared of sand. A race poured steadily through a gap in the sandbank, spreading wider as it drained the lagoon. In the penned and slack upper water the salmon was lying, its fins and tail so still that shrimps rose out of their hiding-places in the sand beside it. While it rested in the water, its gills

opening and closing, a dark squat thing was walking
on the sands towards it, using its fins as feet. It was the
shape of an immense tadpole, covered with tatters of
skin like weed. Its head was as broad as a barrel, gaping
with a mouth almost as wide. Its jaws were filled with
bands of long pointed teeth, which it depressed in the
cavern of its mouth when it came near the salmon. Out
of the middle of its head rose three stalks, the first of
which bore a lappet, which it waved like a bait as it
crept forward. It was a sea-devil, called rod-and-line
fish by fishermen. During the spring-tide it had left the
deep water beyond the bar where usually it lived, and
moving up the estuary, had been trapped in the hurdle
weir.

It crept forward so slowly that the salmon did not
know it for an enemy. The close-set eyes behind the
enormous bony lips were fixed on the salmon. Chains
of bubbles loomed beyond, with otter shapes; the
salmon swirled off the sand, into the cavern of jaws;
the teeth rose in spikes and the jaws shut.

Thrice the old otters worked round and across the
dwindling lagoon in search of the fish, and then they
forgot it, and went down with the tide. Stars shone
over the estuary, the cries of wading birds were wandering as the air. The otters drifted down, passing the
cottage glimmering white on the sea-wall, passing the
beached hulk of the hospital ship, silent and dark but
for a solitary candle in a porthole. The tide took them
to the spit of gravel, crowned by sandhills bound with
marram grasses, called Crow Island, and here they left

the water for a ragrowster. While the cubs were rolling and biting, Tarka and White-tip played the game of searching and pretending not to find. They galloped up the sandhills to slide to the hollows again. They picked up sticks, empty shells of skate's eggs, old bones and feathers of sea-birds, corks from the jetsam of the high tide, and tossed with them in their paws. They hid in the spines of the tussocks, and jumped out at each other.

The lighthouse beams shone on the wet sands down by the water and across the Pool the lights of the village lay like wind-blown embers. *Craa-leek, cur-lee-eek!* The curlews saw them as they swam the shallow water to the top of the Sharshook. White-tip and Tarka ate mussels down by the black-and-white Pulley buoy, and the cubs followed them to the pools of the lower ridge.

Salmon, feverish to spawn in the fresh waters of their birth, were 'running' up the fairway, and with the flow came a seal who tore a single bite from the belly of each fish it caught, and left it to chase others. Tarka brought one of the wounded fish to the rocks, and the otters scratched away scales in their haste to eat its pink flesh. They sliced from the shoulders, dropping pieces to feel the curd squeezed from the corners of their mouths. Tarka and White-tip ate quietly, but the cubs yinnered and snarled. Their faces were silvery with scales when they left the strewn bones. Being clean little beasts they washed chins and whiskers and ears, and afterwards sought water to drink in the pond behind the sea-wall cottage.

Among the reeds the four otters lay, dozing and

resting, while rain pitted the grey sheet of water and wind bent down the stalks of the wild celery that grew in the marsh. When the clouds became duller they left the pond, and saw the tide lapping almost over the top of the wall, coloured with the fresh from the rivers.

Mullet had come up with the tide, and a school of nearly a hundred found a way through a drain-lid under the sea-wall of the pill. At the end of the night the otters, who had been gorging on eels in the mires – reed-fringed dykes in the grazing marsh, filled with fresh drinking-water from the hills – found them in the pit in the corner of Horsey marsh. For two hours they chased and slew, and when every fish was killed Tarka and White-tip stole away on the ebb to the sea, leaving the young otters to begin their own life.

The next night was quiet and windless, without a murmur of water in the broad Pool, on which the lights of the village drew out like gold and silver eels. Sound travels far and distinct over placid water, and fishermen standing in groups on the quay, after the closing of taverns, heard the whistling cries of the young otters, a mile away on Crow Island, lost on the shingle where the ring plovers piped. They were heard for three nights, and then the south-west gale smote the place and filled the estuary with great seas.

Black bits of old leaves turned and twirled in the flooded weir-pool above Canal Bridge, like the rooks turning and twirling high in the grey windy sky. The weir in flood was an immense loom in sunlight; the

downfalling water-warp was whitey-yellow with bubbles; to and fro across the weir moved the air-hollows,
a weft held by a glistening water-shuttle. Below, the
bubble-woven waters were rended on the shillets; they
leapt and roared and threw up froth and spray. A
branch of a tree was lodged on the sill; the rocks had
stripped it of bark. Sometimes a lead-coloured narrow
shape, longer than a man's arm, would appear in the
falling water-warp, moving slowly against the torrent
with sideways flaps of tail until washed back into the
lower river again, which roared and heaved like fighting polar bears. The sun lit the travelling air-hollow
under the sill of the weir.

The salmon never reached the sill. Some fish tried to
swim up the fish-pass, but the pound of the flood was
mightier on the steps. Above in the weir-pool a bird
was swimming, low in the water, watching with small
crimson eyes for trout. Its beak was sharp as a rock-
splinter. Above the water it was brownish-black, foam-
grey beneath – a Great Northern Diver, or loon, in
winter plumage. When Tarka saw it first it was rolling
from side to side and stretching out first one wing then
the other. The otter on the bank alarmed the bird,
which tipped up and vanished quick as the flash of a
turning fish, hardly leaving a ripple. When it appeared
again the otter was gone. It lay in the water, nearly a
yard long, with head and neck stretched out, and swam
rapidly up-river. At the top of the pool it saw another
otter, and uttering a wailing cry of alarm, splashed
along the water to rise, making a dozen oar-like dips

with the tips of its wings. With neck outstretched it took the air and flew round the curve of the river, with wing-beats quicker than a heron's.

Tarka and White-tip had come from the wood in daylight, lured to play by the sun and the flood. Tarka dropped over the sill, the whitey-yellow turmoil bumped and tossed him below. A minute later a narrow lead-coloured shape pushed slowly up the concrete spill-way, and behind it the darker sturdier shape of an otter. Fish and animal made slow and laborious headway; they seemed to be hanging in the warp; and then White-tip dropped over in the smooth and glistering water's bend. They instantly disappeared. The racing churn carried them on its top to the bank thirty yards below, and there left them on stones; and there, an hour later, a thirty-pound fish, clean-run, its gills crusty with ocean shellfish, was found by the water-bailiff, with bites torn from behind its shoulder – the mating feast of otters.

November, December, January, February, were past – but otters know only day and night, the sun and the moon. White-tip and Tarka had followed the salmon up the big river, but at the beginning of the new year they had come down again. Drifting with the ebb under Halfpenny Bridge, they crossed the marsh and came to the Pool of the Six Herons, out of whose deep middle reared the black iron piers of the Railway Bridge. Just below the Railway Bridge, the muddy mouth of the Lancarse Yeo was washed and widened by the sea, and in here, on the flood tide, the otters turned. White-tip was way-wise in this water, having known it in cubhood. She was going back to the Twin-Ash Holt above Orleigh Mill, where she had been born.

With the tide the otters drifted under the road-bridge to a holt in an old rabbit-bury above high-water mark. It was fallen in, and the home of rats, so they left it, and travelled on in daylight. A mile from the pill-mouth the water ran fresh and clear. After another mile they came to the meeting of two streams. White-tip walked up the left stream, and soon she reached the slide where she had played during many happy nights with her cub-brothers; and climbing up, she was in the remembered weir-pool. It was narrow, and nearly hidden by trees. Past six pines, and round a bend, where two ash trees leaned over the brook. Ivy grew on one, moss on the other. Floods had washed the earth from their top roots, carving a dark holt under the bank. White-tip had forgotten the baying and yapping and thudding one day long ago, when an iron bar had broken a hole in the roof and scared the five of them into the water. She had remembered the bass at night round the bridge piers in the Pool of the Six Herons, the frogging places in the Archery Marsh, the trout and the mullyheads in the Duntz Brook, the eels in the millpool; and she had come back to them.

The soft elderberry tree broke into leaf, with the honeysuckle; the wild cherry blossom showed white among the oaks. The greed shovels of the celandine dug pale gold out of the sun, and the flowers were made. Oak and ash remained hard-budded; these trees, enduring and ancient, were not moved to easy change like lesser growths.

On the first day of March Halcyon the kingfisher, speeding up the brook, hit the sandy bank with his beak and fell away. His mate followed him, knocking out another flake of earth, and thus a perching place was made. They picked out a tunnel with their beaks, as long as a man's arm, with a round cave at the end in which seven round eggs were laid, shiny and white, among bones of fishes and shucks of water-beetles. Then the river-martins came back to their old drowned homes in the steep sandy banks above the springtime level of the brook. In the third week of March the carrion-crow, secure in her nest of sticks atop one of the six pines growing over the pool below the Twin-Ash Holt, watched the first chipping of her five eggs, watched the tip of a tiny beak chip, chip, chipping a lid in a green black-freckled shell. The crow sang a song, low and sweet, in the tree top. White-tip heard the song as she suckled her cubs in the Twin-Ash Holt. Every night Tarka came up from the Pool of the Six Herons to see her.

March winds brought the grey sea-rains to the land, and the river ran swollen, bearing the floods of its brooks and runners. Salmon, languid from spawning, dropped tail-first over the sills and down the passes of the weirs, and Tarka caught them easily in the eddies and hovers, and dragged them on the bank. He took bites from the infirm and tasteless flesh, and left the fish uneaten. Many of the salmon that reached the sea alive were taken in the nets of fishermen rough-fish-catching, in the estuary Pool, to be knocked on the head and thrown back – for the fishermen hated the water-bailiffs who upheld the Conservancy Bye-laws protecting salmon out of season, and secretly killed the fish because of their hatred. The fishermen did not believe that salmon spawned in fresh water, where the rivers were young, but regarded it as a story told to prevent them fishing for salmon throughout the year.

Oak and ash broke their buds, and grew green; the buzzards repaired their old nests, and laid their eggs. The heron's young, after days of flapping and unhappy crying, flew from their tree-top heronry in the wood below Halfpenny Bridge. And one evening in June, between the lights, Old Nog and his mate sailed down to the pool by the Railway Bridge to give the four fledgelings their first lesson in fishing. Curlews saw the dark level wings gliding over the mudbanks, and cried the alarm, being afraid of the sharp beaks. Every year Old Nog and his mate taught four fledgelings to spear fish in the pool, which lay placid when the sea had lapsed.

Six herons stood in a row eighty yards above the bridge, in the sandy shallow at the head of the pool. *Kack! Kack! Kack! Kack!* – the young birds squawked with eagerness and delight. Dusk deepened over the wide and empty river, the pool shone faintly with the sky. Down by the round black piers of the bridge something splashed. Old Nog raised his head, for he had been awaiting the splash. It was a sign that the bass in the pool were beginning to feed.

Splash, splatter, splash. Soon many fish were rising to take the shrimp-fly on the surface. They were hungry after the daytime rest, having gone up with the tide to Halfpenny Bridge, and returned to the pool without feeding, while men on the banks fished with lines of rag-worm-baited hooks. Usually the men went home to supper, with empty baskets, before the fishes' feeding time. Then to the quiet pool came that wise fisher, Old Nog, with his family, standing motionless while the bass swam into the shallow water; – splash, splatter, splash, as they turned on their gleaming sides to take the shrimp-fly. Old Nog peered with beak held low, and snicked – *Kack! Kack! Kack! Kack!* cried the four small herons, beating vanes and falling over long toes in their eagerness to gulp the silvery fish.

Gark! said Old Nog, swallowing the bass, and thrusting his beak and long feathered neck at the four. *Gark!* They got out of his way; never before had he spoken so severely to them. One saw the flicker of a fish in the water, and stepped towards it; the bass saw the enemy, and sped into deeper water. *Gark!* said Old Nog, sharply, and they stood still.

Sucking noises arose out of the pool as it grew darker. These were the feeding noises of male eels, thin and small and mud-coloured, whom the larger blue females would meet in the autumnal migration. In wriggling rushes the eels sought the shrimp-fly in the shallows, and whenever one passed near a beak – *dap!* it was snicked, lifted from the water as a writhing knot, and swallowed.

The Railway Bridge loomed low and black against the glimmer of sky and water. Splash, splatter, the bass were moving about the pool. Two or three lay trout-wise, in the slight downward current by each round iron pier, watching the surface above them for the dark moving speck of a shrimp. The splashes of their jumps echoed under the girders.

A summer sandpiper flew over the bridge, crying in the darkness, for it had been alarmed while feeding under the mud slopes of the empty pill. It was answered by a curlew on the gravel bank above the herons.

Immediately below the bridge the brook poured its little fresh stream into the pool; raising up little ridges of sand, sweeping them away again with sudden little noises. Splash, splatter, the bass were feeding in the weed on the stone piling below the bridge-end. Patter, patter, five dark shapes moving on the soft wet sand of the pill's mouth – the pattering ceased, and the brook slurred its sand-sounds as they slid into the pool. White-tip had brought her four cubs from the Twin-Ash Holt.

The vigorous splashing of the bass was lessening, for many fish were gorged with fry. A whitish shine by the stone piling, and one had risen to seize a shrimp in its large mouth – splash, flicker, splatter, bubble. A dark shape crawled out of the water with. the bass. Three lesser shapes followed, yikkering on the stone piling. White-tip turned back into the pool.

Krark! Kak! Ark! Kak! Kack! Kack! Kack! Kack! Kak!
Kak! Gark! Kack!

With heads upheld and watching the herons talked among themselves. They saw three cubs fighting over the fish on the piling; and two heads in the water between the first and second pier. Tarquol, the eldest cub, was following White-tip, for he liked to do his own hunting; and it was in the Pool of the Six Herons that the strange big otter, who chased him in and out of the piers, never biting or sulking, was to be found. Tarquol, who had two white toes on one of his paws, was stronger than the other cubs, and often hurt them in play without knowing it.

The bass, staying in the flumes around the piers with fin and tail, watched the dim forewater above them. All was dark beside and below them. Tarquol and White-tip swam one on either side of a pier, deeper than the bass, whose narrow shapes were dark and plain above them. A fish darted around the pier before White-tip, and was taken by Tarquol. He ate it on the quicksand of the right bank, away from the cubs. The sharp point of the back fin pricked his mouth.

The otters caught eels in the shallow edges of the pool, watched by the hungry herons, whose harsh continuous cries told their hunger. When the cubs had eaten enough they played on the sand, running on and on until they were behind the six birds, on the ridge of gravel where snags were part buried. Curlews – the unmated birds which had not gone to the moors – flew off the glidders, and away up the tidal reaches of the river.

Hu-ee-ic!

Tarquol, playing with the rotten crown of an old bowler hat – fishermen always kept their bait in old Sunday chapel-going hats – heard the whistle, and dashed back to the pool. *Krark!* cried Old Nog, flying up before him, his toes on the water. *Kak! Kack! Kack! Kack! Kack!* as his mate and youngsters followed. Old Nog flew over the bridge, but seeing and hearing the tide flowing up, he wheeled and beat up the Yeo valley. The five herons followed him, but he dived at them, screaming *Gark! Gark!* Old Nog was weary after many weeks of hunger, of disgorging nearly all he caught into the greedy maws of four grown fledgelings, and often, the greedy maw of his mate. *Krark!* a cry of satisfaction. Old Nog flew alone.

Every night for a week the otters came to the pool at low water, until the tides, ebbing later and later, and so into daylight, stopped the fishing. One evening, when the Peal Rock in the river below Canal Bridge was just awash after a thunderstorm, Tarka and White-tip and the four cubs followed a run of peal as far as the weirpool, staying out until after sunrise, when several fish were taken in the water, then low and clear again. The Twin-Ash Holt was far behind them, so they slept in a holt under an oak, which was entered by an opening two feet below the water-level. The next night they went on up the river, catching and eating fish on the scours and shoals, then hastening back to water again.

Tarquol swam near Tarka; the cub was lithe and

swift as his parent, and sometimes snatched fish from his mouth. They rolled and romped together, clutching rudders and heads and pretending to bite; their joyful whistles went far down the river, heard by Old Nog as he sailed by in the wasting moonlight.

Paler the moon rose, and at dawn White-tip went down with the cubs and Tarka wandered on alone; but he turned back again, calling her to Canal Bridge to play one last game.

Hu-ee-ic!

They played the old bridge game of the West Country otters, which was played before the Romans came. They played around the upper and lower cutwater of the middle pier, while the lesser stars were crowned in the heavenly tide flowing up the eastern sky, and the trees of the hill-lane grew dark, and larks were flying with song.

Hu-ee-ic!

Tarquol followed Tarka out of the river and along the otterpath across the bend, heedless of his mother's call. He followed up the river and across another bend; but, scared of the light, returned to water and sought a holt under a sycamore. Tarka went on alone, up three miles of river, to a holt in a weir-pool shadowed by trees, where peal were leaping. The sun looked over the hills, the moon was as a feather dropped by the owl flying home, and Tarka slept, while the water flowed, and he dreamed of a journey with Tarquol down to a strange sea, where they were never hungry, and never hunted.

CHAPTER 18

*A*t half past ten in the morning a covered motor-van stopped at the bridge below the Dark Pool. From the driver's seat three men got down, and at the sound of their footfalls deep notes came from the van. Hearing the hounds, the two terriers – Biff and Bite'm – held by a girl in a jacket and short skirt of rough blue serge, yapped and strained against the chain.

Motor-cars were drawn up on one side of the road. The men, women, and children who had come to the meet of otter-hounds stood by them and talked or lounged against the stone parapets of the bridge. Some men leaned on long ash-poles, stained and polished

with linseed oil and shod with iron and notched from
the top downwards with the number of past kills, two
notches crossed denoting a double-kill. The women
carried smaller and slenderer poles, either of ash or
male bamboo. There were blackthorn thumbsticks,
hazel-wands, staves of ground-ash; one boy held the
handle of a carpet-sweeper, slightly warped. He had
poked the end in some nettles, lest the wooden screw
be seen by other boys. It had no notches.

Faces turned to the hound-van. Huntsman and his
whipper-in each lifted a rusty pin from the staples in
the back of the van and lowered the flap. Immediately
hounds fell out and over each other, and to the road,
shaking themselves, whimpering, panting with pink
tongues flacking, happy to be free after the crush and
heat of the journey from kennels. They were admired
and stroked, patted and spoken to by name; they
scatched themselves and rolled and licked each other's
necks; they sat and looked up at the many faces – old
Harper solemnly, with eyes sunk by age, the younger
hounds, still remembering their walking days, going to
seek their human friends, and sniff and nuzzle pockets
where biscuits, cake, and sandwiches were stored. The
kennel-boy and whip called them by name and flicked
gently near the more restless with his whip: Barbrook
and Bellman, Boisterous and Chorister, Dewdrop, Sailoress, Coraline, and Waterwitch; Armlet, who lay
down to sleep, Playboy and Actor, Render and Fencer;
Hemlock the one-eyed, with Bluemaid, Hurricane,
Harper, and Pitiful, the veterans; Darnel and Grinder,

who sat behind Sandboy. Then two young hounds of the same litter, Dabster and Dauntless, sons of Dewdrop and Deadlock.

And there Deadlock, his black head scarred with old fights, sat on his haunches, apart and morose, watching for the yellow waistcoat of the Master. His right ear showed the mark made by the teeth of Tarka's mother two years before, when he had thrust his head into the hollow of the fallen tree. The swung thong of the whip idly flicked near Deadlock; he moved his head slightly and his eyes; from upper and lower teeth the lips were drawn, and looking at the kennel-boy's legs, Deadlock growled. The hound hated him.

People were watching. The whipper-in felt that the hound was making him ridiculous, and flicked Deadlock with the lash, speaking sharply to him. The hound's growls grew more menacing. Between his teeth the hound yarred, the dark pupils of his eyes becoming fixed in their stare. Then seeing Dabster trotting off to the bridge the whipper-in gladly went after him. Deadlock looked away, ignoring all eyes.

Other cars descended the hill above the bridge and stopped on the left of the road. For a week in the early summer of each year, known as the Joint Week, a neighbouring hunt visited the country of the Two Rivers, bringing their own hounds with them, so that the home pack might rest every other day of the six hunting days. Other otter-hunters came from their rivers which flowed into the seas of Britain west and south and east. Their uniforms were coloured as the dragonflies over the river. There were grey pot-hats, dark blue jackets and stockings, and white breeches of the Cheriton; the grey hats and breeches, and stockings and red coats of the Culmstock; the cream-collared bright blue coats and stockings and cream breeches of the Crowhurst from Surrey, Kent, and Sussex; men of the Dartmoor, all in navy-blue, from pad-pinned cap to black brogues, except for white stock round the throat; the green double-peaked caps, green coats, scarlet ties, white breeches, and green stockings of the Courtenay Tracey from Wessex. A man like a great seal, jovial and gruff among laughing friends, wore the gayest uniform, in the judgement of two ragged children. It blazed and winked in the sunlight, scarlet and blue and brass.

Shortly after half past ten o'clock eleven and a half couples of hounds and two terriers, nearly throttling themselves in eagerness to press forward, were trotting behind the huntsman through the farmyard to the river. The huntsman repeated a cooing chant at the back of his nose of *C-o-o-o-o-orn-yer! Co-o-o-o-orn-yer! W-wor! W-wor!* with names of hounds. They trotted with waving sterns, orderly and happy, enjoying the sounds, which to them were promise of sport and fun if only they kept together and ignored the scent of duck, cat, offal, mouse, and cottage-infant's jammy crust. They pattered through the farmyard in best behaviour; they loved the huntsman, who fed them and pulled thorns out of their feet and never whipped them, although he sometimes dropped unpleasant medicine at the back of their tongues, and held their muzzles, and stroked their throats until they could hold it there no longer, but had to swallow. The *W-wor! W-wor!* and other cooing dog-talk was understood perfectly; they caused even Deadlock to forget to growl when young Dabster, avoiding a kitten, bumped into him. For the two strongest feelings in Deadlock, apart from those of his private kennel life, were bloodthirst for otters and his regard for the huntsman.

They jumped down the bank into the river, leaping across the shallows to the left bank, and working upstream to the occasional toot of the horn. Almost at once Deadlock whimpered and bounded ahead. Tarka had touched there, on the shillets, six hours before.

They came to the groove in the right bank, between two hazel stoles, where Tarka had climbed out to cross the meadows to the weir, for the river-course was like a horseshoe. The grasses still held enough scent for the hounds to own, and they followed the trail to the wood that grew steeply up from the water. A crow, that had been waiting on the weir-sill for beetles and little fish to pass in the gentle film of water near its feet, heard them as they splashed up the leat and flew to the top of a tall tree to watch hidden in the leaves. The crow had seen Tarka as he swam from the leat into the Dark Pool at five o'clock in the morning. Then he had loudly cawed, calling his mate to annoy the otter; now he kept quiet. Hounds swam up the pool.

A furlong above the weir was a ford, where, in summer, horse-drawn butts go for the gravel heaped up by winter floods. By the ford was a tree, and under the roots of the tree was a holt. Deadlock, Render, and Fencer swam to the tree, whimpering, splashing, scratching, and tearing at roots with their teeth. Soon the pack was trying to break into the entrance. They did not obey voice, horn, and whip at once, but had to be urged away by taps of whip-handles on ribs, and by individual commands. *Go'r'n leave it! Go'r'n leave it!* cried one of the honorary whips, in a yarring voice, to Deadlock and Render, who remained. A little shivering sharp-nosed terrier, uncollared, peered with cock-ears and whined on the bank above. The entrance to the holt was under water, and Biff's collar was slipped round her neck again.

The honorary whip, a retired senior officer of the army, prodded with his pole among the roots, and finding soft earth, tried to force the pole to the back of the holt. The water moved away in a yellow muddy wound. He worked until he was hot. He stopped, pushed his hat back from his forehead, and rubbed it with his goatskin glove. 'Where's that chap with the bar?' Below the holt, at intervals of ten to fifteen yards, men were gazing into the sun-dappled water of the Dark Pool. Voices sounded high above, where on the road cut in the rock many of the cars were waiting.

A man came hastening down the cart-track with the iron digging bar. A hole was worked in the ground over the holt, while a sportsman in the Cheriton uniform banged the turf with the length of his pole. The hole was made deeper, the bar worked backwards and forwards, and plunged hard down.

The Master, leaning his chin upon his hands clasping the top of his pole, saw a chain of bubbles rise a yard from the bank, and steadily lengthen aslant the river. Sweeping off his grey hat, he scooped the air with it, crying *Tally-Ho!* Hounds poured down the track and splashed into the river, giving tongue and stirring up the gravel silt. Through shadows of trees lying on the water the lit dust drifted. Many hounds swam mute, striving hard to take the lead, urged by the cries and gestures in front of them.

The chain drew out from one bank to another, in stretches of fifty and sixty yards, until by the sill of the weir a ripple was made by a brown head that sank immediately; but was viewed.

Yoi-yoi-yoi-yoi! Ov-ov-ov-ov-ov-ov-over! Tallyho-! He's gone down the leat!

The dark green weeds were bending and swayed silently by the slow glide of the water. The leat was deep, with a dark brown bed. It had been dug to carry water to the elm wheels of the two mills by the bridge a mile below. Now the larger wheel had been replaced by a turbine, which used less water. Leaves rotted on the leat's bed, the water brimmed almost into the meadow. Tarka swam through the dark green swaying weed, and over the dark brown bed. When he swung up to breathe his nose showed in the ripple like a dead leaf turned up in the current, and settling down again. He swam under the crinkled top-scrum by the heavy oaken fender, which was raised to let the water through.

A trout darted by him as he passed under the fender, and he caught it with a sudden turn of his body.

Trees made the leat shadowy; ferns hung over it, the taloned brambles stretched down to the water. It flowed in the low ground of the valley, bending like the river below it. It left the meadows, the tall grasses, and the reddening sorrel, and flowed through a jungle of rushes and grasses, briars and hazel bushes, where the webs of spiders were loaded with bees, flies, and grasshoppers. Only a weasel could run on the banks. The blue flowers of borage and comfrey grew in the jungle, where the buds of the dog-rose were opening.

Sometimes a swift, cutting the air with alternate strokes of its narrow black wings, dashed a ripple as it sipped and sped on. Willow wrens flitted in the ash-sprays lower down, taking insects on the leaves. A chiffchaff sang its two-note song. By a briar raking the water the otter's head was raised; he listened and swam to the bank. Hounds spoke remotely; he knew Dead-lock's tongue among them. He climbed out of the leat, the trout still in his mouth, and pushed through the undergrowth, among nettles and marsh-wort, and over soft damp ground. Robins ticked at him, wrens stittered. Burrs and seeds tried to hook to his hair, finding no hold. Warble flies tried to alight on his back and suck his blood; the rushes brushed them off. He ran in a loop back to the leat, and slipped into the water above the hounds, who had gone down. He swam up for a quarter of a mile, then rested by an alder-root and listened to the pack running over his land-trail. He looked round for stone whereupon to eat the fish, but hearing Deadlock's tongue, he lay still.

From the wooded hillside above the distant bank of the river came the knock of axes on the trunk of an oak tree, the shouts of woodmen, a sudden crack, the hissing rush and thud of breaking branches, and then quietness, until began the steady knock of boughs being lopped. After a while Tarka did not hear these sounds – he was listening in another direction. He scarcely heard the shooting buzz of sun-frisked flies over the heat. He felt no fear; all his energy was in listening.

Chiff-chaff, chiff-chaff, chiff-chaff sang the bird among the ash trees. And soon the voices of men, the tearing of brambles against coats, boots trampling and snapping the hollow green stalks of hog weed and hemlock. Tarka saw their heads and shoulders against the sky, and swam on up the leat.

His scent was washed down by the water, and the hounds followed him. He crept out on the other bank, on soft ground littered with dead leaves, which lay under crooked oak trees. He ran swiftly up the slope and entered a larch plantation, where the sky was shut out. The narrow lines of thin straight poles stood in a duskiness as of midsummer night. All sound was shut out; nothing grew under the trees. A wood owl peered down at him as he ran among the brittle fallen twigs; it peered over its back and softly hooted to its mate. The plantation was silent again.

Tarka sat by the bole in the middle of the Dark

Hams Wood, listening through the remote sough of wind in the branches to the faint cries below. The smell of the sap was strong in his nostrils. He dropped the fish. Sometimes he heard the querulous scream of a jay, and the clap of pigeon-wings as the birds settled in the tree-tops.

For nearly twenty minutes he waited by the tree, and then the hunting cries swelled in the narrow groves of the wood. The owl flapped off its branch, and Tarka ran down the leat again, passing the hounds nine lines of trees away from them. Sunlight dazzled him when he ran out of the plantation. Then he saw many men and women before him.

Tally-Ho!

Tarka ran round them and dived into the leat. When first he had swum down, the water had brimmed to the meadow, floating the green plants in its slow-gliding current; now the bank glistened with a sinking watermark, and only the tags of the starwort were waving. Trout darted before him as he swam against the water flowing faster. Often his head showed as he walked half out of water beside the starwort. He reached the square oaken fender, where only a rillet trickled. It rested on the bed of the leat, penning the water above.

Tally-Ho!

Tarka turned and went down the leat again. He reached water deep enough to cover him before he met the hounds, who, hunting by the sense of smell, did not see him moving as a dark brown shadow through the channels in the weeds. Hounds passed him, for the wash – or scent on the water – was still coming down.

Tarka swam down to the mill end of the leat, which was dark with the brown stains of stagnant life on its muddy bed. Trees kept the sun from it. A runner, or streamlet, from other woods joined it at this end, and waited in the pool to pass through the grating to the mills. Tarka swam under the culvert of the runner, but finding shallow water he returned and looked for a hole or drain in the banks. Shafts of sunlight pierced the leaves and dappled the water. A broad shade lay before the grating, where oak planks, newly sawn, were stacked over the water. The ringing rasp of a circular saw cutting hard wood suddenly rang under the trees, overbearing the shaken rumble of millstones grinding corn. Specks of wood settled on the water beyond the shade, where Tarka rested, staying himself by a paw on a rusty nail just above the water level.

He waited and listened. The sawdust drifted past him, and was sucked away between the iron bars of the grating. The noise of the saw ceased. He heard the hounds again, coming down the leat. A voice just over his head cried, *One o'clock!* Footfalls hurried away from the saw. The hatch was closed, the trundling wheel slowed into stillness. Tarka heard the twittering of swallows; but he was listening for the sound of the horn. Deadlock speaking! Up the leat waterside plants were crackling as feet trod them down. Voices of the whips, one harsh and rating, were coming nearer. Heads and shoulders moved over the culvert. When the leading hound swam into the pool, throwing his tongue, Tarka dived and found a way through the grating, where one iron bar was missing – a space just wide enough for an otter. He drew himself on to the hatch and walked slowly up the wet and slippery wooden troughs to the top of the wheel. He squatted low and watched the grating. Hounds swam along it and Deadlock pushed his black head in the space of the missing bar. His flews pressed the iron and stopped him. He bayed into the cavern where the ancient water-wheel dripped beside the curved iron conduit of the modern water turbine. The place was gloomy; but in a corner, framed in a triangle of sunlight, three ferns hung out of the mortar – spleenwort, wall-rue, and male fern. Five young wagtails filled a nest built on the roots of the male fern; the nestlings crouched down in fear of the baying.

Drops from the elmwood trough dripped into the plash hollowed in the rock under the wheel. Tarka sat on the topmost trough, his rudder hanging over the rim of the wheel. He heard the shrill yapping of terriers on leash; the shuffle of feet on the road over the culvert; the murmur of voices. Poles were pushed among the layers of planks; feet of hounds pounded the deep water as they swam under the timber baulks. He listened to their whimpers; smelt their breath. After a time the noises receded, and he heard *chik-ik*, *chik-ik* – the cries of the parent wagtails, waiting on the roof with beakfuls of river flies. Tarka licked his paws and settled more comfortably in the sodden elmwood trough. Sometimes his eyes closed, but he did not sleep.

At two o'clock he heard voices in the gloomy wheel-house. The men were returning to work after dinner. The hatch was lifted. Water gushed in and over the trough. The wheel shuddered and moved. Water gushed in and over each trough as it was lowered on the rim, and the wheel began its heavy splashing trundle. Tarka was borne down into darkness and flung on the rock. Under the troughs he crept, to the shallow stream that was beginning to flow through a lower culvert to the river. Sunlight dazed him. The bridge was ten yards below.

The parapet before and above him was a smooth line across the sky, except for a wagtail's pied body, the tops of three polypody ferns, the head and shoulders of an old grey-bearded man in a blue coat, and a black empty beer-bottle.

Tally-Ho!

CHAPTER 19

*T*arka became one with the river, finding his course among the slimy stones so that his back was always covered. He rose beside the middle pier, whose cutwater was hidden by a faggot of flood sticks. Under the sticks was dimness, streaked and blurred with sunlight. Tarka hid and listened.

His paws rested on a sunken branch. The water moved down, clouded with the mud-strings of the leat. He lay so still that the trout returned to their stances beside the stone sterlings.

B'hoys, b'hoys! Com' on, ol' fellars! Leu in, ol' fellars. Com' on, all 'v yer!

The stain spread into the pool below the bridge. Hounds whimpered and marked at the stick-pile. Their many tongues smote all other sounds from Tarka's ears. He knew they could not reach him in his retreat, and so he stayed there even when a pole thrust into the heap rubbed against his flank. Then over his head the sticks began to crack and creak, as a man climbed upon them. The man jumped with both feet together on the heap. Tarka sank and turned downstream. Cries from the lower parapet; thudding of boots above. The chain of bubbles drew out downstream.

Tarka swam to the left bank, where he touched and breathed. He heard, in the half-second his head was out of water, the noise that had terrified him as a cub – the noise of an iron-shod centipede crossing the shallows. Way down the river was stopped by a line of upright figures, standing a yard apart and stirring the water with poles. Tarka heard the noise under-water, but swam down until he saw before him the bright-bubbled barrier. He swung round and swam upstream as fast as three and a half webbed feet could push him.

He swam under the heap of sticks again, enduring the massed tongues of marking hounds until the creak-ing and thudding over his head drove him to open water again. He swam under an arch, turned by the lower sterling, and swam up another arch, to a back-water secluded from the main stream by the ridge of shillets made by the cross-leaping waters of the runner in flood. An ash tree grew over the backwater, but

Tarka could find no holding in its roots. He swam past the legs of swimming hounds and went down again.

Tally-Ho!

He swam through the plying poles of the stickle, and ran over the shallow, reaching safe water before the pack came down. He was young and fast and strong. Hounds were scattered behind him, some swimming, others plunging through the shallows below the banks, stooping to the scent washed on scour and shillet, and throwing their tongues. He could not see them, when swimming underwater, until they were nearly over him. He swam downstream, never turning back, touching first one bank to breathe, and then swimming aslant to the other. Once in the straight mile of river under the Town on the Hill, he emerged by a shallow almost by Deadlock's feet; instantly he turned back. Farther down, by a jungle of balsam, whose top drought-roots were like the red toes of a bird, he left the river and ran on the bank, under trees. He had gone thirty yards on the hot land when Render and Deadlock crashed through the jungle of hollow sap-filled stalks after him. Although his legs were short – it was difficult to see them when he ran – he moved faster than any of the men hunting him could run. He left the land a hundred yards above Taddiport Bridge, by a bank where shards of Roman tiles were jutting.

Below the bridge was a ridge of shillets, long and wide as the broken hull of a sailing ship. Alders and willows grew here, and tall grasses that hid the old dry twigs and reeds on the lower branches of the trees.

Floods had heaped up the island. The wet marks of Tarka's feet and rudder soon dried on the worn flakes of rock; but not before the larger pads of hounds, making the loose shillets clatter, had covered them.

Leu-in! Leu-in, b'hoys. Ov-ov-ov-ov-over!

Tarka's feet were dry when he took to water, after trying to rid himself of scent on the stones so hot in the sun. He passed plants of water-hemlock and dropwort, tall as a man, growing among the stones, some sprawling with their weight of sap. He swam on down the river, passing Servis Wood, over which a buzzard, pestered by rooks, was wailing in the sky. The rooks left it to see what the hounds were doing, and wheeled silently over the river. Their shadows fled through the water, more visible than the otter.

A thousand yards from Taddiport Bridge, Tarka passed the brook up which he had travelled with his mother on the way to the Clay Pits. He swam under a railway bridge, below which the river hurried in a course narrow and shaded. An island of elm trees divided the river-bed; the right fork was dry – hawkweed, ragwort, and St John's wort, plants of the land, were growing here. Tarka swam to the tail of the island, and climbed up the dry bank. The place was cool and shady, and filled with the stench arising from the broad leaves and white flowers of wild garlic growing under the trees. Tarka trod into a thick patch, and squatted low.

Hounds passed him. He listened to them baying in the narrow channel below the island.

Deadlock clambered up the dry bank, ran a few yards among the grasses, threw up his head, sniffed, and turned away. Tarka held his breath. Other hounds followed, to sniff and run down the bank again. Tarka listened to them working among the roots under the island bank, and across the river. He heard the haunting voices of huntsman and whippers-in; the noises of motor-cars moving slowly along the hard-rutted track-way, the old canal-bed, above the right bank of the river; the voices of men and women getting out of the motor-cars; and soon afterwards, the scrape of boots on the steep rubble path down to the dry, stony bed.

Tarka had been lying among the cool and stinking garlic plants of Elm Island for nearly five minutes when he heard gasping and wheezing noises at the top of the island. The two terriers, Bite'm and Biff, were pulling at their chains, held by the kennel-boy. Their tongues hung long and limp, after the two-mile tug from the mills over sun-baked turf, dusty trackway, and hot stones to Elm Island. Just before, while tugging down the path, Bite'm had fainted with the heat. A lapping sprawl in the river had refreshed the couple, and now they strove against the collars pressing into their windpipes.

Tarka started up when they were a yard from where he lay. The kennel-boy dropped the chain when he saw him. Tarka ran towards the river, but at the sheer edge of the island he saw men on the stones six feet below. He ran along the edge, quickening at the shout of the kennel-boy, and had almost reached the Island's tail when Bite'm pinned him in the shoulder. Tissing through his open mouth, Tarka rolled and fought with the terriers. Their teeth clenched. Tarka's moves were low and smooth; he bit Bite'm again and again, but the terrier hung on. Biff tried to bite him across the neck, but Tarka writhed away. The three rolled and snarled, scratching and snapping, falling apart and returning with instant swiftness. Ears were torn and hair ripped out. Hounds heard them and ran baying under the island cliff to find a way up. The kennel-boy tried to stamp on and recover the end of the chain, for he knew that in a worry all three might be killed. White terriers and brown otter rolled nearer the edge, and fell over.

The fall shook off Bite'm. Tarka ran under the legs of Dabster, and although Bluemaid snapped at his flank he got into the water and sank away.

Tally-Ho! Tally-Ho! Yaa-aa-ee on to 'm!

By the bank, fifty yards below Elm Island, stood the Master, looking into water six inches deep. A fern frond, knocked off the bank upstream, came down turning like a little green dragon in the clear water. It passed. Then came an ash-spray, that clung around the pole he leaned on. Its leaves bent to the current, it stayed, it swung away, and drifted on. A dead stick rode after it, and a fly feebly struggling – and then the lovely sight of an otter spreading himself over the stones, moving with the stream, slowly, just touching with his feet, smooth as oil under the water. A twenty-pound dog, thought the Master, remaining quiet by the shallow water listening to the music of his hounds. There was a stickle below Rothern Bridge.

The hounds splashed past him, stopping to the scent. Tarka's head showed, and vanished. He swam under Rothern Bridge, whose three stone arches, bearing heavy motor-transport beyond their old age, showed the cracks of suffering that the ferns were filling green. A sycamore grew out of its lower parapet. Deeper water under the bridge; the frail bubble-chain lay on it. A cry above the bridge; a line of coarser bubbles breaking across the stickle, where six men and two women stood in the river.

Tarka's head looked up and saw them. He lay in the deep water. He turned his head, and watched hounds swimming down through the arch. He dived and swam up; was hunted to shallow water again, and returned, making for the stickle. The water was threshed in a line from shillet-bank to shillet-bank, but he did not turn back. As he tried to pass between a man in red and a man in blue, two pole-ends were pushed under his belly in an attempt to hoick him back. But Tarka slipped off the shillet-burnished iron and broke the stickle. The whips ran on the bank, cheering on the hounds.

Get on to 'm! Hark to DeadLock! Leu-on! Leu-on! Leu-on!

A quarter of a mile below Rothern Bridge the river slows into the lower loop of a great S. It deepens until half-way, where the S is cut by the weir holding back the waters of the long Beam Pool. Canal Bridge crosses the river at the top of the S.

Where the river begins to slow, at the beginning of the pool, its left bank is bound by the open roots of oak, ash, alder, and sycamore. To hunted otters these trees offered holding as secure as any in the country of the Two Rivers. Harper, the aged hound – he was fourteen years old – knew every holt in the riverside trees of Knackershill Copse, and although he had marked at all of them, only once had he cracked the rib of an otter found in the pool. Leeches infested the unclear water.

Tarka reached the top of the pool. Swimming in the shade, his unseen course betrayed by the line of bubbles-a-vent, he came to the roots of the sycamore tree, where he had slept for two days during his wandering after the death of Greymuzzle. He swam under the outer roots, and was climbing in a dim light to a dry upper ledge when a tongue licked his head, and teeth playfully nipped his ear. Two pale yellow eyes moved over him. He had awakened the cub Tarquol.

Tarka turned round and round, settled and curled, and closed his eyes. Tarquol's nostrils moved, pointing at Tarka's back. His small head stretched nearer, the nostrils working. He sniffed Tarka's hair from rudder to neck, and his nose remained at the neck. It was a strange smell, and he sniffed carefully not wanting to touch the fur with his nostrils. Tarka drew in a deep breath, which he let out in a long sigh. Then he swallowed the water in his mouth, settled his ear more comfortably on his paw, and slept; and awoke again.

Tarquol, the hairs of his neck raised, was listening at the back of the ledge. He was still as a root. The ground was shaking.

Go in on'm, old fellars! Wind him, my lads! B'hoys! B'hoys! Come on, b'hoys, get on to 'm.

The otters heard the whimpers of hounds peering from the top of the bank, afraïd of the fall into the river. They watched the dim-root opening level with the water. Footfalls sounded in the roots by their heads; they could feel them through their feet. Then the water-level rose up and shook with a splash, as Deadlock was tipped into the river. They saw his head thrust in at the opening, heard his gruff breathing, and then his belving tongue. Other hounds whimpered and splashed into the river.

Pull him out, old fellars! Leu-in there, leu-in, leu-in!

Tarka squatted on the ledge; he knew that Deadlock would follow him wherever he swam in water. Tarquol, twisting and weaving his head, ran down on roots to the water, dragging his rudder for a dive; but a whitish light alarmed him and he ran up to the ledge again. The whitish light was reflected from the breeches of the wading man. A voice sounded near and hollow. Then a pole pushed through the opening between two roots. Its end was thrown about, nearly striking Tarquol's head. It was pulled out again, and the whitish light moved away. Tarka heard the whining of Bite'm.

Hands held and guided the terrier past the outside root. Tarquol tissed again as the dim light darkened with the shape of the enemy, whose scent was on the hair of Tarka's neck. Bite'm whined and yapped, trying to struggle up to the otter. His hindfeet slipped off the roots, and he fell into the water below. *Plomp, plomp, plomp*, as he trod water, trying to scramble up the side.

Again the opening grew dark with arms holding and guiding another terrier, and Biff began to climb. *Wough! wough! wough!* Soon she fell into the water. The terriers were called off. Tarka settled more easily, but Tarquol could not rest. Hounds and terriers were gone, but still the voices of men were heard. The sound was low and regular, and Tarka's eyes closed. Tarquol squatted beside him in, and for many minutes neither moved. Then the murmur of voices ceased with footfalls along the bank coming nearer, and stopping above.

Heavy thuds shook down bits of earth on the otters' heads and backs. The huntsman was pounding the holt-top with an iron digging bar. Tarquol tissed, moving to and fro in fear of the great noises. Tarka slipped into the water, climbed out again, then submerged himself, only his nose and whiskers being out of the water. On and on went the pounding, until he could bear it no longer. He rolled over, and swam out of the holt. Tarquol followed him. He saw Tarka's chain rising bright before him. He turned upstream and was alone.

Seventy yards from the holt he rose under the bank to rest, and heard the baying of hounds. He dived again and went on upstream at his greatest speed. At his next vent he knew that the terrible beasts were following him. He swam out of the pool, turned back again, saw their heads in the water from bank to bank, became scared, and left the river. Galloping across the meadow faster than he had ever run in his life, with the hunting cries behind him and the thudding hooves of bullocks cantering away from hounds on his left, Tarquol came to sheds where farm machines were stored, and going through a yard, he ran through a gap in a hedge into a garden, where an old man was picking off the tops of his broad beans in a row, muttering about the black-fly on them. Tarquol passed him so near and so swiftly that the granfer's short clay pipe dropped from between his gums. He muttered in the sunshine and pondered nearly a minute. Hardly had he stooped to pick up his pipe when a great black-and-white hound crashed through the hedge and ran over his tetties and sun-dried shallots, followed by three more hounds, and after them a couple, and then his garden was filled with them.

Git'oom!

The hounds were gone, leaving him staring at his broken beans.

Git'oom — get home — go away.

Tarquol was trying to get home. He ran round the walls of the cottage and into a farmyard, scattered fowls in terror before him. One of the hens, who was broody, ran at him, and leapt at his back, pecking and flapping. Tarquol kicked a little dust behind his straight rudder. At full speed he ran into a pigsty, where a sow was lying on her side with a farrow of eleven tugging at her. Seeing him, they stopped tugging, stared together, squeaked together, and scampered away into corners. The sow, too fat to get up quickly, tried to bite Tarquol as he rippled from corner to corner. The baying of the pack grew terribly loud, and still Tarquol darted about the sty, seeking a way of escape. The sow, after many grunts, flung herself on her trotters and bundled her flabby mass to the door, unlocking her dirty teeth to bite Deadlock, who had just arrived. Squealing with rage, her bristly, mud-caked ears flapping on her chaps, she chased him out of the sty, followed him back into the yard, and scattered the rest of the pack. Tarquol had run out behind the sow. He gained three hundred yards before the hounds found his line again. He ran with the sun behind him for two hundred yards over grass, then he turned and went through a thorn hedge, climbed the railway embankment, and ran up over Furzebeam Hill, leaving an irregular trail. He ran for three miles on land, hiding among the dry spikes of gorse, and under branches. Sometimes he mewed in his misery.

Hounds ran far ahead of the men and women. Eventually the pack – with the exception of Pitiful, who was lost – hunted him back to the railway line, to where he was crouching low in the thorn hedge. A bird with a loud rasping voice, and a beak like a bent iron nail, clacked and chattered on a briar rising out of the hedge. It was a bird of property, or red-backed shrike, and Tarquol was squatting by its larder of bumble-bees, grasshoppers, and young harvest mice impaled on thorns. The mice were dead, but the bees still moved their legs.

Tarquol ran out of the thorns just before Render's muzzle pushed into his hiding-place; but hounds leapt the low hedge and overtook him, before he had gone very far on his short, tired legs. Deadlock seized him and shook him and threw him into the air. Tarquol sprang up as soon as he fell, snapping and writhing as more jaws bit on his body, crushed his head, cracked his ribs, his paws and his rudder. Among the brilliant hawkbits – little sunflowers of the meadow – he was picked up and dropped again, trodden on and wrenched and broken, while the screaming cheers and whoops of sportsmen mingled with the growling rumble of hounds at worry. Tarquol fought them until he was blinded, and his jaws were smashed. He had gone home before Tarka.

CHAPTER 20

Meanwhile Tarka, swimming out of the sycamore holt, had turned to deeper water and gone under the railway bridge twenty yards below – the line with its embankment and three bridges cut the S from south to north. He kept close to the left bank, in the margin of shade. The copse ended at the bridge; below was a meadow. He rose to breathe, heard hounds, and swam on underwater. He passed a run of peal, which flashed aside when they saw him and sped above the bridge at many times the pace of a travelling otter. Sixty yards below the bridge, by the roots of a thrown alder, Tarka rose to listen. Looking around, he saw neither hound nor man, and knew that he was not being followed. He thought of the holt under the oak tree above the next railway bridge, and swam on down.

Where the river's bend began to straighten again, the right bank lay under oak trees growing on the hill-slope to the sky. Tarka dived and swam across the river to the holt he had remembered as he left the roots of the sycamore. This holt had a sunken opening, where no terrier could enter. Here Tarka's sire had been asleep when hounds had found him two years before. Tarka swung up, coming into a dark cavern lit by a small hole above, and stinking of the paraffin poured there the previous afternoon. He sniffed the oil film on the water, and turned back into the weir-pool.

Again he made a hidden crossing, to listen under cover of flag-lilies for more than a minute. The river was quiet. He heard the sound of falling water, and swam slowly down, after touching under the bank. He passed under the middle arch of the railway bridge, and reached the weir slanting across the river. The summer water tumbled down the fish-pass, but glided thin as a snail's shell over the top end of the concrete sill. The lower end by the fender at the head of the leat was dry. Tarka walked along the sill, nearly to the end, which was two inches above the level of the pool. He stretched his weary back on the warm concrete and sprawled in the sun.

He lay basking for more than an hour, enjoying the sound of water tumbling in the pass and sliding down the face of the weir. Swallows dipped in the pool, and sometimes a peal leapt in the shadow of the bridge. Tarka's head was always raised before the fish fell back, but he did not leave the sill. Warm and brilliant sun-flickers on the shallows below dazed his eyes, and made him drowsy, but when a hound, working along down the left bank, climbed on the sill by the pass and shook himself, he was instantly alert. Half lying down, he remained quite still, while the hound lifted its muzzle to sniff. Something moved on the bridge – otter and hound turned their heads together, seeing a man behind the railing. At first the man saw only the hound, but when it walked along the sill and ran down the face of the weir, he saw the otter it was following. The man had come along the railway to see if many fish were in the pool; he was a poacher nicknamed Shiner, and the top of one of his fingers was missing. He had no love for otters. Along the railway line he hastened, and shouted to the otter-hunters.

Followed in silence by the hound Pitiful, Tarka swam leisurely. He watched from under a tree, a single enemy working down the shallow, crossing a deeper water to seek his scent along the banks. He let it come within a few feet of his head, then dived and swam away. Pitiful never saw him, or the chain of bubbles. Often she followed the wash carried down with the current; and when it grew weak, she would amble along the banks until she found where the otter had touched.

Tarka felt neither fear nor rage against the hound.

He wanted to be left alone. After several hidden swims from bank to bank, and finding no holding where he might lie up and sleep until evening, he walked out by a cattle-trodden grove in the right bank, and ran away over land. He followed the otter-path across a quarter of a mile of meadow, and came to the river again by the third oak above Canal Bridge.

Tarka drifted under the high lime-spiky arches of the bridge, and the white owl, roosting on a ledge below the parapet, beside the briars of a dog-rose growing there with hawkweeds, saw him going downstream.

Bees came to the wild roses, crammed more pollen into their laden thigh-bags, and burred away over the bridge. A petal dropped, a swallow played with it as it fell, clipping it with first one wing and then the other, until it dropped into the water, and was carried away, past the gap in the bank where the Owlery Oak, Tarka's birthplace, had been held by its roots two years before.

Then Pitiful swam under Canal Bridge, and after her the pack came down, and many men, and the owl was driven into wavy flight down the river. It pitched in the tree of Leaning Willow Island, as a dull clamour broke out half a mile up the river. Hounds had marked the otter under a hover, and driven him out.

The water of the pool was swimming-deep from the shallow above Canal Bridge to the shallow above Leaning Willow Island. The surface above Tarka mirrored the bed of the river – the dark rocks, the weed, the sodden branches, with the legs and bodies of hounds –

until ripples broke the mirror into shades of light. In this underwater realm, where sounds were so distinct – the crush of nailed boots on stones, the tip-tap of poles, the thresh of hounds' legs, and even the flip of cyclops and waterflea – Tarka swam until he was forced to vent, which he did at the river verge, under the banks, or by clumps of yellow flags. Sometimes he crept on the stones, hiding himself under overhanging roots as he sought a refuge, until dreading the nearness of hounds he slipped into the river again, covered with a silver skin of air. As he swam, twin streams of bubbles came out of his nostrils, raced over his head and neck, and shook off his back to lie on the surface in a chain, watched by many eyes. Up and down the pool he went, swimming in midstream or near the banks, crossing from side to side and varying his depth of swimming as he tried to get away from his pursuers. Passing under the legs of hounds, he saw them joined to their broken surface-images. From underwater he saw men and women, pointing with hand and pole, as palsied and distorted shapes on the bank. However hard he swam with his three and a half webs, always he heard the hounds, as they spoke to his scent lying in burst bubble, in seal on muddy scour, on leaf and twig. Once in mid-river, while on his way to a clump of flags, his breath gave out, and he bobbed up to breathe a yard from Deadlock. He stared into the eyes of his old enemy; and dived. During forty seconds, he swam a distance of seventy yards, to a bed of reeds, where he breathed and rested. No one saw him; but they saw the chain.

Up the river again, past the Peal Rock, and under the middle arch of Canal Bridge to the shallow, crossed by a line of men and women, white and blue and green and red and grey, standing close together.

Tally-Ho!

He turned and reached covering water just before hounds.

Get on to 'm! Leu-on! leu-on! Wind him, old fellars!

The huntsman was wading up to his waist in the water, scooping the air with his grey hat. Bellman, a small-footed hairy black-and-tan, cross between a drafted harrier and a Dumfriesshire rough otter-hound, yelped his impatience, seeming to snap the water as he swam. Sometimes the huntsman gave an encouraging spit-note on his horn. Tarka went down-river, but a blurred and brilliant colour band stretched from bank to bank above Leaning Willow Island. He tried to get through the stickle, but stocking'd leg was pressed to stocking'd leg, a fixed barrier behind plying poles. The owl flew out of the willow, miserable in the sunlight with small birds pursuing it.

Tarka turned and swam upstream again, leaving hounds behind. For five minutes he rested under a thorn bush. Deadlock found him, and on he went, to Canal Bridge once more, where he lay in the water, weary after the long chase. At the beginning of the sixth hour he tried to pass the higher stickle, but his enemies stood firm on the stones. The tongues swelled under the bridge. He was nearly picked up by Hurricane, the Irish staghound, but the blunted canine teeth could not hold him.

The chain became shorter. Tarka was too weary to seek a holding in the banks. He breathed in view of his enemies. Seven and a half couples of hounds swam in the pool, their sterns throwing behind them arc-lines of drops on the surface. Others splashed in the shallows under the banks. The huntsman let them work by themselves.

During the sixth hour the otter disappeared. The river grew quiet. People not in uniform sat down on the grass. The huntsman was wading slowly upstream, feeling foothold with pole and keeping an eye on Deadlock. Stickle stood slack, but ready to bar the way with pole-strokes. Look-outs gazed at the water before them. It was known that the otter might leave the river at any moment. The boy with the warped pole, on whose cheeks were two patches of dried otter-blood, was already opening his knife, ready to cut another notch on the handle in the form of a cross.

But for more than an hour the sun-thongs flickered across the placid water; and in softening light the owl returned, flying high over the bridge, to the mouse runs in the quiet meadow beyond.

A fallen bough of willow lay in the pool near one bank, and Tarka lay beside it. His rudder held a sunken branch. Only his wide upper nostrils were above water. He never moved. Every yard of the banks between the stickles was searched again. Poles were thrust into branches, roots, and clumps of flag-lilies. The wading huntsman prodded Peal Rock and the rock above it.

Hounds sat on the banks, shivering, and watching Deadlock, Render, and Harper working the banks. The crack of a whip, a harsh voice rating – Rufus had turned a rabbit out of a bramble and was chasing it across the meadow. He returned to the river in a wide circle, eyeing the whip.

At the beginning of the eighth hour a scarlet dragon-fly whirred and darted over the willow snag, watched by a girl sitting on the bank. Her father, an old man lank and humped as a heron, was looking out near her. She watched the dragonfly settle on what looked like a piece of bark beside the snag; she heard a sneeze, and saw the otter's whiskers scratch the water. Glancing round, she realized that she alone had seen the otter. She flushed, and hid her grey eyes with her lashes. Since childhood she had walked the Devon rivers with her father, looking for flowers and the nests of birds, passing some rocks and trees as old friends, seeing a Spirit everywhere, gentle in thought to all her eyes beheld.

For two minutes the maid sat silent, hardly daring to look at the river. The dragonfly flew over the pool, seizing flies and tearing them apart in its horny jaws. Her father watched it as it settled on the snag, rose up, circled, and lit on the water, it seemed. Tarka sneezed again, and the dragonfly flew away. A grunt of satisfaction from the old man, a brown hand and wrist holding aloft a hat, a slow intake breath, and,

Tally-Ho!

Tarka dived when the hounds came down, and the

chain showed where he had swum. Many saw his dark sleek form as he walked by the edge of a grassy islet by the twelve trees. The hounds ran to him, and Tarka turned and faced them, squatting on his short hindlegs, his paws close against his round and sturdy chest. He bit Render in the nose, making his teeth meet. In an instant he drew back, tissing, and bit Deadlock in the flews. The narrow lower jaw snapped again and again, until the press of hounds hid him from sight.

He squirmed away through legs and under bellies, biting and writhing a way to the water; and the chain drew out on the surface of the pool while hounds were still seeking him on the stones where he had sat and faced them.

Leu-on, then! Leu-on! Ov-ov-ov-ov-over!

Tarka's pace was slow and his dives were short. In the water by the Peal Rock he lay, glancing at the faces along the banks, across the river, and in the river. His small dark eyes showed no feeling. He turned away from the human faces, to watch the coming of the hounds. He was calm and fearless and fatigued. When they were his length away, he swung under, showing the middle of his smooth back level with the surface, and swimming past their legs. He saw the huntsman's legs before him joined to the image of legs, and above the inverted image a flattened and uncertain head and shoulders. Up and down he swam, slower and slower.

At the beginning of the ninth hour an immense fatigue came over him, greater than his fatigue when in the long hard winter he had lived for over a month on seaweed and shellfish in the estuary. He was swimming up from the lower stickle when the water seemed to thicken at each thrust of his webs. He ceased to swim and drifted backwards. Barbrook touched his neck as he dived. He reappeared two poles' length away, and lay still, looking at the huntsman wading nearer.

For ten minutes he rested, between dives of a few yards only, and then he rolled from Deadlock's bite and went downstream. He swam with his last strength, for upon him had come the penultimate desire of the hunted otter, the desire that comes when water ceases to be a refuge, the desire to tread again the land-tracks of his ancestors. He crawled half up the bank, but turned back at the thudding of many feet, and swam down to the stickle. The sideway ply of a pole in a turmoil of water struck him on the head. He pushed past the iron point, but it was brought down on his shoulder, to hold him against the shillets. Hounds were fifteen yards away, urged on by hat and horn and the yarring cheers of the whippers-in. Thrice Tarka's teeth clicked on the iron pressing his shoulder as he strove against the weight of the sportsman trying to lift him back. A second pole was brought down from the other flank, crossing with the first. The wooden pincers held him; he twisted like an eel and bit into a leg. With furious strength he writhed from the crossed poles, and through the stickle, as Deadlock bore down upon him and pulled him back by the rudder. Amidst the harsh cries of men and women and the heavy tongues of hounds Tarka was overborne by the pack. The Master looked at his watch – eight hours and forty-five minutes from the find in the Dark Pool. Then the screeching, yarring yell of one of the honorary whips: *Yaa-aa-ee-io! Leu-in on 'm! Yaa-ee-oo!* for again Tarka had escaped from the worry, and had merged into the narrow stream of water that hurried to Leaning Willow Island.

Below the island the river widened, smooth with the sky. Tarka swam down slowly, bleeding from many wounds. Sometimes he paddled with three legs, sometimes with one, in the water darkening so strangely before his eyes. Not always did he hear the hounds baying around him. At the beginning of the tenth hour he passed the banks faced with stone to keep the sea from the village, and drifted into deeper water, whereon sticks and froth were floating. Hounds were called off by the horn, for the tide was at flood.

But as they were about to leave, Tarka was seen again, moving with the tide, his mouth open. The flow took him near the bank; he kicked feebly, and rolled over.

Tally-Ho!

Deadlock saw the small brown head, and bayed in triumph as he jumped down the bank. He bit the head, and lifted the otter high, flung him about and fell into the water with him. They saw the broken head look up beside Deadlock, heard the cry of *Ic-yang!* as Tarka bit into his throat, and then the hound was sinking with the otter into the deep water. Oak-leaves, black and rotting in the mud of the unseen bed, arose and swirled and sank again. And the tide slowed still, and began to move back, and they waited and watched, until the body of Deadlock arose, drowned and heavy, and floated away amidst the froth on the waters.

They pulled the body out of the river and carried it to the bank, laying it on the grass, and looking down at the dead hound in sad wonder. And while they stood there silently, a great bubble rose out of the depths, and broke, and as they watched, another bubble shook the surface, and broke; and there was a third bubble in the sea-going waters, and nothing more.

HERE ENDS TARKA THE OTTER BY HENRY
WILLIAMSON, BEGUN IN JUNE 1923 AND
FINISHED IN FEBRUARY 1927 IN THE
VILLAGE OF HAM IN DEVON

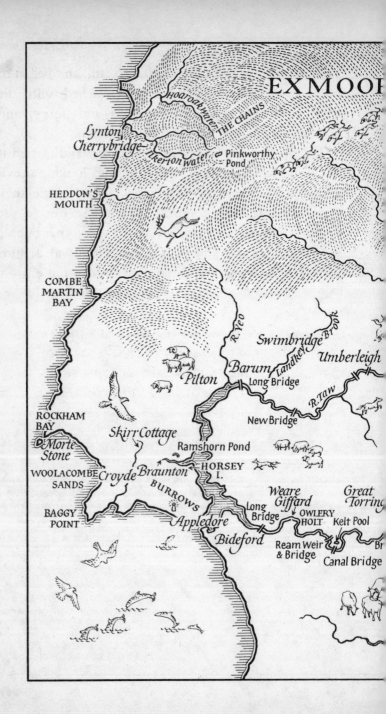

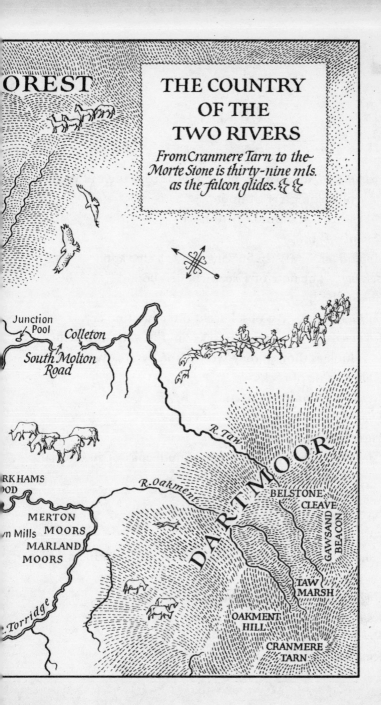

THE COUNTRY
OF THE
TWO RIVERS

From Cranmere Tarn to the
Morte Stone is thirty-nine mls.
as the falcon glides.

OREST

Junction
Pool

Colleton

South Molton
Road

R. Taw

RK HAMS
OD

R. Oakment

BELSTONE
CLEAVE

MERTON
MOORS

n Mills

MARLAND
MOORS

D
A
R
T
M
O
O
R

GAWSAND
BEACON

TAW
MARSH

Torridge

OAKMENT
HILL

CRANMERE
TARN

GLOSSARY

Ackymal   An onomatopoeic word from the call of the blue and great titmouse.

Aerymouse   Common British bat

Ammil   Frost

Appledrane   A wasp buzzing inside a ripe apple

Belving   The note of a deep–chested hound

Brock   Badger

Bubbles-a-vent   An obsolescent otter-hunting cry

Channered   Wandering tracks in the salt turf which look as though they were made by great worms

Clitter   Pile of rocks

Crackey   Common wren

Dimity   Twilight

Fitchey or *fitch*   Stoat

Glidders   The smooth, sloping mudbanks of an esturial creek

Oolypuggers   Bulrushes

Pill   Esturial creek

Pollywiggle   Tadpole

Quapping   The sound made by a duck with its bill when feeding

Ragrowster   To enjoy boisterously

Ram-cat   Tom cat

Ream   A wave

Ruddock   Robin

Shillets   Flat stones of the river bed deposited by flood
    waters

Shippen or *shippon*   A roofed shed with one side open
    for cattle to shelter in

Spurring   Following the track of a wild animal

Stag-bird   A cock among domestic hens

Sterlings (Pronounced *starlings*)   The stone piling round
    the base of a bridge

Tacker   Small child, usually a boy

Twired   Slow and shallow flow of river water moving
    past a heron's legs

Vair   Weasel

Vuz-peg   Hedgehog

Yinny-yikker   Noisily aggressive

AFTERWORD

Tarka the Otter is a true story – as true as a man's account of the life of a wild animal can possibly be. It was revised as a whole and rewritten many times, always and only for the sake of greater truth. The truth, the whole truth and nothing but the truth was the author's deliberate aim and ambition. Mere polishing for grace of expression or literary style did not interest him. He plodded on, striving 'always to be more truthful, to write or render a scene or incident with the authentic sunlight of life, learning at each scrutiny and revision', teaching himself to be truthful, not to exaggerate, to unlearn all the prejudice he had learned from other people since childhood, always 'cutting out untruths and inaccuracies, facile descriptions, inventions not of true imagination'.

How he came to understand so much about the life of the otter is a story in itself.

After the First World War, Henry Williamson found himself out of love with mankind, at odds with his family, weary and nerve-wracked. He left London and, on a racing motor-cycle, came to the West coast where he found a cottage in North Devon for one shilling and sixpence a week. It was a tiny place built of cob (that is trodden clay and straw) in the days of King John. For three hundred years owls had nested under the thatch and soon Henry Williamson had painted his totem of a barn-owl in white and gold on the door. The same owl he uses as a sign-manual at the conclusion of his books.

He lived there alone, hermit-fashion, tramping about the countryside, often sleeping out. The doors and windows of the cottage were never closed, and his strange family of dogs and cats, gulls, buzzards, magpies – and one otter cub – were free to come and go as they chose.

He had, up to that time, seen only two otters in his life – the first as a boy in Norfolk and the second in an old German field-gun emplacement near the River Ancre in 1916 or '17. He encountered the third, which was to play such a significant part in his life, three or four years later, when a stranger looked in at the cottage one day, asking for help in digging out some otter cubs whose mother had been shot by a farmer as she was crossing one of his fields by a stream, on a rabbiting expedition. Williamson went willingly and they got out two cubs, one alive, the other dead. He wrote that he took the living one back to his cottage and offered it milk in a fountain-pen filler with a hole nipped in the rubber tip, but it refused this strange teat and sprawled helplessly on the table, opening its mouth in feeble, voiceless mewing.

The cat, who was still nursing one kitten, leaped up, full of curiosity, to see what was going on. She walked round the strange creature, sniffed it and returned unconcernedly to her basket. The cub was put in with her, but she ignored it until Williamson had taken it and the kitten and rubbed them together, mouth on mouth, tummy on tummy. Then she accepted it and let the otter suck side by side with her kitten.

The cub throve and learned to lap from a saucer. It took to fish and ate partly-cooked rabbit mixed with dog biscuit and vegetables. Soon it entered into happy games in a zinc bath when water from a hose was played on it. It grew big and followed Williamson about, played and frolicked with him on twilight walks by the banks of the stream. It came to his call.

On one of these walks, Williamson heard suddenly a dreadful hissing and chattering, and turned to find the otter caught by a paw in a rabbit gin. It was in a frenzy of pain and fear, struggling frantically to free itself, biting at the steel spring and gnawing its imprisoned foot. Three toes were almost severed. Williamson threw his coat over it and so managed to hold it between his knees while he freed the paw from the serrated steel jaws. As he braced himself to a firmer hold of the writhing body, so that he could carry it home, the otter wriggled out of his grasp and disappeared. He called after it and searched along the river banks, but it never returned. Up and down stream he sought it for weeks, examining mud and sand for a trace of that maimed paw. He went further afield, leaving his own neighbourhood and following the otters' haunts to the Estuary of the Two Rivers, on up the Torridge and the Taw from mouth to source – but he never found it again.

His solitary way of life had brought him to feel more at one with wild things than with human beings.

Now, as he haunted the rivers which came down both from Exmoor and Dartmoor, searching for the seal of an otter with three of its front toes missing, the story of *Tarka* began to take shape.

He went out with the Hounds, though always fearful of seeing his own otter harried and killed – yet as that, too, was the common experience of an otter of the Two Rivers, he had to face and comprehend the hunt and the kill if he was to present the whole of an otter's life truly.

So he entered the otter's world for a time and it became more real to him than the world of men. He learned the small experiences of the otter's daily life and interpreted what he saw with such truth that, after many years, *Tarka* is still endorsed by naturalists, hunts-men and other observant countrymen.

With a good map (one inch to the mile) the whole movement of the story can be followed minutely, up and down the Two Rivers, round the coast of the Severn Sea from Lynton to the Estuary, along Braunton Sands or the 'Pill', a creek where ketches lie at their moorings. The descriptions of moor and river, grass, water, and stone, are seen at otter level, nose a few inches from the ground, and not often with the wider sweep of eye at man's upright height. He was never satisfied unless he had seen things for himself and had watched closely enough to get the letter as well as the spirit of reality. He went back over and over again to the scenes of his story.

While still at work on *Tarka*, he married and had a

son. He still lived in the little cottage, was poor and had difficulty in finding even that small rent. His wife fell ill and had to spend many weeks in bed. The baby was not strong and cried incessantly, for they could not find the proper food for it. Williamson looked after the house, cooked, tended and fed both wife and baby – and still went on revising *Tarka*, mainly at night with the baby crying in the crook of his left arm.

When the book was finished and first published, a copy was sent out to India to T. E. Lawrence, Lawrence of Arabia, who wrote back a long detailed criticism for the author, adding later that 'Had I known you were so established a writer, I'd never have had the cheek to write down my 'prentice ideas about the book. By the care and passion of the text I'd assumed you were a beginner, half in love with his first effort, and probably now heart-broken by its failure to come anywhere near the perfection dreamed of . . . As you saw, I'm glad to say, by the length and elaboration of my remarks, the book did move me, and gratify me profoundly. It was the real stuff . . . Tarka, to anyone who's tried to write, is a technical delight, all the more perfect for being imperfect here and there . . . I wonder what you'll do about money. Tarka will not have made much, and the more carefully you write, the less you are likely to earn.'

But literary friends were at work, particularly Sir John Squire, who had published the long winter chapter in *The London Mercury*. The book was warmly and publicly praised by Thomas Hardy, John Galsworthy,

and Arnold Bennett. It won the Hawthornden Prize –
and there were no runners-up for the award that year.
It was a very great success.

'What the critics say about its being too tightly
packed is right,' the author wrote in retrospect, adding
that during that final revision he had been exhausted,
working grimly, doggedly, with no pleasure left. 'Yet
I enjoyed it all. I knew the prose was straight, keen and
true – facts, you know. It is all here in Devon, if you
just happen to see and hear or smell it.'

Eleanor Graham

Since Eleanor Graham wrote this Afterword in 1949,
more detailed information has come to light about
Henry Williamson's life. If you would like to find out
more about him, please contact the Henry Williamson
Society at the following address:

Mrs Margaret Murphy
The Henry Williamson Society
16 Doran Drive
Redhill
Surrey
RH1 6AX

Some other Puffin Modern Classics

THE SILVER SWORD
Ian Serraillier

This is the story of four children's struggle to stay alive throughout the years of Nazi occupation and, afterwards, their epic journey from war-torn Poland to Switzerland in search of their parents.

Based on a true story, this is an extraordinarily moving account of life during and after the Second World War.

WATERSHIP DOWN
Richard Adams

Fiver felt sure that something terrible was going to happen to the warren – and Fiver's sixth sense was never wrong.

Yet the fleeing band of rabbits could never have imagined the terrors and dangers they were to encounter in their search for a new home.